CHARMING MY BROODY BILLIONAIRE BOSS

A HOT ROMANTIC COMEDY

JOLIE DAY

ABOUT THIS NOVEL

He's the devil himself:

Damon Copeland (he practically carries a pitchfork).

Fiery-hot and a killer smile (if he ever smiled).

He's also the top dog at my father's company,

And my brother's best friend.

Oh, and someone I accidentally slept with.

In my defense, that was before I knew who he was—

And before he hired me.

Now, my one-night stand has turned into my boss.

What's worse, he's Mr. Bosshole Superior: brutish, broody, and impatient.

He's also 6'4".

With a perfect jawline.

None of this will break my resolve.

The girl who resists her irresistible boss? That's me.

I will not fall for controlling, short-tempered Mr. Hot Shot.

1

DAMON

"Just bourbon for me." I waved to the bartender, Gracie. "Hurry up, doll. I don't have all day."

I preferred to avoid all the extra sweeteners and artificial shit you'd find in most cocktails.

She sauntered down the length of the bar with a wide grin, two drinks in hand. "Well, Damon, aren't you in a mood today? Did you lose a deal?" She was in her thirties, but her voice was deeper than one would expect. A result of a lifetime career of bar work, I suspected.

"Who's in a mood?" I raised a questioning brow. "Nobody's losing deals over here."

"Life is about the good things. Didn't anybody ever teach you that?" she asked with a wink. "Also, honey, I've only got two hands."

"Better cheer up," I heard the bouncer say behind me.

"Hey," I said, "there's nothing but positivity over here."

"Uh-huh, sweets. I can see all that positivity just *dripping* from you." Gracie was on one today, with her sarcastic humor. She handed my buddies the drinks they'd ordered, a Long Island Iced Tea for Oliver, and a classic Martini for his brother Miles. "Careful, you guys, the alcohol content is enough to knock you both on your asses," Gracie joked.

The two cheered and raised their glasses. "Keep 'em coming!"

She pivoted on her heel and glanced over her shoulder. "Get ya that drink in a sec."

"Appreciate it, Gracie," I said, giving her a nod.

A long ride on my motorcycle through the countryside with my best two buddies, followed by a few drinks at one of our favorite bars back in the city—Talia's was an old school biker bar, not a Highlands yuppie watering hole. No attitudes, except maybe for the bouncer. It was unchanged since it had reopened in the early 80s, with several pool tables in the back and the next room. Seating was somewhat limited, but that was part of the charm. It was the perfect place to celebrate the big deal we just closed at work. The best part about it? I was the key player. And soon, a *lot* of people would see a *lot* of profit.

It felt good.

Needless to say, my mood was good as well.

Oliver and Miles motioned to find a table, drinks in hands. I nodded as I waited for my drink. But by the time the bourbon arrived, and I turned around, they were out of sight.

Where the hell did they go? I scanned the crowded room and couldn't see them. *Maybe they moved into the next room,* I thought, setting out to find them.

The moment I rounded the corner—I felt a jolt of human flesh slam into my chest. Soft human flesh.

What the f—? My drink didn't survive the collision.

I glanced down at my jeans and shirt, noting the damage of the spill, before my gaze drifted up.

That's when I saw her.

The hottest girl in the bar. Clearly, she had to be.

Maybe even the hottest girl in New York City.

Magnificent freckles, the most adorable I'd ever seen. Her big blue eyes sparked with anger, but I was too caught up in observing her tempting, long tan legs extending from her denim miniskirt. I followed the sight of them up to her gorgeous tits beneath a white blouse, that was now drenched in the rest of my drink—and completely see-through. I couldn't help but stare at the black lace push-up bra and two hard nipples that the fabric clung to, torturing me.

"Son of a gun!" she hissed, attempting to fan out the soaked shirt, causing her tits to jiggle.

"My bad. Didn't see you there." I wasn't *really* sorry, but I hadn't seen her.

However, I *did* like what I was seeing now.

She was petite, with curves in all the right places. Her honey-blonde hair sparkled with glitter, framing her flawless freckled face, and her plump crimson lips were curled in what appeared like spite. They were soft and inviting. Maybe it was just in my head, but I could have sworn her lips had that color naturally, rather than being coated in lipstick.

"Then maybe you should have been paying closer attention." She eyed me angrily, still fanning her shirt.

"Oh, believe me, I am now," I said, still taking in an eyeful of her drenched top and luscious curves underneath.

A brunette girl appeared at her side, taking her by the arm before tossing a dirty look my way. She shoved me against the wall. "You pig," she huffed, before dragging her friend off toward the bathroom.

Pig? No. What man wouldn't look?

Well, normally, I wouldn't be so obvious when checking out a woman. Normally, I'd be the asshole who didn't give a flying fuck about a random chick in a bar. But she'd hit me like a lightning bolt. I couldn't help myself.

After they'd stormed off, I straightened myself, noticing that my right contact lens had hit the eject button. With one eye still intact and clear, I spotted Miles and Oliver taking a seat at a table on the opposite end of the bar. Even if I was walking away with a spill down the front of my clothes, an empty glass in hand, a missing contact lens, and a scorned woman who now hated my guts, I couldn't be too upset about it.

I slid onto the stool next to them.

"There you are," Oliver said.

"Hey." In a swift motion, I popped the left lens out, tossed it, reached into my side pocket, and put on my glasses. Usually, I wore glasses on a daily basis, but contacts were easier when riding a bike, what with the helmet and all.

"Did you see that girl I ran into?" I asked them, scanning the bar to see if I could spot her again.

They started looking around, too.

"No," Miles replied, turning his attention to my shirt. "Was it a girl or a waterfall?"

I grimaced and waved the bartender over to order another. "I've never seen a girl like her."

"What exactly are we dealing with here? Be more specific." Miles snorted. "I'm a tits *and* ass man, and the bartender, Gracie? Yeah, she's got a great ass. That's the first thing I notice about a woman."

"Jesus, *man*, stop staring," I told him. "She's coming."

Gracie handed me my drink and some napkins.

"Me, I'm an ass guy through and through." Oliver nodded, taking a drink of his cocktail.

"You two are fucking creeps," I said, shaking my head. "Don't you have girls?"

"That's why we're only *looking*. And hey, you're the one who started it," Miles pointed out. "So, let's hear it. What was so special about that mystery chick?"

"She had it all. I've never seen her here before," I said. "She knocked the breath out of me. I literally lost my breath for a second. I'm telling you, I've never had that happen before."

"Dude. Never? Really?" Miles asked, surprised.

"Never. Why? Have you?"

"Sure." Miles chuckled. "That's exactly how I felt when I accidentally ran into Jason Momoa the other day."

"You wanted to impregnate Jason Momoa?" I asked, keeping my face impassive. "Thought you were a tits and ass man."

Miles shoved me, almost pushing me off my stool. "Fucker."

"And where the fuck did you meet Jason Momoa?" Oliver asked him.

Miles shook his head. "Dude, I'm just kidding. We have a biker buddy who looks just like him, though."

"Sure you have," I said, calling bullshit. "Who? Don't say Malcolm Gladwell."

"Malcolm Gladwell."

Oliver smirked at me, ignoring Miles. "But by the way you got all worked up, sounds like somebody's in love."

"Oh, Jesus." With my new drink in hand, I glanced at my watch, ready to change the subject. "Don't you two have a game to catch?"

"Yeah. That's why we sped all the way here like motherfuckers," Miles grinned.

"We made it back here on schedule. A little ahead of schedule actually," I said.

"You don't say?" Miles shot back with sarcastic enthusiasm. "That calls for an *extra* level of celebration. How about a toast?" He held his nearly overflowing martini glass in the air. "To Damon's excellent planning skills. Not only does it choke the fun out of everything we try to do, but it puts us everywhere ahead of schedule and prevents us from ever being, God forbid, a minute late. Much less accidentally doing something...*spontaneous!*" He gasped like it was the most scandalous word in the English language.

To me, it kind of was. Spontaneity wasn't a part of my repertoire.

Oliver patted me on the shoulder. "Don't mind him. But hey, you got our asses out of the office on time and in a hurry. Nothing wrong with that. And, you got a girl to spill your drink all over you. Good job, man."

"Shut the fuck up." I rolled my eyes and leaned forward with a shameless air. "First, you two don't complain when I help make the company millions. And second, if not for my 'meticulous planning,' you ass-hats wouldn't know when to scratch your ass or wind your watch."

Miles looked down at his watch and grinned. "Oh, shit. He's right, actually. Okay, your next drink is on me."

"How about we do a round of shots instead?" I suggested.

"Good to see you loosen up a bit, man." Miles raised his hand into a bro-fist.

Really? Bro-fist? Was that still a thing? I bumped my fist against his, stopping myself from pointing out the inevitable, namely that I was too old for that shit and ready to call it a night. If he only knew my real motivation.

I wasn't as uptight as they liked to believe, but I did like having a plan. And whether they wanted to admit it or not—my plans had gotten us where we were today. Without me, they'd be lost. So would half of our profits on this last deal. I knew there was a limit to how much of a hard time they'd give me, at least for tonight.

"You're just trying to get drunk enough to go hit on that hot-ass mama you ran into," Oliver said.

"I don't have to be drunk for that," I argued. But I did take another glance around the room, searching for her. She appeared to be long gone. Too bad.

"Still, I know it's typically not your style," Miles said. "You should change things up a bit, though. Go find her, take her home, hit it *hard*, and leave."

The thought made me smirk, but I rolled my eyes at his enthusiasm. He was right.

Unlike Miles (well, before he started seeing somebody), picking up women in bars had never been my style. It was too big of a gamble. You had no time to really get to know them and figure out what kind of crazy you were inviting into your life.

Of course, romance wasn't exactly my style, either. I preferred something in the middle. A friend-with-benefits situation. Or, a chance encounter, packed with a lot of chemistry and attraction, followed by an on and off again casual affair. Somebody to call on when you were lonely or horny. Okay, I was always horny, but that's how I played the game: upfront and without any promises for more. Anything beyond that was too complicated. Lying around and snuggling—not my thing. Women and relationships were too unpredictable, and I'd seen too many poor schmucks get their lives and routines all fucked up over the trouble that came with them. Not for me.

Noting the time, I grew impatient. I didn't give two shits if they missed the game, I just didn't want to stick around for longer than absolutely necessary. I gestured to the clock on the wall. "Fair warning...you two have less than one minute before you have to leave, if you want to make it home in time for the game." In all seriousness, if they actually wanted to make it back in time for the game, they'd have to chug their drinks, or they'd have to leave them behind, half-finished.

"Fuck, Damon's right," Oliver began to chug his drink.

Miles shot me a crooked smile. "And just what are *you* planning to do when we head home?"

I was going to call it an early night. I wanted to get in a good run the next morning before doing some work at home, along with everything else I had to do to prepare for the week ahead. But that was exactly the kind of response Miles expected, and I wasn't about to encourage the smug grin on his face. I also wasn't in the mood to argue.

"I'm going to find her, take her home, and hit it." I motioned for Gracie, asking for a refill. "And now, you two should leave me the hell alone about it so I can get down to business," I added with a smirk—for dramatic effect—ready to make my exit the moment they were out the door.

"No shit." Miles seemed impressed, tipping his glass. "Well, okay then. Damon really *is* cuttin' loose tonight. How about we all—"

"Oh, no, you don't." Oliver cut him off. "Not tonight. You're not dragging me into another one of your wild evenings. I'm not looking for a hangover from hell because of some stupid-ass decisions and not having enough time to recover before Monday morning. We're going to my place to watch the game with Laney, just like we planned."

"You're no fun," he grumbled.

Oliver and I shot each other a knowing look. Miles said that now, but I knew him. Five minutes into the game he'd be carrying on, cheering for his favorite team, forgetting he ever thought of doing anything else.

They cashed out and said goodnight, leaving me to finish my final glass of bourbon.

Usually, I was the first one to leave, not the last. Sure, sometimes I'd pop in for a beer on my way home once or twice a week, but I generally had my laptop and a stack of papers by my side to keep me company. This time was different. I was empty-handed and buzzed, and unfortunately, the chick with the perky tits was nowhere in sight.

After tossing back the rest of my drink, I headed for the men's room. I had to piss like a motherfucker.

Pushing through the swinging door, I froze.

2

DAMON

*C*oming out of one of the stalls was none other than the blonde chick I'd spilled my drink on earlier. She had found a button-up shirt, either from her friend or another guy in the bar, and slipped it over her see-through white blouse. For a second, I wondered if I'd accidentally walked into the women's bathroom, but looking at the urinals, there was no doubt: I was in the men's room. What was she doing in here?

Her eyes caught mine with an unapologetic smirk. "Oh, look who it is," she said with her angelic-sounding voice.

"You do know this is the men's room," I said casually.

"The ladies' line was too long." She shrugged.

I shook my head and strode toward the line of urinals. I wasn't about to piss with her standing just a few feet away, was I?

"Don't worry. I won't look," she teased, moving to the sink to wash her hands. Truthfully, I wouldn't mind if she did. She'd likely be impressed. Not that I thought she'd waltz over and stare at my dick.

Just then, the door swung open again. This time it was one of the bouncers, and he didn't seem too happy to see her in there.

"What the fuck? Didn't I just tell you?" He gawked, clearly ready to grab her and drag her out and kick her ass out of the bar. I knew the guy. He was what some people would call "easily irritated." In other words, he was an aggressive prick. You couldn't reason with him. He also wasn't the smartest guy you'd ever meet—making him a ticking time bomb. I'd seen him kick out girls for lesser reasons. Probably didn't get his dick sucked enough, or he hated women in general. He towered over her, his tone loud and aggressive. "You can't be in here, lady. Out. Now!"

She looked like she was gearing up to tell him off, which I knew wouldn't help matters.

"Stop! Sorry, my fault." I interjected. "She's my sister. She came in here to...help me."

His face twisted with a hint of disgust. "Help you?"

"Toilet paper," I said, nodding to one of the stalls.

"Well, okay, Mary Poppins, if you're finished with your TP delivery, get the hell out," he barked. "And don't come in here again."

She finished washing her hands, blowing a sassy fuck-you kiss to the dude. Then, she flashed a smile over her shoulder and sauntered out, leaving me to finally relieve myself in peace. Only now I had the bouncer staring at my dick.

What the fuck?

"Dude, back off," I said, giving him a sidelong glance. "I'm trying to take a piss. I don't need an audience. I've got this. Thanks."

The bouncer held up his hands with a smirk. "My bad. I got the wrong vibe. I'll leave you to it then."

The fuck? He thought I was gay? Not that there was anything wrong with it, but did I really trip the gaydar?

Wait. Shit. It was because I'd used the sister story.

I just hung my head and finished my business.

*W*hen I emerged from the bathroom, I was pleased to see the blonde waiting out in the hall.

"Thanks, *brother*," she said.

"You owe me, *sister*."

She laughed and shook her head. "I thought *you* were the one who owed *me*. You *did* ruin my shirt after all. And my bra."

Images started flooding my mind at the mention of her bra. Could a little spill of bourbon ruin a bra? Do bras fucking dissolve on contact with alcohol or something? I was clueless. "You ran into me, if memory serves."

"I did *not*," she said, changing her posture and putting her hands on her hips.

"And for the record, I didn't make it out unscathed, either, you know." I glanced down to my pants and shirt. The previously darkened spill had already faded, but I didn't divert. "How about you buy me a drink?"

"Nope." She stepped away from the wall. "You'll buy *me* a drink, and we'll call it even."

Ha. Game on. This was going better than expected. Again, I appraised her appearance from head to toe, not moving an inch as she approached me. "You need a better grasp on your bargaining power. I can buy the drinks, and the bonus is you join me for one round."

She raised a brow. "Just one?"

"For starters."

Those magnetic blue eyes of hers sparked mischievously. "Deal."

Whoa. That was almost too easy. I'd expected more resistance after all that bullshit bitchiness she'd given me earlier. But hell, okay. She was ready to play, and I was ready to win. Perfect. She reached out her hand to shake on it, keeping her gaze locked on mine. For someone so small, she sure did have a bold, disarming allure to her. It hadn't exactly been planned, no. But fuck, I'd be an idiot to just walk away from her.

"Deal." I pressed my palm to hers, the touch of her skin sending a jolt of arousal straight to my dick. "Pick your poison."

~

*B*efore I knew what was happening, my back hit the mattress, and I was staring up at the naughty chick's bright smile as she loomed above me. Part of my vision was blurry. I realized that my glasses had come askew. When I reached to correct them, she lightly slapped my hands away, before removing them and placing them on the side table.

She leaned back down, pressing her lips to mine. She kissed me for a long while, slowly and sensually, the length of her perfectly naked body resting against mine, with her legs parted over my hips, where her wetness soaked onto my stomach. She provided a delicious friction as she moved her hip lower and began to grind her center against me, all hard from her. I wanted to fuck her senseless.

I growled into her mouth and reached up, stilling her hips with the clench of my fingers. "Are you trying to kill me, babe?" I grumbled. She grinned, nuzzling her nose against mine.

"Maybe," she purred, pressing another kiss to my bottom lip.

I growled again, turning to press her back into the mattress, my body on top of hers now, my weight pushing her down. Her hair fanned out around her head like a blonde halo. I wanted to whisper her name into her ear when I felt her getting closer—fuck, we hadn't exchanged names—so instead, I husked sweet praises into her hair, continuously brushing against her perfect little clit. She whimpered and wriggled, her nails digging into the base of my spine as I teased her little bud. I tugged and played with it until her breathing became more desperate.

"Oh, you like that, huh?" I breathed against her neck.

"Mmm-hmm, I'm so close..." was all she managed.

Her nails dug deeper. She moaned and buried her face into my neck, wiggling under me while her second climax washed over her. Her body felt limp even though her thighs continued to quiver around my hand. My body was still warming hers as I leaned over toward my bedside table and began rifling through the drawers. She knew exactly what I was looking for.

"Hurry please," she gasped as my hips rubbed against her.

"I've got you, babe," I mumbled. She couldn't wait to have my cock in her. My kind of girl.

I was back soon enough. I gave myself several strokes while her hands grasped at the bare skin of my ass, and my hard length settled at the vee of her legs. She heard the crinkle of the wrapper and reached out, enclosing her fingers around the package in my hand.

"I'll do it."

She made quick work of the foil wrapper, ripping it open effortlessly and reaching down to unroll it over my cock, before stroking it a few times with her hand.

I positioned my tip at her opening, my cock hard as steel. Ah, she was nice and wet. This felt fucking great already.

I waited until she met my eyes.

~

*W*hen I started awake, it was close to 2:30 a.m. Soft tits were pressed against the left side of my body. I found myself appreciating the feeling, before I even looked down at the blonde beauty tucked under my arm. Her hair covered half of her face and was splayed across the pillows beneath her head. She looked like an angel. Gently, I raised one hand to brush the locks away, smiling as the glitter in her hair caught the moonlight. She wrinkled her freckled nose adorably in her sleep. I leaned down to kiss one of the freckles.

When the woman shifted and turned over, the heat of her body left me slightly chilled, and I found myself reaching out for her—before thinking better of it. No. She deserved to have her rest. Instead, I silently stripped the sheets from my naked body and slipped out of bed, grabbing my glasses and sweatpants—yep, gray ones—on the way.

My steps were silent as I moved through the apartment. My muscles were sore, and I stretched my arms above my head, feeling a twinge in my lower back—it wasn't unpleasant, though. I reached back to rub my shoulder and felt the shallow indentations from where her nails had scored my flesh. They hadn't broken the skin, of course, but I could bet that they'd left their mark, at least for a day.

I easily located a glass in one of the upper cupboards and filled it with cool water from the fridge. As I took a long sip, my throat felt like it had been stripped raw tonight. There was gravel in the back of it that I couldn't quite rid myself of, no matter how many times I cleared my throat. I assumed it had something to do with the way the woman had been ripping groans and naughty little nothings from my vocal chords for the past several hours.

Glass in hand, I entered my home office and opened my laptop. One hour. One hour would be enough to refine the presentation I needed to get ready. Then, I would quietly sneak back to the beautiful nameless woman in my bed and catch up on sleep.

3

MY NAME? NO IDEA

*H*e'd literally screwed my brains out—and I couldn't be happier. I'm not kidding you. When I opened my eyes, I was glad I even remembered where I was.

But my own name? Nope. Gone.

I didn't know his name, either, but who cares, right?

The man's chest was moving up and down at an even pace. His heartbeat was under my ear, and my entire body seemed to ache with both pleasure and pain. Good *heavens*. Whoever *this* man was, he looked like someone sculpted by the gods themselves, delivered straight to me for the taking. While tall and intimidating, and an inhumanly furiously chiseled perfection of a jawline, the stranger was—without a doubt—one of the most handsome men I had ever laid eyes on. I wanted to stroke his jawbones, rub my soft cheek against them, and kiss them over and over again. Both sides. Oh, and those lips! I hadn't been too drunk the night before to forget how delicious his kisses were, or how my heart fluttered each time those dark, stormy eyes met mine.

Sure, he had pissed me off with the whole drink spilling thing... But then, suddenly, out of the blue, there he stood, imposing person at 6'4" with thick, jet black hair—wearing glasses!—black frames that made his chiseled face even more chisel-y.

I had a theory on men with glasses. A pathetic one. My gal-pal Zoe thought it was ridiculous. Maybe it was, but I had a shitty ex. That's how you come up with all these sorts of crazy things.

Stretching like a cat next to him in bed, I admired his naked sleeping body.

Anyhow, of course, it wasn't just the glasses. What had really won me over was how smoothly he'd handled the TP bouncer douche situation! Not gonna lie, he was clever as hell. Quick-witted! And not the least bit scared of that brick of a gorilla. He'd outsmarted him without even thinking. What's hotter than that?

I could have laid there and stared at him forever.

Or at least I could have, *if* I didn't have to pee. My legs still felt like jelly after hours of having the—*cross my heart and hope to die*—best sex ever. He was just the right amount of rough passion (so hot) mixed with heart-melting tenderness and intimacy (even *hotter*). But the animalistic force he'd attacked me with had taken its toll, despite how in shape I thought I was.

It was still very early morning—I knew that much.

I forced my tingling, sore body to roll out of bed with every intention of sneaking back in to wake him up for round two—*or four*—I'd lost count after the third orgasm. Stretching my arms high above my head with a satisfied smile on my face, I stopped to admire the gorgeous view of the city from his huge floor-to-ceiling bedroom windows. Manhattan. Manhattan was the heart of the city that never slept. I'd learned that the first night I'd gotten back to New York.

Scooping up my panties, shirt, and phone, I crept to the bathroom. I knew a place that size had to have more than one, and I didn't want the toilet flushing to wake him up. No, I had other plans for bringing him back to life. Much better plans. I stopped at the door one last time to observe him in bed.

I'll be back for you in a minute, Mister Hot Pants.

His place was nice, too. A super-expensive penthouse decorated in masculine deep blues, blacks, grays, and whites. I tried to take in as much of it as I could on my way to locating the other bathroom. I was so freaking happy I took the time to find it before waking him, because when I stopped and saw myself in the mirror—holy *hell*. Hello *hair*? It was even more frazzled and crazy looking than it usually was in the mornings. I had the freaking *worst* bedhead in the history of *ever*. I turned on the faucet and started smoothing it down, raking my fingers through the tangles, turning myself back into the put-together vixen I'd felt like the night before. Well, at least I tried to—I looked rough to say the least.

The countertops around the sink were lined with just the right number of products for both men and women—enough to accommodate guests, but not so much that I got the feeling he had random women coming and going from his place night after night.

Everywhere I looked, I checked off a pro or con in my head for the potential of seeing him again. So far, it was at least two to three more times in the win column as far as I could judge by his belongings. He was obviously an exceptionally clean, neat, and organized kind of guy, which was harder to find than you'd think. I never asked what he did for a living, but he was *obviously* more than just well-off. Throw in those devastatingly good looks of his and that very impressive, charming, big...*I.Q.*—I'd be crazy not to want to see him again.

Just so I wouldn't be walking around a stranger's house naked, I slid back into my panties and shirt and glanced at the notifications on my phone. Three texts from Nate, which sent my eyes rolling so far into the back of my head, it hurt.

Nate: Can we talk?

Nope. We did all the talking we needed to do days ago when I dumped your ass.

Nate: I miss you.

You sure as hell weren't missing me, when you did what you did.

Nate: I'm so sorry. I fucked up. Please answer me.

You're only sorry you got caught. You definitely fucked up. And you weren't sorry about all the ugly, ugly things you said to me. And I won't ever be speaking to you again if I can help it.

That was exactly what landed me in this guy's bed in the first place.

Yep, rebound sex to the rescue. After three years of being with Nate, only to find out he had a side chick, I was in a weird head-space and needed to get out with my best friend, Zoe. I normally wasn't a "one-night stand" kind of gal, but I decided the occasion called for even more spontaneity than usual. Cue the mysterious tall, dark, and handsome stranger collision—and here I was.

I promptly deleted Nate's texts and muted all notifications from him in my contacts, then turned my attention to another startling alert on my phone. My heart sank a little at the email from my boss in all caps—and bold letters—followed by several exclamation points and question marks (my pet peeve).

Deadline For This: Was Friday...

WHERE ARE YOU!?!?

Okay, sure.

If I'd answered his first three emails, or actually finished the project on time to begin with, he wouldn't be so mad. *Oops.* But it hadn't been a lack of time management or ability that always put me behind, despite what he insisted in all of my performance reviews.

It was the fact that he and the whole company were so stuck in their ways that all my ideas and initial drafts had been rejected from the get-go.

But I'd worry about that later.

At the moment, I was much more interested in digging up a little more information on Mr. Hottie through scanning the framed photos he kept on display in his living room. I didn't see any women, other than an older lady posed next to him, who was most likely his mother. She looked sweet and adorable in her pastel-pink blouse and wide smile.

Good, so he wasn't married and likely didn't have a girlfriend.

There was a photo of him standing next to a heavy, shiny motorbike, helmet in hands. Sexy! Okay, so without a shadow of a doubt, in about ten seconds, I was going to give him the best wake up surprise he's ever had in his whole life (wink-wink).

I was just about to saunter my ass back into bed when I froze.

A familiar photo sent sirens blaring off in my mind.

No. No, it can't be.

Please.

I leaned in closer to study the picture of him and two other guys posing with their motorcycles. *Noooooooo!* I'd seen that very photo before. Because the two other guys in the photo were none other than Oliver and Miles.

My brothers!

"*Shit,*" I quietly squeaked, throwing a hand over my mouth.

They're going to kill me.

I couldn't stop staring at the photo, no matter how badly I wanted to look away. What a train wreck—only I felt like I was still on the train and needed to find some way off of it, and *fast*! Really, really fast!

My body glitched for a moment, flailing in every direction all at once as my brain tried to catch up to tell it what to do. I knew all about my brothers' best friend Damon. I'd just never met him, and I certainly never expected to unknowingly tumble into bed with him.

Here was what I knew from them. Damon Copeland was the Chief Technology Officer of their company—extremely smart and driven, though maybe a little too driven. They always teased him for being even more obsessed with work than they were, which was saying something. The way Oliver and Miles described him, Damon sounded straitlaced and not very impulsive. His only "vice" would be his motorcycle. For some reason, I imagined him as an arrogant ass who was no fun. Well, let me tell you: he didn't feel "not very impulsive" to me. The man I'd been in bed with the night before certainly didn't have any trouble unwinding—or unwinding me in *all* the right ways.

Okay, calm down, Aria. This is simple. I took a deep breath. I knew I couldn't see him again—now that I knew who he was. I needed to get the hell out of there as fast as I could and forget this (*incredible*, best *sex* of my *life*) ever happened.

Then maybe your family will never find out.

Half of my clothes were with me, but the rest was still in his bedroom. The morning sun shining in through the windows was growing brighter by the minute, and I was terrified it might wake him up before I had time to make my not-so-grand exit.

I needed to act. Fast.

4

ARIA

Tiptoeing more carefully than I ever had in my entire life, I crept back into the bedroom like a stalker. I wanted Dorothy's red slippers to wish myself back home. This was *so* bad... How hard and fast everything had unraveled! Minutes ago, I thought I'd be sneaking back in here to seduce him into sweet, yummy morning sex, but now it was all about getting my stuff and hightailing it the hell out of there.

I opted for snatching everything up and putting on my clothes in the living room before bolting out the door. But, it proved to be a *teensy bit* harder than I expected to juggle my skirt, shoes, phone, and purse without making a sound. I managed—even after dropping one of my shoes and falling to the floor in a crouch, wide-eyed, and nearly dying of a heart attack—to grab everything and scramble back to the door without waking him.

After catching my breath, I stopped and glanced back at him one last time on my way out. *Why the hell did you have to turn out to be Damon Copeland?* Out of all the random men I could have had the hottest sex with, he just *had* to be my brothers' best friend! Dammit!

Shaking my head in disappointment at my bad luck, I slipped out the door. Tossing my phone and purse onto the floor, I reached for my skirt. But just before it touched my fingers, a terribly loud song started blasting through the whole apartment. Not just any song. *Stupid Love* by Lady Gaga, a ringtone remnant of my and Nate's relationship, which I hadn't had time to change yet, and now hated more than ever.

In a freaked-out shuffle, I grabbed everything, including my bag with the ridiculously loud phone, and darted out the front door. It wasn't until I'd made it into the hallway, the door slamming shut behind me, that I remembered I was wearing nothing but my T-shirt and panties. And with horrendous timing, I heard a door open, and a mother and her two children emerged from a room at the other end of the hall. Great. At least my phone had stopped ringing.

I threw myself back at the handle, only to realize it'd locked behind me. *Shitshitshitshitshit! Just my luck!*

The lady and two kids were rapidly approaching. Fortunately, they hadn't noticed me yet. They were too absorbed in the ball, the kids were kicking back and forth, and mum's nagging as she tried to dodge it.

I had two choices: either toss the rest of my things onto the middle of the hall and scramble to put on my skirt, at least, or I could take off running.

Having Damon poke his head out and catch me in that position (bent over with my naked ass cheeks on full display) was far more mortifying of a possibility than anything else, so I decided to take off running. I dipped into the alcove of the elevator and did a mad dash to throw everything on. I'd just managed to zip up my skirt when the mother and her kids appeared around the corner. They froze at the sight of me standing there, only half-dressed with my shoes and everything else in my arms, along with my disheveled hair and smudged makeup.

I *so* had sex hair (even though I'd tried to tame it) and last night's mascara down to my cheekbones.

That would or *should* have been bad enough. But no... The elevator doors *whooshed* open behind me, revealing a whole other cluster of people standing there, gawking at me.

Could this get any more embarrassing? Why, yes. Yes, it could.

Fuck. My. Life.

Laughing awkwardly, I shuffled to the side, mumbling "rough night," letting the woman and her kids get on.

They all appeared somewhat amused. Except the mom. She started pushing the button over and over, as many times as it took to get the doors to close as quickly as possible, protecting her children from witnessing more of what was clearly my walk of shame.

And what a walk of shame it was. *Kill me now.*

"Oh, you go on ahead." I smiled and waved as nonchalantly as possible. Like it was no big deal. Like I did this every day. "I'll catch the next one."

After I'd slipped into my shoes, I stood facing the corner until the next elevator arrived, just in case Damon came wandering out looking for me.

He didn't.

*T*hankfully, I managed to make it down and out into the lobby without any further humiliation—just in time for Lady Gaga to start belting out *Stupid Love* all over again.

"Hey, Zoe," I answered with a groan, still in shock over everything that had just happened.

"Yikes. You sound terrible, hon. Not what I was expecting."

"Yeah, me either," I huffed, still completely mortified from hopping on one leg to get my damn shoe on in front of a gaggle of spectators. I was a freaking disaster. "You won't believe the morning I had."

"Okay, gimmie *all* the details."

As I walked home, I explained everything that'd happened since she'd left me last night at the bar. It was disappointing for both of us. Everything had felt so promising, after Damon surprised me in the men's room. Of course, I hadn't known he was Damon then. I'd just thought he was *the* perfect cure to all things Nate.

And he had been.

The witty conversation full of sultry looks and suggestive tones. Then all the mind-blowing sex. His nice *rocket ship*. Boy, had he flown me over the moon and then some. *Dammit*. His *glasses*. I didn't bring up his glasses in front of Zoe. Like I said, she was no fan of my theory. She also wasn't a fan of my ex either, or all of the mean things he'd said to me. I'd really thought he was the one. I'd really loved him. I'd thought he was a *real* man. He was not. Zoe was the only one who knew how much my self-esteem had crumbled—a lot—after he left me for a much prettier girl. The asshole. I'd even started to think maybe I'd caught Nate with the other woman just in time. It was all supposed to land me in that bar, on that night—just so I could meet the man I was *really* supposed to be with. (Okay, not saying I was *supposed* to meet my dream guy in a bar, but you get what I mean.) *Well, thanks, universe!*

"I don't understand," Zoe said after I finished my story. "If this guy is such a big part of your brothers' lives, then wouldn't they love to see their little sister in his hands? Well, you know, not literally in his hands. Not like that. But, they know he's a good guy, or they wouldn't be best friends, right?"

"You don't understand, Zoe. I'm not just the little sister. I'm the *baby* sister. You know how overprotective they are of me. Especially Oliver. And this guy isn't just their friend. He works with them. Which means he works *for* my father. That's a serious conflict of interest on *so* many levels."

"How did you *not* know it was him?"

"Well, you know I was at that one job in LA for a few years. I've heard my brothers talking about him, but our paths just never crossed. Or if they have, I don't remember meeting him. Although looking at him now, it's hard to believe I could forget somebody like him."

"Haven't you ever seen a picture of him before?"

"Maybe I have. I never paid attention. No close ups for sure. I've seen photos of all the guys together in sunglasses with their bikes," I explained. "I didn't recognize him in the photo until I saw it at his place. Besides, it's not like I follow Miles or Oliver on Insta or Snap. Heck no. Then they'd follow me back and be that much more in my business."

"You could just tell them what happened," she suggested. "Maybe they'd think it was funny. And they might be cool with you seeing him again."

"Are you *kidding* me? After three years, they never warmed up to the idea of me being with Nate," I reminded her.

"Yeah, but that was Nate. Everybody hated him."

"They did not. Not everybody!"

"They did."

"Well, thanks again for telling me that *after* we broke up." I rolled my eyes, even though she couldn't see me. "I just don't see my brothers being too happy about me dating the guy. No brother likes their best friend screwing their little sister. Come on."

"Okay, fine, I get it. It's just a bummer. I thought getting down and dirty with a hot bad boy would be good for you," she said with a hint of a whine.

"Oh, believe me—so did I." I unlocked my front door, tossing my stuff inside. Just thinking about last night still gave me the warm fuzzies and hot tingles—all the feelings that would be amazing had this morning not pooh-poohed all over it, destroying my day-dreamy fantasies with a fury.

"You gonna be okay?" she asked in a serious tone.

I may have been determined to bounce back quick, but the whole thing with Nate really had taken its toll on me—on top of my preexisting misery from hating my job with a burning passion.

"I'll be fine." I sighed. "The whole point was to move on and get him and that bubbly dental hygienist of his off my mind. And I think the shock of this morning was enough to do just that."

"Okay. As long as you're all right. It'll probably be best if you try getting under another guy tonight. You know, to get over this one."

"Zoe!"

"*Kidding.* I gotta run, but call me later."

"You're a nut! Will do. Love you. Bye."

I ended the call and took a long look around my apartment. At least it was still spotless from the mad cleaning spree I'd gone on a few days ago—a desperate move to scrub away every last trace of my cheating ex. My phone dinged again with another angry message from my boss. Too bad I couldn't have scrubbed him away, too.

Grabbing a pint of ice cream from the fridge, I thought Ben and Jerry's *Chocolate Salted 'n Swirled* would be the perfect breakfast remedy for my horrible morning. And it was.

I would force myself to sit down and work on my overdue project, after I'd finished the ice cream, and then everything would feel better.

Just as long as my brothers *never, ever* found out about last night.

I only wished I could be as oblivious as they were.

As I sank onto the couch, digging another spoonful into my ice cream breakfast, I marveled over the fact that knowing Damon was the big forbidden fruit, and suddenly, it only made my memories of the night before even hotter.

Sigh.

I'd just have to take that as the one good souvenir from the entire traumatic experience.

Sitting all alone on my couch, I imagined how he was still asleep in bed, and hadn't yet noticed my disappearance. We'd both barely slept that night, so it was possible he wasn't up yet. Would he think of me when he woke up? Would he be disappointed that I'd left? Or would he be mad? Or glad? Oh Jesus, what if he was glad that I'd left? Relieved?

A man like him couldn't probably have cared less.

Cut your losses, Sweet Cheeks, I thought to myself, and with the flavor of the ice cream still on my tongue, I headed for the shower.

5

DAMON

I woke up with a dull pounding in my head from sleeping less than usual. One night of mind-blowing sex had robbed me of all of my senses. Even in my sleep-deprived state I had no problem remembering how fantastic the sex had been. The thought alone stirred my cock into a semi.

The chick had been feral in bed, so willing, like a wild animal ravaging me. I was happy to match her enthusiasm, and judging by the lingering soreness in my body, I not only made up for missing my morning workout, but I wouldn't need to visit the gym for at least another week.

Even more than the sex, I remembered how intriguing she was.

She was the kind of woman I could look forward to having breakfast with and learning more about. We hadn't talked about much of anything substantial the night before, and I was curious to know who she was. Eyes still closed, I rolled over in anticipation of a nice morning BJ followed by more morning-after sex, where I'd have to introduce myself since we skipped right over that part.

Not that I had minded. Not in the least. Actually, that'd been part of the thrill. Like I said, I'd never been a long-term guy.

But now, I was interested in finding out who she was.

When I opened my eyes, I was met with the sight of an empty bed.

That was new.

Where'd she go?

She wasn't in my en suite bathroom, so I went searching through the rest of my penthouse. But she was gone. She had disappeared just as quickly as she'd caught my eye and fallen into my bed.

Standing in the middle of my empty place, I scratched my head and tried to shake the tinge of disappointment I felt. I'd been known to do that sort of thing to women a time or two in my youth —ducking out early to avoid early morning small talk or the unbearable conversation about when we might see each other again.

But it'd never been done to me. Karma was a bitch. A bitch with principles.

Okay, so I hadn't gotten her name, much less her phone number. That was that. She wasn't a regular at the bar. I'd just have to accept the smoking-hot encounter for what it was, along with the reality that I'd likely never see her again.

Oh, well. Fuck it.

I cut my losses and hopped in the shower.

6

DAMON

*T*hree months later

*O*liver, Miles, and I were walking through the lobby of our company headquarters when Miles stopped suddenly and nudged my arm.

"How can you *not* see the way that chick checks you out every time we walk by?" he mumbled to me.

"Shut up." I glared at my watch and stepped inside the elevator. "It's not that I don't see it. It's that I don't shit where I eat."

"But she doesn't work directly for you. And *look* at her," Miles grunted.

I knew Miles. Always up for some fuckery. I knew he was just talking shit to rile me up—and I wasn't going to get into it. Why would I? None of us would ever touch an employee, working directly or indirectly for us. It was an unwritten rule. Using our positions to hit on our employees was a hard, fucking no, and we all respected that.

"That's why *she* doesn't look at you like that," Oliver piped in, pressing the button for our floor. "She knows it'd be game over. So...no fun. No chase."

"She doesn't pay attention to me because I'm taken," Miles said. "And happily so. That's the vibe I'm sending."

"With Damon here, she can look and flirt all day, and nothing will happen," Oliver continued, ignoring Miles's comment. "And it's not just because of our principles. But, if he ever *did* make a move, hypothetically, it'd be that much more exciting because she gave up on it ever happening."

I rolled my eyes at them and was relieved when the elevator doors closed, blocking the woman's body from our view. Out of sight, out of mind, out of stupid comments.

"Are we going out tonight? With our ladies?" Miles asked, and Oliver gave him a "sounds good" nod. "There's a new spot opening up across town, or there's that one place we liked over by—"

"I'll most likely be working late tonight," I said, cutting him off. "And every night this week. There's too much happening on my end with this new construction for Young Industries. Until we get all the plans finalized and turned over to our client, the contract is on hold. And no contract means no money. At least not for certain."

"Fair enough." Miles shrugged as the elevator doors opened, and we strolled onto the main floor. The top floor, to be exact, where our personal offices were located. "But when you close the deal," he continued, "we're hitting the clubs."

"We'll see." I waved over my shoulder, heading straight to my office, and leaving the two of them behind.

Truthfully, the whole disappearing act that chick pulled on me a few months ago had left a sour taste in my mouth. More than I wanted to admit. After the months or years of focusing on work and just dating casually, I had decided that something serious just wasn't in my plans—only to finally meet a girl who piqued my interest, and she ran for the hills without even telling me her name.

Of course, I'd gone back to that bar. Several times, in fact.

Never saw her again.

Don't get me wrong, I hadn't been heartbroken about it by any means. It'd just been another reminder that women were too complicated, and I was better off without them. At least without expecting anything more than the occasional romp in the sack when the need arose.

But for the time being, I was preoccupied enough with work. And when I wasn't working, the gym and my morning runs had been sufficient in helping me blow off steam. Of course, I was human and could only go so long without sex, and since I hadn't gotten any action for too long, it *was* about time to change my circumstances. But, the only thing on my mind right then was the progress report meeting with my chief engineer.

$\mathcal{I}$ pulled out all the relevant files and waited for Bernadette, my admin assistant, to buzz him in. Bernadette was a married woman; short and in her early fifties, she was originally from Edinburgh. She did her job well, was persistent and always on-the-nose.

Thankfully, my chief engineer arrived five minutes early rather than five minutes late.

Cornelius Cackowski was a younger guy, a bit on the scrawny side, but he was whip-smart and indispensable to my team. He seemed a little nervous as he came in and took the seat in front of my desk, but I didn't think anything of it. He'd always been socially awkward. Nothing uncommon in a team of talents. In fact, a good sign, mostly. Grinders typically didn't spend all day socializing. Cornelius was one of our top people. I could only hope that nothing else had triggered his agitation. I wasn't eager to hear him report another set of delays.

"Whatchya got for me, Cornelius?" I asked, popping my knuckles and preparing to dive right in.

He fidgeted in his seat and cleared his throat. "Yes, sir, uh, well... I know you requested a progress update... So, I put everything together in this report for you." He slid a white binder across my desk.

Furrowing my brow, I slowly picked it up.

The binder was thick—it wasn't just a simple printed report. He'd clearly put a lot of time and effort into his work, but it would take days to go through it. "What's this? Why a printed report? You could have sent me a digital file in less than half the time it took to put this together, or better yet, just review the important information with me in person. Which is why you're sitting across from me right now."

"I thought the folder would be helpful when you review potential candidates," he explained, not making the least bit of sense to me. "The thing is...I needed to meet with you today because...I'm turning in my notice."

What the fuck? "Notice?" I blinked.

"I received a job offer in Belgium," he continued, "which as you may remember, is where my fiancée is currently working. I start next week."

"Next week?" I sat back in my chair, scrubbing my hand down my face, annoyed. "That's hardly a notice at all. Come on, Cornelius. You can't do this to me right now. You know we have our hands full with finalizing these plans for Young, and you're my chief engineer.

We barely have time to finish everything and meet the deadline, much less put the project on hold and find a replacement for you."

"I do understand," he said awkwardly, avoiding eye contact. "And I'm sorry for the position this puts you in. But you know I've wanted to transfer so I could be closer to my fiancée for a while now. She's the one, you know? The opportunity came up for me to do it, so I'm taking it. Some things are more important than work..., you know..."

"And?"

"And, the offer I got is quite generous."

I perked up at that, catching a glimmer of hope. "How generous? I'll double whatever they're offering. At least for the remainder of this project."

"That would be amazing, Mr. Copeland...if only we were in Belgium. As I said, it's not just about my career and money."

"Tell me how much you want." I tried again, assuming this was only a haggling tactic he'd planned out ahead of time. "With enough money, you could relocate your girlfriend here."

"Fiancée, sir..." He cleared his throat again and sat forward in his seat.

"Your fiancée. Hell, you could fly out to see each other every weekend."

He shook his head, dropping his chin. "Sorry, Mr. Copeland. She made, I mean, *we* made this decision together, and our minds are made up. This is the best move for our future, even if it's not the best move for you or this project. I apologize."

I let out another groaning sigh, but I knew there was no chance in hell I'd convince him. He was whipped. Clearly. Was he even wearing pants? No matter what I said, this kid wasn't going to budge. "Okay then. Keep working throughout the remainder of the week. I'll try to get a few candidates in before your last day so you'll be able to transfer what you can to them firsthand."

Even as I said it, I knew it would be impossible. We had a month of wiggle room—at best—to push the deadline before the client started getting antsy and looking elsewhere. A hefty amount was on the line. If we could get the job posting up by the end of the day, there'd be a mountain of candidates to sort through. And only a slim fraction would be qualified enough to meet my standards, much less pick up a project of this magnitude so late in the game, when we were already behind to begin with.

Fuck.

I had to bite my bitter tongue to keep from warning Cornelius about how stupid it was to uproot his entire life just for some girl.

No pussy was worth losing your balls.

Instead, I maintained my professionalism and got to my feet, buttoned my suit jacket, and extended a firm handshake to him across my desk. "Well, that's that then. I wish you the best of luck. We'll see what we can come up with this week."

"Thank you, sir. And...sorry again." He nodded, shaking my hand before bolting out of my office.

Poor kid. I knew I made him nervous, but that was a stupid-ass decision, pulling some shit like this on such short notice.

The moment he skulked around the corner, I smashed the button on my phone to page Bernadette. "We need a posting for Cornelius's job on the website immediately," I barked. "Get with HR to make that happen. Pronto."

"Okey-dokey, Mr. Cope—"

I ended the call before she even had a chance to finish her sentence. She'd been working for me long enough to know the tone of my voice meant to get to it, no questions asked, and no fucking around. "Okey-dokey?" Yeah, no. That was a response I *never* wanted to hear.

Settling back into my chair, my mind reeled with a massive list of issues that would now compound and become neglected, while I attempted to put out this dumpster fire of a situation.

42

7

DAMON

*B*y the following afternoon, the fire had reached massive proportions. It was fucking huge. I'd scrambled to review the resumes as they trickled in and conducted a few phone interviews. They'd gone from epic fails to comically tragic. The clock was ticking. If I didn't come up with something quick, the whole deal would be dangerously close to imploding.

I had Bernadette set up a meeting with our CEO, Mr. Humphries, Miles and Oliver's father.

Going to him for help was not something I enjoyed. I *hated* it. But I knew he'd understand, given the circumstances. Thankfully, he seemed to be in a good mood when his secretary showed me into his office.

"Damon! Good to see you. Have a seat." He waved me over to the expensive mahogany leather chair across from him, before walking to his minibar and pouring us a drink.

"How's the wife?" I asked.

"Couldn't be better. My PA filled me in on your troubles. I'd say you could use one of these."

Charles Henry Humphries was your classic family man. He and his wife had been together for over thirty years and still had a good marriage. In fact, I'd never seen the man without his wedding ring —some men in his position liked to take it off on occasion as I'd witnessed more often than I would have liked—and he always kept a picture of Helen on his desk. He was charming, smooth, and debonair with a taste for the finer things in life. It was what'd driven him to build his empire, Humphries Properties, and I never let myself forget the leap of faith he'd taken in hiring me. Disappointing him didn't just mean failing at work, it meant letting down a family friend.

More than that.

He was like a second father to me.

I eyed the glass of top-shelf whiskey he held out in front of me and considered politely turning it down. I needed to be sharp-minded to stay ahead of the game, and I still had a shit-ton of work to do before I could leave for the day.

But damn, did it ever look good.

"Actually, yeah," I relented, blowing out a long breath. "I think this is exactly what I need, now that you mention it."

He took the seat next to me as opposed to meeting with me from behind his desk. It was another part of his personality that I admired. His seemingly blasé approach to life and business could fool you into letting your guard down, but I knew he was just as ruthless and determined as I was.

"I hoped you might have a referral for me. Something to go off of beyond these padded resumes and dead-end candidates."

"You know, Damon, I just might," he said after a few seconds, tapping his index finger on his chin. "Have you ever met my daughter, Aria?"

"No, I don't believe I have. Miles and Oliver have mentioned her over the years, though."

"Kids these days." He chuckled. "Don't ever have kids, Damon. Find a girl, get married. Hopefully, you meet a wonderful one like I did. My Helen has been with me through thick and thin. But don't have kids. They'll turn your hair gray." He laughed and smoothed his hand across his slick silver hair. "My Aria is so smart it's almost frightening. She finished high school at sixteen and had her undergrad completed by the time she was twenty. A master's in computer engineering in only eighteen months, then she ran off to LA to work for a while. Now here we are several years later, and she still can't hold down a job. Says she can't find a company that's the right fit." He waved his hand in a dismissive gesture.

"I can't say I understand."

"It's the same thing with this Cackowski guy. Abandoning a job like his? After a few years he could have landed any position in the world at a salary damn near close to what you're making."

"Or more," I teased.

"Why did he quit?" he asked.

"He's moving to another city. He's got a fiancée waiting there."

Mr. Humphries chuckled again and shook his head. "I can't say that I haven't committed my share of foolery in the name of love when I was young." He glanced at the picture of his wife holding a bouquet of red and white flowers. "But, I'm proud to say that I've never lost my head. Today, the young folk, they're all heart, no brains. Although Aria has the brains, she doesn't use it to her full potential. She just up and quit her job as head of engineering at Cyrus Enterprises. I warned her it would be a reckless decision, but of course, she doesn't listen to her old man. She's always been spontaneous like that."

I tried not to tap my foot as I sipped my drink. I could sympathize for his position with his daughter, but it didn't exactly help my situation. And if he was going where I thought he might be—trying to pawn the young woman off on me... *Fuck.*

It would be a perfect pain-in-the-ass situation.

That was the last thing I needed. I wasn't happy about it to say the least, but sitting face-to-face with Mr. Humphries—what choice did I have but to hear him out?

None. Zero.

"*A*nyway," Mr. Humphries continued, shifting forward in his seat. "Being as stubborn as she is, she wouldn't work for my company after school because she had this grand idea about building a name for herself on her own. But we haven't discussed it in a couple of years. I finally gave up. Maybe now that she's had some time out there in the workforce, she'll change her tune. Especially after this last fiasco. I'll approach her about your position," he grinned, "and see if she's willing to consider it. It's an excellent idea. But don't get your hopes up, Damon. I doubt she'll have an interest in a long-term situation, seeing as not much of anything seems to hold her interest for long periods of time. But, it would get you by in the interim for this project at least."

He looked at me, waiting for a response.

"That'd be great," I answered, attempting to mask my doubt.

Not that he painted the worst picture of her as a reliable employee—she at least sounded *somewhat* qualified. Still, I didn't want to delude myself into thinking I'd manage this curveball somehow. I should do the opposite, in fact. Being the boss of the

CEO's daughter? That was a bag of "what the fuck" I didn't want anywhere near me.

If anything, I should be preparing for the worst.

In my mind, I sighed. What kind of shitshow was I getting myself into?

But, there was *one* perk.

Mr. Humphries had recommended her and openly admitted she had a penchant for job-hopping. So, if she didn't work out, then he wouldn't be surprised.

"Please," I said, "let me know if she's interested."

8

DAMON

a few days later, I was stuck in yet another insufferable interview. I watched as the candidate flipped through the binder Cornelius had put together on Young, trying not to appear completely lost. But I could see it in his eyes—and by the sweat running down his temple. Too many applicants had an expensive education, but no firsthand experience. Jumping in on a project like this was way over their heads.

"This would...this would be no problem at all," the guy stuttered, not sounding the least bit convincing.

"Really? Well, that's great." I humored him. "Why don't you give me a run-down of your game plan? I understand it'll take some time to really go in depth but explain your initial thoughts."

I didn't expect anything detailed. In all fairness, it wouldn't be reasonable to expect him to grasp and come up with a perfect scenario after reviewing the information for only a few minutes. But it'd give me an indication if the overall idea of the project even made sense to him.

Ding.

Just as the mortified expression washed over his face, an instant message from Bernadette popped up on my computer screen.

Mr. Humphries had informed us yesterday that his daughter Aria was interested in temporarily taking on the position, so I'd asked her to set up a meeting.

Apparently, she'd just arrived. Obviously, she could skip the preliminary screening, seeing as the CEO of the company vouched for her.

I had been expecting her at 11 a.m. It was ten past.

I shifted my attention back to the guy sitting across from me, who was still rambling on about general bullshit, with no specifics or anything meaningful regarding how he'd actually tackle picking up the project. It was time to end this interview. Clearly the guy wasn't qualified, and I didn't want to waste his time—or mine.

Holding up my hand, I stopped him. "Thank you. That'll be enough for now. I hate to cut this short, but I have something urgent that's come up." I stood to give the customary send-off hand-shake. "We'll be in touch if we decide to move forward."

He thanked me and rushed out of the room like he was running for his life. I think he knew he was in way over his head and likely felt relieved to be off the chopping block.

I pressed the button to buzz my assistant. "Go ahead and send Ms. Humphries in, Bernadette."

Sitting back in my chair, I didn't expect much. She was likely out of shape, dull as shit, with thick unfashionable glasses, and wearing her hair in a boring style. Not that it mattered to be honest. I sounded like an asshole. The stress was getting to me. Still, this meeting with Mr. Humphries' daughter, given everything he'd said about her education and background, would hopefully turn out to be a more productive use of my time than the unqualified appli-cants I'd been interviewing for days.

Knock. Knock. Knock.

Bernadette opened the door, ushering the young woman in.

She entered with her head down at first, her honey-blonde hair hanging in her face.

"Aria Humphries," I got up to greet her. "Thank you for—" My mouth dropped open as she lifted her face and brushed her shiny hair to the side.

Freckles.

Millions of them.

It was *her*.

The woman from the bar.

The knockout with gorgeous tits and ass to match.

The disappearing act one-night stand.

Fuck.

My brain short-circuited with shock as the factors at play settled in, one at a time.

For one, what were the odds that she'd show up here for a potential job after what'd happened between us?

Second, I was even more taken aback by her beauty than I'd been that night at the bar.

Third, my cock twitched. Twice. Okay, three times.

She'd be stunning at any hour, in any room. Nobody could argue with that. But seeing her in the daylight, in our regular professions, *and* with both of us stone-cold sober, she was even more impressive. No. Not just impressive. She was a goddess. The glow of her skin. The way she held herself. The way she looked at me.

My eyes reached her bright blue gaze, waiting for any hint of recognition to wash over her.

"Mr. Copeland." She smiled, reaching out her soft and graceful hand I remembered so well. "It's so nice to meet you."

What the fuck?

She apparently remembered nothing about me.

The brush of her skin set off the same rush of electricity—straight to my dick—like I'd felt that night. Was she really immune to it? Had she been so drunk back then she recalled nothing about our evening? I'd never been one to take advantage of women once they were past a certain point of drunkenness.

How could she honestly not remember me at all?

When she let go of my hand and repositioned, my eyes landed on her chest, and I could see her nipples pressing against the fabric of her blouse.

"Thank you, Bernadette." I nodded to excuse her, clearing my throat.

As I returned to my seat behind my desk, my brain fired off a million lines I could throw out to break the ice. Maybe she was just feigning blissful ignorance to save us both the embarrassment. I thought addressing the matter right away would be a better approach, but then the third and final, most important, realization sank in.

She was Charles Henry Humphries's daughter. The founder and owner of the company.

For fuck's sake.

Not just that, she was the baby sister of my two best buddies. And I'd unknowingly fucked her (and by fucked her I didn't mean that I made sweet sappy-ass love to her—no, I meant I fucked the shit out of her. For hours on end. Hell, she'd almost passed out she came so hard. Multiple times.).

To make matters worse, I was interviewing her to potentially be her fucking boss.

I swallowed hard and tried to regain my composure. Any flirtation suddenly seemed like the worst possible way to proceed. Especially since she didn't seem to remember me. She stared back at me expectantly, waiting for the interview to begin like I was any other man.

What the hell?

"I'll just take a look at your resume," I decided aloud, trying to recover as smoothly as possible. If she was going to carry on like nothing happened, I'd have to do the same. "Mr. Humphries..." I cleared my throat. "Your father has already informed me of your qualifications." I slid Cornelius's binder across my desk, desperate for a bit of relief from trying to find words. "Maybe you can just jump right in and start reviewing this. Let me know your thoughts. It seems to be the most intimidating part of the process to my previous interviewees. I understand jumping in on a project at this stage can be challenging."

She reached for the binder and started flipping through it.

I cut my eyes from her resume and noticed her taking her time. She scanned through each page, occasionally going back and forth before moving forward again. Her expression was unreadable, which was more promising than the look of intimidation everybody else had displayed. I smirked to myself when she accidentally dropped a pen and lunged to retrieve it, almost letting the binder of papers slide from her lap. She quickly recovered and continued reading.

"If you know what you're doing, the stage of the project really shouldn't matter," she suggested, cool and calm. "And it looks like your previous engineer knew what they were doing. It'll be a time crunch, for sure. But he left us in a good spot to proceed."

It was the first reassuring thing I'd heard all week.

That was reason enough to want to forget any awkwardness and decide that she was hired on the spot.

"So, you could meet the deadline?" I asked, remaining somewhat skeptical. "We could possibly move it forward by a week or so, but much further would be risky. A bigger risk than I'm willing to take at this point."

Those damned eyes met mine again, just as disarming as ever. Even without all the crazy circumstances, she was the most promising—no, the *only* promising candidate to cross my path so far.

"It *will* be challenging, but it's certainly doable," she assured me with confidence, closing the binder and setting it back on my desk. "I could have a revised timeline and plan of approach drawn up for you by the end of the day."

Sounded fucking perfect to me.

I carried on with the interview, trying my damnedest to treat her like anybody else and ignoring her gorgeous curves that'd been teasing me relentlessly. I didn't address the elephant in the room. Why would I? Just as she'd been in the bar—and in my bed—she was honest and straightforward. Nothing seemed to throw or faze her. It was just as refreshing in a professional setting as it'd been when I was just talking to a beautiful woman over drinks.

And yet, as I listened to her speak, casual as ever, I couldn't shake my annoyance with her seemingly absent memory of me. That night had definitely stood out in *my* mind as more mind-blowing than your average hookup.

Something was off, but I was in no rush to question it. At least not right now. There were more pressing matters to attend to.

9

ARIA

I was *dying.*

I'd always been good at remaining calm and collected on the outside, no matter how I was feeling on the inside. It was one of the reasons why some people thought I could be overly confident. But that skill was being put to the test more than ever today.

Positioned across from Damon in the interview, I felt like I was in the spotlight—literally—as the sun streamed in on me from his impressive office view. He had a glow around his tall, muscular body—intimidating in size, even when he was sitting behind his desk, huffing and puffing, all broody and unapproachable. I tried to focus on his words as he explained the details of the current project, but instead, I found myself staring at his lips. *God, those lips.* The same ones that'd been between my legs, bringing me such mind-numbing pleasure.

Just forget it ever happened, Aria.

I wouldn't acknowledge that this man had been inside me. All night.

I wouldn't acknowledge that I knew what his O-face looked like and what sounds he made when he came.

Least of all, I wouldn't acknowledge that I hadn't come so hard in my life.

Be professional, I chided myself. *Don't bring up what happened. He didn't mention it—and you're sure as* hell *not mentioning it.*

He was my boss now, assuming everything went well today.

I swallowed the lump in my throat, as he continued to catch me up on everything.

Damon's voice had a sexy, dragon-y, deep rasp to it, and the sound flowed from his mouth like the taste of melted chocolate. *Yum...* It made everything he said that much more appealing to listen to. One of the sexiest men on earth speaking at length about a topic that just so happened to be one of my biggest passions in life? *Yes, please.*

"We hooked Mr. Young on the basis that our team had developed some of the most innovative design software available on the market today." As he spoke, his voice sent another wave of desire straight to my core. "It's meant to deliver higher-quality results on a much faster timeline. So, you can understand why it's important that we deliver by the deadline."

"Of course," I replied, trying my best to keep my tone smooth and steady. "You wouldn't want to break any promises with a prospective client at this stage. Not only would they look elsewhere, but it'd also damage your reputation with potential future clients."

"Precisely," he said with a nod.

A strange expression washed over his face—one I knew I had to capitalize on. As much as I wanted to avoid the obvious—the fact we'd been in bed together not too long ago—the more focus that was drawn to our night, the less I'd be able to concentrate around him.

Do not drop that pen again.

"Something wrong?" I asked, raising a brow, acting like his presence didn't faze me at all, like the sound of his voice wasn't causing beats of pressure to thrum against my center. Yep, I was *perfectly* fine. *Totally.*

"No, it's just that..." He cleared his throat, shaking his head. "Nothing. So, how does everything sound? Think you're up for taking it on?"

"I'm up for it," I told him, recrossing my legs and squeezing my thighs together. "You won't be disappointed."

"I trust you're right." He stood from his seat, buttoning his suit jacket. Damon towered over me, and my mind started drifting back into a lust-filled haze. So much so that I could feel my chest becoming flushed and my hands getting clammy.

Did he just look at my boobs? No, it must be my imagination.

I attempted to subtly slide my palms along the front of my skirt as I rose to my feet, wiping away the dampness before shaking his hand. His handshake was firm and dominant, sending a jolt of electricity racing down my spine and between my legs.

"Thanks for meeting with me today," he said. "Can you start tomorrow?"

"Tomorrow it is." I smiled politely. "And I'll send over my initial notes by the end of the day, as promised."

Damon stepped from behind his desk to show me to the door. I could feel the heat emanating from his body as he followed me. *Is he staring at my legs?* To make matters worse, when I reached for the doorknob, so did he. I jerked my hand back the moment I felt his close around it, but that only sent me bumping straight into his chest. With his arm still stretched out around me, I was trapped.

Brushing a strand of hair behind my ear, I tried not to reveal how flustered I was by his closeness.

"Sorry," he murmured, finally opening the door and setting me free.

I could feel his eyes burning into me as I walked down the hall and back to the lobby. As long as my stilettos didn't slip on the slick marble flooring, I'd be in the clear. Soon, I would be safely tucked inside the elevator, away from his gaze, and the sight of that deliciously muscular body.

"*A*ria!" my brother called out to me just as I reached the elevator, stopping me dead in my tracks.

Dammit. I knew it was a likely possibility that I would run into one of them at the headquarters of Humphries Properties. I just hoped I wouldn't be so flustered, hot, and bothered when I did.

"Oliver." I pivoted with a smile. I glanced back to Damon's office, but his door was already closed.

"I heard you'd be here interviewing today. How'd it go?"

"Great. I start tomorrow, but I promised I'd turn in my initial report by the end of the day...so I really can't stay and chat long," I explained, reaching out to press the button to call the elevator.

"Damon didn't give you too hard of a time, did he?"

"Hmm?"

"He's all work and no play at times. It can be a *little* off-putting when you first meet him. But he's the *best* at what he does."

My brain started firing off in a thousand different directions I didn't want it to. *Damon. Hard...hard parts of his body... Oh, he definitely knows how to play... Yep, in all the best ways. And I don't know about off-putting, but he sure does know how to get* me *off*.

My cheeks were hot and my darn freckles likely bright red by the time the elevator dinged.

"Are you all right, Sis?"

The doors slid open. "Nope, can't do lunch today," I replied in a sing-song voice, attempting to breeze right past him. "But hey, soon I'll be around every day. I'm sure we'll have a chance to grab lunch soon."

"What? I didn't even—"

I thought I was getting away free and clear, but then I noticed my other brother rushing toward us. "Wait up!" Miles called out from across the lobby. "Hold the elevator."

Oh, no. I said "soon" twice and talked about lunch? Geez, I wanted to slap myself. *Just make it obvious, why don't you.* So much for remaining calm and collected on the outside. I was getting on my own damn nerves. I had to get away from them and fast!

"We'll ride down with you," Oliver decided.

There was no feasible excuse as to why they couldn't, but just when I thought it couldn't possibly get any worse, our father came around the corner. Did the three of them always go to lunch at the same time like clockwork?

The universe hates me today...

"Hey, Aria." Dad gave me a happy nod.

I guessed there was nothing *that* absurd about it, but being trapped in a small box alongside both of my brothers *and* my father with wet panties, while my body was *still* on fire from Damon's presence was my worst nightmare. Well, okay...maybe not the *worst*. That would be them catching on to what'd happened between us or just how turned on I was.

So. Freaking. Embarrassing.

"I just saw Damon's message about your interview," Dad said

with a satisfied smile. "I'm glad to hear it went well. You'll be in good hands with him."

"I know I will." *Jesus Christ. This was getting worse and worse.* I couldn't be sure if a bug flew in my mouth or if I was just choking on my own spit, but suddenly my throat seized up and sent me into a coughing fit. I managed to recover quickly enough, but not without all three of them staring at me like I'd lost my mind.

"Excuse me." I covered my mouth, hacking again. "Allergies. My throat's been dry."

"He's a rough boss," Oliver added. "But he rewards his staff when they come through for him. It makes up for the rest of it."

I was *screaming* on the inside. After keeping myself together so well while I'd been in the same room with Damon, here I was unraveling at the seams with incessant vivid fantasies of just how rough he could get—and the promise of a reward after. Bending me over his desk and spanking me, followed by mind-blowing orgasms? *Sign me up. Just not while I'm crammed in a tight elevator, surrounded on all sides by my brothers and father. I think I'm going to die of a heat stroke in here... Or a heart attack. It could go either way.*

"I'm confident you'll find him satisfactory and agreeable," Dad continued. "Just be sure to give him your best."

"Good advice," Miles said. "You should listen, Aria."

If you guys only knew... But I wished they'd stop talking and get out of my bubble. I wanted to run and hide before I said something stupid—or worse... No. That would be bad.

What the hell was wrong with me? There was no way seeing Damon had destroyed my sanity to a level where I couldn't carry on a freaking conversation. *Come on, Aria, get your shit together.*

The elevator jerked, causing my family to sway and slightly close in on me. I cringed at the brush of their arms against me and couldn't have been more relieved when it dinged. *Finally*, the doors opened again. Maybe now I would really, *truly* be free, since my first escape had been foiled.

"Bye, you guys." I started to bolt between the sliding doors and make a mad dash across the lobby. "Gotta run. I'll talk to you later."

But I was foiled *again*. "Aria, wait a moment." Our father reached out and grabbed me by the arm, snatching me back a step just as everybody filed out. *Ah, shit.* I wanted to stomp my feet. *And dammit!* I couldn't catch a freaking break. Had I given myself away? Did he pick up on how weird I was acting?

"If you're not free right now," Dad continued, "let's all have dinner tonight. To celebrate you coming on to work with us."

"It's only temporary," I reminded him. *Phew. I'm seriously sweating now. Can they not leave me alone?*

"Drinks and dinner sound good to me," Oliver agreed.

"Especially the drinks." Miles chimed in, too.

Oh, for shit's sake. I wanted to strangle my brothers.

Surrounded by their expectant expressions, I knew I had no *real* reason to turn them down. The "encounter" that had happened with Damon was undoable, as was my commitment to this project. The damage was done. I couldn't let that make me weird around my family. But, I'd definitely need to change my, um, *clothes*.

"Fine." I sighed. "Dinner."

"Six o'clock?" Dad asked.

"Yes." I gave him a quick nod.

"Meet us here, and we'll go together when we're finished with work," Dad suggested. "Maybe Damon could come along, too."

"No!" I blurted, eliciting a wide-eyed response from all three of them.

I softened into a blushing smile and an awkward laugh. "I mean...I just don't want any strange rumors to start about me being all buddy-buddy with my boss, you know? It's bad enough that you're all in positions of authority here, and he's a family friend."

"I'd put my neck out for him, he's not the gossip-creating kind," Oliver said, and Dad and Miles nodded.

"Let's keep it just us," I insisted. "For now." *Or like...forever*, I thought to myself.

"You're overthinking it, but suit yourself. See you tonight, sweetheart!" my dad called out as I started racing for the front doors.

I caught a glimpse of their confused expressions as I "fled" the scene. I'd have to master the art of balancing their presence with the effect Damon had on me if I was ever going to survive this gig.

10

ARIA

I could only hope my ruffled, unsettled state hadn't been as noticeable to everybody else as it was to me.

But my exit had been less than graceful to say the least.

The moment I stepped through the revolving doors of the building and the rush of fresh air slapped me in the face, I felt like I could breathe again. I had to formulate some kind of plan to keep myself together in the days to come.

When my father had first called and proposed the meeting with Damon, I'd immediately decided I wouldn't acknowledge what'd happened between us.

I forgot that I knew what he looked like naked beneath that suit.

I forgot how his lips tasted and how his tongue felt in my mouth —and other places.

I *was* a professional after all.

And anyway, why should guys get to be the only ones to have one-night stands, be man-whores, and it be perfectly fine and acceptable? It was a complete double standard! By marching into his office, pretending like the whole thing never happened, I'd keep the upper hand *and* my power. It may even throw him off his game a little. I'd thought it to be the best approach. *Supersmart idea, right?* It was my way of breaking down the double standard. At least that's what I told myself to calm my nerves.

Too bad my march *out* of that office hadn't gone quite as smoothly. In fact, it'd gone rather *un*-smoothly. Okay, I'd been a bull in a china shop.

So much for *supersmart.*

Taking a cab to my side of town, I decided to grab lunch there to avoid running into anybody else from Humphries Properties (in particular, somebody wearing sexy glasses). Getting my food to go gave me the opportunity to eat at home and start going over the project. It was easier to forget about everything (again, that person) as I threw myself into work, and I could only hope that would continue to prove to be true.

And hey, it did!

The project itself was challenging, no doubt. But that's what made it interesting. A highly successful nonprofit had secured funds from a big-time investor, Mr. Christopher Young, for the sake of a new state-of-the-art facility. Their mission was to provide resources to people of all classes and backgrounds—regardless of social or financial standing—to start their own businesses. Their vision for their new building was to include affordable office space and meeting rooms for lenders and investors, among other things.

The idea was that anybody who wanted to pursue the capitalist dream and branch out on their own, no matter where they came from or what they were starting with, could access the building and learn everything they needed to know—including introductory business courses and financial guidance. Their counselors would even set up tailored meetings with investors and bankers once the participant's pitch was ready.

It was a beautiful idea. Even though I'd grown up with every advantage in the world, it'd never been lost on me that others weren't as fortunate. And I'd always been acutely aware it was much harder for those same people to make any headway in the world, much less start their own businesses. My mind immediately sparked with ideas that I was excited to share and implement, although it would be demanding to revise the work the previous engineer had already completed.

I knew I was up for the challenge, and it was exactly the level of passion and interest that my previous job had been lacking. It only made me that much more eager to get past this whole thing with Damon and just focus on the task at hand.

*W*hen I was finished drawing up my plan of action, I resisted adding any flirtation into the email to Damon. Even if it was tempting to stoke the flame of my desire, and potentially torture him in the process, I didn't want anything to hinder his view of my proposal. And then there was the pressing need to let our attraction die off rather than making it worse—no matter how appealing the latter may be.

Keeping my own mischievous, impulsive tendencies in check through this might prove to be more challenging than the project itself. But I sent the brief, professional email and proposal on its way, then headed back across town to meet my family for dinner.

. . .

*I*t was like any other evening with my father and brothers. They spent the entire dinner talking about work, and then, during dessert (a yummy strawberry cheesecake—I had two slices, okay three), we moved on and started talking about Mom. She'd excused herself from coming because her old acquaintance had surprise-visited, and she didn't want to break the almost eighty-year-old woman's heart. Dad updated us on her gardening and other hobbies, then excused himself after paying the check so he could get home to her.

Miles and Oliver coerced me into staying for one more round with them at the bar. I only agreed because I hoped it would lessen the likelihood of inviting me out after work the following night when Damon could end up tagging along.

Much to my dismay, it didn't take long for him to come up in conversation.

"You've got to help Damon get this project back on track," Miles pleaded, which was kind of out of character for him. "If for nothing else than freeing up some of his time. He's been so busy at work, he never hangs out with us anymore."

"I don't fucking buy it." Oliver shook his head. "He blames work, but that's not it. Pretty sure it's got more to do with whatever happened a few months back when he stayed out later than we did."

"Mystery girl turned his head." Miles lifted his glass with a smirk.

"What do you mean?" I asked, unable to curb my curiosity. Surely, they weren't talking about...

"He hooked up with some chick who ghosted him the next morning." Miles chuckled. "He's been an even bigger stick-in-the-mud and fucking grump-ass since."

I was perplexed for a moment. There was no way they were talking about me. Was there? If they were, at least I knew they hadn't made the connection between me and his "mystery girl." Likely because Damon hadn't either until I walked into his office for the interview. But why would that one little encounter throw him to such a degree?

"What did she look like?" I ventured to ask, all innocence.

"Why?" Miles furrowed his brow.

"It's just that...she must have been pretty great. For him to be so bent out of shape about it, you know?"

"He didn't hookup with her until after we left, so we've got no clue." Miles shrugged. "He said she was hot as fuck, though."

"Is he just upset because some girl didn't fall all over him after one night?" I prodded. "Surely he has one-night stands all the time." Not that I wanted to hear details about his or *their* sex lives from my brothers—because, *gross*. But I assumed all men did that sort of thing regularly, unless they were in a happy relationship.

"Nah, Damon isn't that type of guy," Oliver said.

"He ain't no virgin either," Miles said. "Whoever that girl was, she really got him wound up," Miles noted with a shake of his head.

I went back to sipping my drink, attempting to play it off. But the prospect was nagging at me. I had to know for sure. "When did this happen?"

They looked at each other for a moment, muttering to themselves. "When was that? Two, no three months ago?" Oliver finally nodded.

"Where?" I asked.

"Sis? How come you're so interested all of a sudden? What up?" Miles' eyes pierced mine.

"Nothing. I'm just wondering," I lied, shrugging all casual, the cool self I always am.

"We went out to that one spot...Talia's." Oliver snapped his fingers. "Yeah. Miles talked us into checking it out."

My chest nearly imploded.

Talia's. Three months ago. They *were* talking about me. Which only made it that much more imperative to change the subject.

"Oh, who's playing tonight?" I asked suddenly, turning toward the big screens that lined the wall behind the bar.

My brothers were big sports fans, and I knew that would get them going on a lifesaving tangent, which I so desperately needed.

But as I finished my drink and pretended to listen to them, my mind drifted back to Damon. It was one thing when I thought he couldn't have cared less that I disappeared after we hooked up. Not only was this revelation a major ego boost, but it also gave me room to mix a bit of business with torture—the sweet heavenly kind.

Sure, I wanted to focus on the project. I really did care about its success. But I didn't see any reason why I couldn't have a little fun with the guy in the process. I couldn't sleep with him again, but knowing he was so hung up on that night (with good reason, by the way, because it *was* just so damn hot), I could at least enjoy my stay at the company. Maybe even tease my irresistible boss a little in the meantime? The best thing about that: He wouldn't suspect a thing.

Grinning to myself, I sipped the last of my cocktail, suddenly looking forward to the next day at work, even more than I had been before.

11

ARIA

*S*till in the office, I was working late, when my inbox chimed with Aria's email. I hadn't been able to shake her from my mind since the interview, and I resented another reminder of her. But, I was eager to see what she was proposing for the project.

My eyes were burning from staring at too many screens and printed reports all day long, but I pushed through and dove into her report. Fuck me. Right off the bat, I was impressed. Not only was she offering realistic strategies for tackling the entire venture and meeting the deadline, but she was also full of ideas of how to make it even better. She had *it*—the big-picture thinking that was somewhat out of scope for her title. That was the hardest attribute to find in an employee. How often had I nagged my team about thinking outside of the box and contributing to the idea as a whole, rather than remaining clammed up in the shell of their job description and duties?

Right out of the gate, Aria seemed to be a natural.

Or, at least, she'd nailed her first impression. Most likely not for me, but for her father. Whoever she'd wanted to convince, I didn't care. It worked.

After reading through the email, I shutdown my computer and felt a strange sense of relief. *Huh, we just might pull this damn thing off after all,* I thought to myself.

Calmness took over my body, along with the momentary release of dread of failing to meet Young's needs and expectations. Being stressed out and overworked had more or less become my new normal over the past couple of weeks. Now, I could walk out of the office knowing we had a plan in place.

If only I could keep my mind from wandering to *other* forms of release I knew Aria was all too capable of providing.

Shaking off unnecessary thoughts—at least for tonight—I headed out of the office, stopping by the gym on my way home. A good workout would be a perfect way to end my day.

*A*s I walked into my penthouse, my phone dinged with several texts all at once.

Oliver: How's it going man?

Miles: You're having a good day?

Damon: I'm having a day.

Oliver: All right, all right. We're out for drinks with my girl-friend and Miles. Join us.

Miles: Let's celebrate your new hire!

Oliver: You coming?

I had a feeling Aria would end up going out with them after I'd seen them leaving together that afternoon, so I declined.

Damon: I'm beat. Maybe next time.

Seeing her around the office was one thing—a struggle I knew

I'd quickly adapt and adjust to. It was worth it to stay on top of the tasks at hand, which I could already see Aria would be an invaluable asset to. But hanging out with her over drinks again, with her brothers lurking around at that? It was *not* a scenario I'd willingly throw myself into. Miles would pick up on that shit in a heartbeat. One look at the two of us in a casual setting, and he'd know something had happened between us. Then Oliver? Fuck that. Hard pass.

After cooking up some grilled chicken and a salad for dinner, I was ready to call it a night. For the first time in a while, I could sleep well knowing that we were in a good place to hit the ground running the following morning.

*T*he next day, I felt refreshed and determined—and horny as fuck after the dream I'd had. Waking up with morning wood was nothing new, but a raging hard-on from a sex dream starring Aria? Yeah, I'd taken a cold-ass shower and had to rub one out. It'd helped "refresh" my state of mind. I'd shaken off the initial surprise of realizing who Aria was, but keeping everything strictly professional? That *might* be an issue. Thoughts of her perfect tits and tight pussy played on a loop in my mind. What had that woman done to me? *Fuck.* It was one damn night.

Today could be *hard.*

Getting to the office early, I'd already been at it for a couple of hours when Bernadette buzzed in to say Aria had arrived. I called Cornelius and asked him to report to me so I could introduce them. Everything was on track until Bernadette showed Aria in, and my jaw almost dropped. *What the h—*

Her skirt was still within professional dress code, but it was tight enough to accentuate every one of her curves. The gray pencil skirt came to a point just above those perfect calves of hers. It hugged her hips and ass all the way up to the light-blue, low-cut blouse that revealed her *generous* cleavage.

Fuck me.

I had no idea how long I'd been checking her out before I noticed the coy grin on her face and realized I'd completely lost myself in the sight of her body in that outfit. Bernadette cleared her throat, brutally snapping me back to reality.

"Good morning, Aria." I quickly recovered. "I hope you don't mind me calling you by your first name. There are enough Humphries around here; it'll be easier."

She lifted a brow. "Not at all. I prefer it."

I noticed her somewhat-seductive tone. Was she doing that on purpose? "Good."

Cornelius appeared over her shoulder—just in time.

"Cornelius, this is Aria. Aria, Cornelius is our current chief engineer, so he'll show you around and get you caught up on everything. He'll introduce you to Josh, the team manager, and Jonas, the lead architect. Bernadette, set her up a tour with HR, too, so they can go over all of the general ins and outs."

"Of course." Bernadette nodded with a polite smile, ushering the pair out of my office.

Blowing out a sharp breath, I crossed the room to shut my door. I couldn't resist moving to the window that overlooked the work floor. My main office was more secluded on the top floor, but I kept this one with the rest of my staff for times like this—when we were on a time crunch, and I wanted everybody to have more direct access to me, and me to them.

The added benefit, or downfall—depending on how you looked at it, in this case—was that it allowed me to watch Aria's perfect ass swaying seductively in that tight-fitting get-up and those fuck-me-stiletto heels of hers as she followed Cornelius around.

The worst part about how damn good she looked, was that I knew what she looked like *underneath* that outfit. The kissable trail of freckles on her shoulders, more on one side than on the other, the adorable little beauty mark I remembered spotting on her inner thigh, or the way her soft, sexy voice cracked when she was crying out from pleasure. How her pussy had clenched me so tight I could hardly move. I knew a few other details about her I wished I could forget.

Shaking my head, I tried to pull myself together. Remnants of last night's dream filtered into my mind, and my efforts were shattered. My dick was hard again.

Working with her was going to be more challenging than I thought. It wasn't going to be a walk in the park—It would be a nightmare.

I wondered if it'd be helpful just to come right out with it and confront her about the whole thing.

She remembered.

I could tell by the look in her eyes and the way she smiled at me that she was fucking with me by pretending not to.

This was all just a game to her.

But to me, it was much more serious. I didn't like the idea of having to resist her all day. I needed to be able to put that night behind us—if I was going to survive the permanent state of blue balls I expected to endure during her time here. Sure, I could go blow my load in all sorts of ways. But I had a feeling it wouldn't scratch the same itch. Seeing her around the office all the time would be a bitch.

As anticipated, Cornelius and Aria rounded the corner into the engineer workroom, leaving me to finally pull my stalking ass away and return to my desk. *Good*, I thought. *Out of sight, out of mind.* At least for the moment.

a few hours later, I was back into the thick of my work and in need of more coffee. Break-room coffee sucked ass. Whoever was in charge had shitty taste. Bernadette was out for lunch, and I didn't want to lose my workflow by stepping out to the shop around the corner. Shitty break room coffee would have to suffice.

I'd just lifted the pot to fill one of the mugs when I caught a glimpse of somebody coming in behind me. I recognized the blur of a gray and light blue hourglass figure instantly. *Aria...her skirt, her blouse.*

"How's it going so far?" I asked without glancing up. "Getting settled in?"

She strolled right up to me—*too close*—and leaned against the counter. I didn't budge.

"Great," she said. "Cornelius gave me the initial intro to everything, and I'm about to meet with HR now."

"Perfect. The sooner we get you acclimated, the sooner we can move forward with your ideas." I stirred creamer into my mug, distracted by her lingering presence. I glanced up and noticed that the way she'd crossed her arms had pushed her breasts together in stunning peaks.

Her eyes grew wide as she stared back at me. "Something wrong?" she asked.

"I was going to ask you the same thing. Did you need something?"

She let out a soft laugh and gestured to the coffee pot. "Just waiting for my turn to grab some of that. If it's okay. I love the coffee here."

"Sure," I said, tossing the stirring straw in the garbage and moving out of her way. I couldn't believe she liked the burnt-mud crap here, but to each their own. She must have drunk some really shitty coffee in her life.

The moment I got to the door, I decided that the only way to get through all the awkwardness between us was to get used to it. *The quicker the better.* I spun around. "Your report was good." I took a casual sip of my coffee, trying my best not to spit it back into the mug. "I'm looking forward to discussing your ideas further."

"I would like that," she said. "I hope we can actually implement some of those." She carried her steaming cup over to the counter, exposing more of her legs as she slid up onto the stool and crossed them. "I know it's late in the game to be making those kinds of revisions."

I stared at her, feeling conflicted.

A woman who looked like that, I'd normally plow into her.

An employee of mine who looked like that? Certainly not. Employees were off the radar, no exceptions. We had standards and principles to uphold. No sex. Regardless of history. But, if anything, and that's a big "if", a little harmless flirt would get a pass—if *she* initiated it.

My boss's daughter and the kid sister of my two best friends?

Hard fucking no. Off-fucking-limits.

The situation was frustrating me more than I wanted to admit.

"But I'm confident we could pull it off." She smiled. "And the project would be better for it."

"You can discuss those changes with Cornelius." I said casually, ignoring her teasing. I took another sip of the coffee. Ugh. It tasted terrible. Was the machine broken? I made a mental note to tell

Bernadette. I adjusted my glasses and looked back up at Aria. "He can send a revised plan over before he leaves."

"Sure, if that's what you'd prefer." She shrugged, cupping her mug with both hands as she drew them up to those perfect, heart-shaped, plump, ruby lips.

Just as she had done in my office earlier, I picked up on a subtle but distinct seductive tone, convincing me more than ever that she knew *exactly* what she was doing to me. *That little minx.* Did she not know I could see right through her? Was she curious how far she could push me? Test the waters and see if she could get a rise out of me (no pun intended).

I considered calling her out right then and there but decided against it. Why spoil her fun? I was interested in how far she was willing to take it. Also, I was in a rush to get work done.

"Come see me if you need anything," I answered curtly before making an exit back to my own office.

I played into her hands by extending the offer, but it was what I'd do for anybody else. The dominant side of me still needed to be hands-on with this project, even if it meant being subjected to whatever game she was playing. Which I was determined to get to the bottom of sooner or later.

12

ARIA

*L*eaning against the break room counter, I watched Damon walk away with a smile on my face. I had to admit, I was feeling pretty smug as I took slow sips of the coffee I'd prepared earlier. Yum. I loved organic decaf. Such a treat. But for some reason, something was off. The brew didn't seem as good as usual, and it was only lukewarm. Had I used the machine incorrectly? Oh well, it still tasted almost as good as normal, and nobody had complained. Not even Mr. C. for Control-Freak.

If I knew anything about my brothers' best friend based on what I'd heard over the years, it was that Damon seemed *completely* unobtainable—also grumpy, uptight, hard to please, and controlling—among other things.

Being the spontaneous, carefree woman I was, I got a thrill out of unraveling a guy like him. Maybe it was a *teensy bit* below the belt, but hey, hard times required hard measures. And since I'd gotten word he'd been out of sorts after our night together, I'd been flattered to know I had left an impression on him. But even if he weren't *my* boss and even if I wasn't the daughter of *his* boss, it would never work out between us. Because: We were complete opposites with zero-point-zero sexual chemistry.

And, do you know what? I could tell it was working. The few encounters we'd had through my first day were brief, but he *was* on edge. He seemed wound up and in turmoil about something—and I could only assume I was at least partly to blame.

After finishing my coffee, I returned to Cornelius in the main engineering workroom. He was reviewing the same proposal I'd sent to Damon the night before.

"What do you think?" I asked, pulling a rolling chair next to his.

"These are great. Really great," he muttered as he continued reading. When he finished, he took off his glasses and tossed them on top of the report before looking up at me. "You know, you could have made things easier on yourself by just coming in and taking over where I left off."

"I know, but..." I hesitated, wondering how to put it mildly.

"No worries. I know my plans were a little predictable." He interrupted my thoughts. "I guess I was distracted by these potential plans for leaving."

"I'm not afraid of the extra work," I said, "and this gives the client something to really get excited about."

"You're right." He shrugged. "You've made a lot more work for yourself by going this route, but...it will be a much better finished package."

"Thank you! I'm glad you think so."

"Of course, I have to be honest. What did Mr. Copeland say?" he asked.

"He said it was good."

"That means he thought it was *fantastic*," he explained.

77

I snorted. "What would he say, you know, if he thought it was good or less than good?"

"He'd say something like, 'so far, so good'."

I chuckled again, but he added, "That wouldn't be to insult or discourage you. He would want to push you. If he thought your work wasn't any good, he wouldn't waste his time. Mr. Copeland encourages his staff to come up with their own ideas. He's tough but fair. He's not the devil or bosshole he's made out to be, not usually, anyhow. You'll learn a lot from him."

Hmm. I liked that. My goal had always been to grow, to get better at my craft.

"Let's get to work on integrating everything together," I suggested. "Tomorrow is your last day here, and I've been told they have quite the going away party planned for you."

"Let's do it," he agreed, pulling up the current plans on the computer screen in front of him.

We spent the next few hours upgrading the old plans to include my suggestions. It was the most engaged I'd felt in the workplace for a while, and I'd never been more certain that I made the right choice in walking out of my old job. It felt good to be taken seriously for once and actually know that my ideas were respected by my coworkers and supervisors. It made me more excited than ever for the rest of the project.

Cornelius and I were just getting to a stopping point for the evening when Damon walked into the room.

"I need to give the client an update today. How's it coming along?" he asked. There was a sternness to his voice I didn't miss. I also couldn't help but notice how he kept his gaze fixed on Cornelius. Was he trying to avoid me?

"Take a look." Cornelius waved him over to my computer.

I spun around to face the screen, waiting for Damon to move

nearer. He stepped closer and leaned down, but maintained his distance. As I clicked through the various screens of plans and talked him through all of the progress we'd made, I got a whiff of his cologne. Mint, pine, and other notes of irresistible manliness that made me tingle with lust. But I kept my head together and explained everything carefully.

Seeming to get caught up in all the information, Damon stared at the screen and moved closer.

"Now that the old plan and the new one are merged, we're all set to move forward," I concluded, facing him. "Cornelius will be a big help in his last few hours here tomorrow, and then I'll be taking over from here. If you approve of everything, of course."

He tilted his head, locking eyes with me, our faces only inches apart. "Yes. Of course. Everything you've done so far looks good. Keep it up."

I felt myself getting lost in his dark eyes for a moment until he pulled away, straightening his tie. He swiveled his gaze back to Cornelius, but I caught his eyes cutting over to me. It was like he couldn't look away, at least that's what I told myself, and I was eating it up. I leaned back in my chair, pushing my boobs out somewhat and crossing my legs with a smile. I was full of coy little moves I'd watched my friend pull on her boyfriend, and they'd worked, but what I was doing was subtle enough to go unnoticed by everybody else in the room.

"I'll let the client know where we're at," Damon said before nodding and strolling out of the workroom.

"Great job," Cornelius told me once he was gone. "Told you he's a hard one to impress."

"Is that why you're leaving?"

"No. I'm going to miss working for him." He smirked. "I'm actually leaving to be with my fiancée."

A big smile spread across my face.

I could see Cornelius's eyes twinkling in anticipation. I couldn't remember the last time I felt that kind of intense, warm rush of love.

"Congratulations. She's a lucky girl." I smiled a genuine smile.

*W*e worked long after the sun had gone down, trying to get as much done as possible. By dinnertime, we were exhausted and ready to call it a night. I gathered up my things and followed Cornelius out into the lobby where we waited on an elevator together. I was relieved not to run into either of my brothers or my father this time. I wanted nothing more than to go home and take a long hot bath with a glass of wine, a bag of ruffles, and get rested up for my second day on the job.

But the moment the elevator doors started to close, a man's arm shot straight through the closing crack, stopping them. I shut my eyes, and my heart jumped. I knew exactly who it was just by getting a glimpse at his expensive cufflinks attached to his beautiful, manly hand.

Damon stepped inside at the last minute and shuffled between us. Just as the doors began to close, Cornelius's eyes grew wide. "Oh, shit. I forgot something. You two go ahead."

He scrambled to press the button until the doors slid open once again. I'd somehow, very quickly, gone from an easy, casual ride down with Cornelius—to a maddening one with Damon. The only downside of the little game I was playing was that it left me in an awkward situation like this (and undeniably thirsty).

He flashed me a polite smile and pressed the button for the main floor. He appeared focused—or was it tense?—just the same as he had all day. But he always managed to keep a certain cool calmness to his demeanor no matter what.

"Good first day?" he asked curtly.

"Yes, and I'm surprised to see you here at the end of it," I said. "Don't you have a private VIP elevator?"

"It's under maintenance," he replied, his voice gruff.

Of course. That was why I'd been subjected to those run-ins with my family the day before.

"But I usually use this one, anyway," he added. "It's closer to my office."

I racked my brain for anything else to say, but the air between us was so thick that I could barely swallow or breathe. We were surrounded by rose-tinted mirrors on all four walls, from floor to ceiling. I glanced over at his reflection, noticing how the color of it made him appear that much more devastatingly handsome.

"Big plans for the evening?" I managed to ask.

"Getting ready for tomorrow," he answered. "Friday is still a full workday, despite what some people around here try to pretend."

"It's Cornelius's going away party," I reminded him. "Or do you not participate in cake and champagne with your employees?"

Damon shrugged. "Depends on how busy I am."

Okay, Mr. Grumpy was *extra* grumpy this evening. I didn't let it get to me. I bit my lip, resisting the urge to make some snarky comment about cocktails and sex, which was apparently fine to share with women before they were your employees. But I decided I'd likely laid it on thick enough for the day. Also, it would be completely unprofessional to talk about sexual habits with my new boss.

He'd probably heard my non-audible sigh of relief when the door finally dinged open to the lobby.

"Have a good night, Mr. Copeland," I said as breezily as possible, gliding past him toward the front doors.

"Good night."

I *swear* I felt him linger behind for a moment, no doubt taking in a long look of me as I walked away. I made sure to put an extra amount of sass in my step—swishing my ass for him like I was strutting down a catwalk—and, I almost fell flat on said swishing ass. *Damn, girl.* I smiled to myself over my own goofiness as I stepped out onto the front sidewalk. That was so *not* what Zoe had told me to do, and so *not* sexy. Yes, I'd worn one of my sexiest skirts and played up my flirting game, but almost falling? I was supposed to be naughty.

Epic. Fail.

Zoe was going to laugh her ass off as soon as I told her how my day had gone.

Bosshole—1. Aria the Klutz—0. *Try harder next time.* I snorted out loud, and people on the sidewalk stared at me like I'd lost my mind.

Yeah, I was a winner all right. I snorted again. Fuck it. I couldn't help myself.

*a*fter my bath, a relaxing ménage à *moi* (with delicious thoughts of *his* rocket ship), two glasses of red wine at home, a bag of ruffles, and a microwave bag of popcorn, I started digging through my closet to find the perfect outfit to slay Mr. Cranky Pants. I'd watched a soap opera (one of my secret thrills— Yes, I loved them. *Sue me!*) where a woman, in the exact situation as me, wanted to tease her broody boss. *Go figure. My life as a soap opera. Ha!* She'd chosen to do so with a sexy power suit. So, I thought, *why the hell not? It'd be fun.* I had to admit, amping up my subtle seductress vibe and dancing around the situation was *almost* as much fun as tumbling into bed with him in the first place.

At least it was a close second.

But, I couldn't be sure who I was teasing more: myself or Damon.

13

ARIA

The next morning flew by as Cornelius and I tried to get as much done as we could with him still around. But by lunch, a group of women barged in and insisted on pulling us both away for cake. I helped myself to a glass of champagne as I watched him make his rounds—accepting everybody's good wishes for the next chapter of his life.

By my second glass, I was deep in conversation with two secretaries named Lulu and Angie. They were telling me all about the ins and outs of the company. The important stuff, like who had slept with who and all the big office scandals.

"Cornelius and I had a fling years ago," Lulu noted resentfully as she watched him from our corner of the room.

Oh, boy. She gave him some serious side-eye treatment. It must have been *bad*.

Angie groaned and rolled her eyes. "Don't try to act all hurt over it. *You* dumped *him*. You said he was lousy in bed."

"Yep. I swear, he's never heard of the word 'clit.' The worst lay of my life. Nope, never again. I heard *all* engineers are," she blurted without thinking, but immediately turned to me with bright-red cheeks. "So sorry! I'm sure it's just the men."

"Not all of them." I laughed. "I've met one or two that could prove that theory wrong. Especially that last one, phewww, he really knew what he was doing."

"Sounds like a clit party!" Lulu snorted.

Angie clapped a hand over her mouth. She'd almost spewed her drink. "Right?"

They both giggled as I glanced up to see Damon emerging from his cave. *Speak of the devil...*

"What about him?" I asked with a subtle tip of my glass in his direction.

The two women looked over at Damon, then back to each other before bursting into laughter.

"Mr. Copeland?" Angie shrieked, her blue eyes widening. "If he's had any office romances, he's kept it on the down-low. I've never even heard of him having a girlfriend. He comes to all the office functions alone."

"I bet he likes it rough in bed," Lulu added with a smirk, brushing her long blonde hair over one shoulder.

Angie studied him over the rim of her champagne glass. "He seems like the type. Primal. Pure animal instincts. He'd devour you with utter primitive desire."

"Too bad none of us will ever know," Lulu said. "Such a shame. I'd love to know somebody I could live vicariously through. Would you just look at him? I bet he has a perfect dick. Girls?"

I inclined my head, envisioning his perfect dick. There was no denying that.

"Oh, yeah, a hundred percent." Angie nodded. "You can tell."

"You can?" I asked, ever the ingénue, and arching a brow.

"Just by the way he walks," Angie said. "His dick gives him that extra push of motion. It's the extra weight. Its lengthy, girthy position sends manly signals to his hips, resulting in a vigorous but floaty step. Most men don't have it. 99.8% don't. He does."

"I can totally see that." Lulu nodded, observing him.

"Yeah. Confident. Bossy. He'll grab your hair forcefully from behind and pull it hard, if you know what I'm saying." She waggled her eyebrows and pushed her dark-brown hair off her shoulders.

"Oh, I know what you're saying. He's all stern and growly while he takes you from behind with his angry cock." Lulu laughed and then immediately sighed.

"And then he'll slap your ass!"

Then both of them sighed.

"You're right, Lulu. We'll just never know." Angie shook her head, and sighed—*again*.

The three of us settled into silent shameless adoration over Damon's tall, fit body as he floated around the room making small talk. I kept my lips sealed. As much as I would have loved to see the way Angie and Lulu lit up if I confessed the truth to them about his indeed, perfect dick, I knew I had to keep it to myself. It was almost more fun having such a big juicy secret all for myself anyway.

Damon was working his way over to the bar near us when two of the guys from my department gathered around us. I couldn't remember their names, but if I recalled correctly, one of the engineers was Larry, the other Jerry (no joke), but I didn't bother asking.

"What are you three gossiping about?" one of them teased.

"Just discussing dicks," Angie said without missing a beat.

Oh, shit. I almost choked but held myself together. These two were something else.

"And the rumor about engineers being bad in bed," Lulu quipped with a shrug.

I heard a small cough and looked up to see Damon shaking his head, before swallowing his first sip of champagne. Did he hear what Lulu said? That was freaking hilarious! Nobody else seemed to notice, but I was trying to keep my huge smile under wraps.

"But Aria thinks—" Angie began.

"Ooookay, girls, time to change the subject." I interrupted, giving her a "let's keep *some* details to ourselves" look.

Angie cleared her throat and directed her attention to Lulu. "Have you given Cornelius the official send-off yet?"

She shook her head "no," and they set off to talk to him.

The two guys, Larry and Jerry, lingered behind, awkwardly drinking from their glasses while scanning me up and down.

"So? What about you?" One of them bobbed their head toward me, his eyes roaming my body. "What *are* your opinions on what engineers are like in bed?"

I winced a little at the creep vibes emanating from him. "None that I care to share." Some men simply didn't know the difference between being playfully flirty and being downright lowlife creepy. *Time to get outta here.* I didn't want them to think I was running away like a dog with its tail between its legs. No, I needed to leave smoothly, elegantly, and with class—but quickly nonetheless.

In one graceful motion I turned to walk away.

But as soon as I pivoted on my feet, I ran smack-dab into a wall of hard muscle and designer fabric. *Shit.* My boobs definitely noticed the collision, causing me to flinch. My brain short-circuited as my gaze slowly traveled up to meet Damon's, staring down at me with a pained smile. *Hello, universe? Do you love torturing me that much? You have me run into him twice? Is this payback for my seductress routine?* Well, at least this time neither of us spilled our drinks. I guessed that was a plus.

"Aria. Can I see you in my office?" he asked, his gaze dark behind his glasses, his voice stern.

My face fell. He wanted to see me in the office. Had I done something to get myself in trouble? Beyond all the *maybe* too-obvious instigating with him, but he couldn't very well call me on that. Or could he? It hadn't been *that* obvious.

"Yes, of course, Mr. Copeland," I replied professionally before starting toward his office door.

Well, *shit*. I felt Angie and Lulu's eyes boring a hole in the back of my head, and I wanted to shoo them away over my shoulder but couldn't. *Dammit.* Oh, boy. I'd be in for an interrogation later with those two. Maybe I could hide from them? Nope. Angie could sniff me out, and then she'd know for *sure* something was up. Then there was Lulu... Uh-oh. I'd have to come up with something quick and in a hurry. I'd just met them, but I could immediately tell from their personalities that they were like hound dogs with a bone. Lovely hound dogs who I couldn't wait to get to know better, but they didn't need a bone.

No, that would be bad. So. Freaking. Bad.

I straightened my posture and held my head high. They couldn't *make* me talk. I wouldn't. *Ever.* I seriously wanted to roll my eyes at myself... How did I keep getting in these situations?

He kept a tight hand hovering above my lower back as he led me in, practically slamming the door shut behind us.

My heart hurtled against my ribcage. "Sorry if I said anything I wasn't supposed to back there," I offered, taking the seat in front of his desk. "I'm still learning what's okay around here and what's not. I just figured since they were all—"

"Suggestive banter isn't my favorite." He cut me off. "But it's not explicitly prohibited—unless someone is uncomfortable. *You* looked uncomfortable."

The corner of my lips curled slightly. Was it me who was uncomfortable? Or him? But then I realized he was talking about the creeps.

"Oh. Yes! Yes, I was a little uncomfortable. Is that why you dragged me in here? To save me?"

"Actually, I didn't think you needed saving. I thought we should address the elephant in the room."

Oh, shit. My heart pounded, but I kept my face straight and unmoved. "The elephant in the room? What do you mean, Mr. Copeland?" *I might faint or fall out of my chair if he mentions the sex. The incredibly, amazing, and all the wonderfully orgasmic adverbs describing his rock-hard... Shut the hell up, Aria. What did he just say?*

"Stop calling me that." He nearly growled. "I mean, yes, call me that during regular work hours, but—"

"It's still regular work hours," I argued. "Friday is a full workday, despite how everybody around here acts." *Isn't that what he told me just last night?*

He closed his eyes and let out an exasperated sigh. "Aria, look around. Everybody out there is half-drunk and halfway out the door. Regardless, for the sake of this conversation, let's forget I'm your boss for a moment."

"I can do that, Mr.—"

"Call me Damon."

I leaned back in my chair, delighting in how frustrated he was getting. He looked so devilishly handsome when he ran his hands through his black hair. "Fine. Damon." And just to irk him, I said, "I'm afraid I don't know what elephant in the room you're talking about."

He chuckled with annoyance, flashing those perfect white teeth of his. "Sure you don't."

"Maybe you could be more specific?" I said, arching a brow.

"You know, up until now it was really easy to see you as a professional, full-grown woman, separate of my ties to your family," he fired back. "But right now, you're really channeling your role as Miles and Oliver's bratty baby sister."

"Is that what this is about?" I returned. "The fact that you're best friends with my brothers?"

He leaned back, lifting his hands from his desk. "Okay. I thought you could be mature about this, but it seems you can't. We need to talk about sex."

I was *dying*.

"Sex?" I asked, innocently, trying to cover my own embarrassment.

"Geez woman. Our one-night stand."

I glanced down at my watch, pretending to check the time. "Wow. I'm surprised it took you nearly two whole days before bringing it up."

He appeared unamused. "No. I knew you were messing with me."

His eyes locked with mine. Gooseflesh pebbled along my skin as I got lost in his dark gaze—he looked so handsome.

The sexual tension that had already been crackling between us was only amplified by my frustration. It burned me up from the inside out, sparking from my eyes to his.

Images of Damon's hot mouth between my legs, giving me the best orgasm of my life; him bending me over his desk and taking me from behind, pulling my hair—all the deliciously naughty ways he could have me, filtered into my mind.

But I couldn't allow it.

He knew it.

I knew it.

There could never be a repeat.

"I was merely trying to be professional," I defended with a shrug and a smile, slowly rising from my seat. "I can assure you it won't be a problem, Mr. Copeland."

"Wait, that's not what I—"

"I mean, *Damon*. Was that all? As you said, everybody else is already halfway out the door, and I'd like to cut out a little early as well. Unless...you need something else from me?"

I could tell he was far from satisfied with the conversation, but he leaned back in his chair and waved me out. "No. That will be all."

Slowly, I headed for the door, stopping to add over my shoulder, "Have a good night."

14

DAMON

*T*apping my foot furiously underneath my desk, I watched Aria saunter out of the room, swaying that perfect hourglass figure of hers that always seemed to be enveloped in the most torturous of tight dresses. Once she was out of sight, I couldn't stand sitting still another second. I leapt up from my desk and started pacing the room.

I knew she'd recognized me. How could she not? But to hear her admit it only made it worse. She was doing this shit on purpose —all the little looks and moves and teasing meant to drive me mad. I didn't think she was trying to get me fired, but maybe she enjoyed the forbidden thrill? Was she testing how far she could push me?

Fuck, it was working.

My inability to be immune to her subtle flirtations was just as frustrating as her doing it in the first place.

Slowly, I swiped my hand across my mouth, my other arm leaning against my desk. Was my perception of that night really so off?

After any night of sex, especially a night as satisfying as that one, I'd have thought it would have left a lasting impression, or at least some deep traces. What the hell? Aria seemed completely content just toying with me. Was I the only one left with that taste in my mouth the next morning...the one that made me want more all the fucking time?

Shaking my head, I tried to stop the barreling train in my mind. Obsessing over it wouldn't fix anything. I loathed wasting time worrying about things I couldn't control. And if anything had been made obvious over the past couple of days, it was that I couldn't control my dick any more than I could control Aria Humphries. Hell, I could barely guess what she'd do or say next half the time—another unfamiliar territory for me.

I shutdown my computer and cleaned up my desk for the day, desperate to get the hell out of there. I needed to hit the gym. I needed to sweat and blow off steam more than ever before. Most of all, I needed to get my cock sucked. I tried to remedy the situation the best way I knew how—pulling out my phone to text a hot chick who was usually down for a booty call. I'd met her a while back, and we'd had a good time. Maybe I could fuck Aria out of my system. No. That wouldn't solve the problem. It'll probably make it worse, so I put my phone back into my pocket. I'd be better off rubbing one out.

It was the weekend. I wouldn't see Aria again until Monday. That was a good thing.

I headed downstairs into the archive. My plan was to grab a few files and read up on a case that could be helpful for the Young project. As I was searching through the folders, I saw Aria making her way toward the elevator, deep in conversation with our two secretaries, Lulu and Angie. I hadn't missed the way both had stared at Aria when I'd asked her to my office a few minutes ago. They were dying for a juicy report, obviously. It wasn't a secret that I disliked the typical water cooler talk. Didn't I keep them busy enough with work?

"Really, *all* men with glasses?" Lulu asked.

"Yes, all men with glasses," Aria said. "So hot. It's the ultimate turn on. Nothing compares, I swear."

They couldn't see me. A bamboo plant blocked me from their sight. *Well, well.* This could get interesting. I decided to stay where I was.

"Huh? How so?" Angie asked. "They take them off for sex! So, then it's what, a mega turn-off?"

"No. That's the whole point. Because once he takes his glasses off, he can't see your imperfections."

"Your imperfections?" Lulu asked. "Like your fat?"

"Yeah. And other things."

"How about turning off the lights?"

"No, I don't want him to think I'm insecure. That's a big turnoff for men. Also, men don't like the whole lights off concept. Typically. But once the glasses are off, they stay off."

"Uhh-uhh, sorry girls," Angie said without missing a beat. "I'm pretty sure he can still see you pretty well. I mean, you're naked and right in front of him."

"Yeah, but he won't see *all* the details. You can feel sexy and confident because he's as blind as a mole. You can be the goddess you've always wanted to be. Uninhibited. Fierce. *Savage*," Aria's tone sounded amused. "You can't be that if he has perfect vision."

"It's not as if he goes 100% blind when he takes his glasses off," Angie replied. "I hate to burst your bubble, but he'll still be able to *feel* your imperfections."

"Girl, are you ruining my No-glasses-No-goddess-theory for me? At least he won't feel these freckles."

"Wait. No-glasses-No-goddess-theory?" Lulu asked. "Sounds legit."

"It *is* legit, at least to me. I've tested and proved it."

"My aunt," Lulu said, "smart gal that one, she's been around the block and back, and she recently told me something really crazy. Don't laugh. She said that men couldn't care less about a woman's "imperfections." As long as she knows how to—her words, not mine—touch his heart—honestly, I assumed she meant, suck his dick—she can have all the fat, and stretchmarks, and moles, and dimples and, air quotes, "body flaws" she wants—possibly even two heads. He'll be coming back for more. Dumb, I know."

Angie cleared her throat and directed her attention to Lulu. "Hmm. That's not dumb. I'm pretty sure there's some truth to it."

"Na-ah, it's a myth. Men don't have hearts. That's a fact. Everybody knows it. How can you touch something they don't have? Or is their heart in their dicks? I mean then I guess all of that would make sense. Isn't there a new study from Princeton that proves that?"

"Are you sure it's Princeton? Not a different school?" Aria asked. "I mean Princeton is one of the most respected universities."

"Exactly. They are known for their groundbreaking research."

Angie sighed. "Women are such nutcases, I swear."

"Yeah, we totally are... Hang on, wait, why?"

"We spend *way* too much time trying to figure men out. It's ridiculous. I don't see no man walking around hoping a woman takes off her glasses so she can't see his hairy ass crack."

"Truer words have never been spoken," Lulu agreed.

"Men are wired differently, that's why."

"And men aren't perfect either."

"Well, some *are*," Aria said.

"Like Mr. Copeland." Angie swooned. "He's *it*, and, girls, have you seen his perfect jawline? And his beard shadow? All the way down to his freakin' Adam's apple. I bet he's got a really hairy chest. So hot. Because of all the testosterone. I swear, every time he as much as looks at me, I almost faint."

"I bet he's got a hairy ass," Lulu snorted.

"Yes!" Angie said, undeterred. "And he probably has that sexy hairline, from his belly button down the middle of his V. He's so perfect. Everything about him screams: man."

"Best of all. He wears glasses," Aria interjected.

"You and your glasses. I'm sure he doesn't take them off during sex, though. He likes it rough and primal—we've established that —*but,* he's a total control freak. He wants to know exactly what he's dealing with. At all times."

Ding-Dong.

I heard the elevator door swoosh open.

"True," Lulu said, her voice growing quieter. "Girls! Glad we got this all figured out, together. We're such an amazing well of knowledge, and Aria, I'm glad Mr. Copeland didn't fire you. It's not as if we talk sex *all* the time."

"It's not?"

Some more cackling followed, and then the sound of elevator door swooshing closed.

I stepped into the hall, a folder in my hand. The women were gone, and the hall was silent. I made my way to the garage. I had started to gain new appreciation for office talk. Not that what I'd overheard mattered. It didn't. It looked as if Aria was just coming off a bad experience and recovering from some asshole prick. Men were shit. I could only guess what the mother-fucker had told her. Women worried way too much—nobody was perfect. But about her freckles? What the hell?

Ding.

A message popped up on my cell. It was from Stella, my younger sister. It looked as if she was surprise visiting this weekend.

Stella: Available for dinner tomorrow, Gummy Bear?

Stella: 7 pm?

Stella: Kiss emoji.

I was. For her, I always was.

Me: Don't be late, Chicken Little.

15

DAMON

*M*onday morning rolled around, but by the time I headed back into work, I was determined not to let Aria get to me any longer. We only had a few weeks to finish drawing up all the plans for the project before meeting with Christopher Young and Mark Castell, the head of the nonprofit. And while she and Cornelius had worked us up to a good spot, there was no time for slacking off.

I had Bernadette organize an impromptu meeting with the engineering team and everybody else working on the project. We'd start the day by reviewing our current status and the progress that needed to be made by the end of the week.

Once they were gathered in the boardroom, with complimentary beverages and donuts, I strolled inside. Everybody quickly quieted down and dispersed to their seats the moment I walked in.

I stopped at the head of the table.

"Good morning, everyone." I nodded.

Sliding my chair up to the table, I flipped open the notepad in front of me and instantly caught sight of Aria on the opposite side of the room. She was in another one of those damned dresses that ruffled around the top, accentuating her voluptuous tits, hugged her hips and ass like a glove before tapering off at a point just above her knees, showing off her perfect legs.

I was pissed. Not only was I pissed that she looked like that, but she was also the only one who didn't scatter into place when I'd arrived. She lingered by the refreshment bar, drawing a piece of donut to her lips as she stirred her coffee.

"Girl, what are you doing?" Angie hissed at her through clenched teeth. "Hurry up and sit down. He's waiting."

Aria froze and glanced at me with wide eyes, her mouth full of donut with crumbs trailing out the side and down her chin. She started chewing rapidly and stumbled toward the empty seat at the table, nearly tripping over her feet as she went. In her haste to scramble into her rolling chair, she knocked a thick binder of project notes onto the floor. It slammed to the carpet with a loud thud, making her jump.

"Oh, so sorry," she muttered.

After picking it up and sliding it back onto the table, she swallowed down the rest of her food and looked at me with a blushing grin. "Sorry, Mr. Copeland. I didn't hear you come in."

Was she for real? Or was she fucking with me?

Acting innocent as ever, she slowly sat down. Finally. Everybody else eyed her and then me. I swallowed, annoyed. I couldn't have this kind of shit. I wasn't about to let everybody who worked for me think that I was taking it easy on Aria because she was the fucking daughter of the president. Or worse, I couldn't let them start thinking of *other* reasons I might be taking it easy on her...like the fact she'd ridden my cock for an hour straight.

My eyes darkened over her as she settled in. Scolding her right then and there just for being a few seconds late to the table would be a bad idea.

I was realizing that so many of my expectations were impossible to articulate, but my team had always been driven to meet them—and not out of pure intimidation. And that was the most nagging annoyance of all—Aria wasn't showing any sign of respect. Not even a little bit.

Clearing my throat, I pushed my thoughts aside to begin. "Thank you, everyone, for meeting on such short notice. I know we will all have full plates in the coming weeks, which is why I thought it would be important for us to get on the same page first thing. We've had some unexpected changes come up. Which brings me to my first order of business for the morning. I'd like to introduce you to Aria Humphries."

Motioning to Aria, I continued, "She's our new lead engineer for this project, taking Cornelius Cackowski's place. Some of you may have already met her around the office." Lulu and Angie nodded excitedly. I narrowed my eyes at Larry Loffer and Jerry McHanderson, who had attempted to "talk to her" at the going away party on Friday, before I dragged her away into my office.

Everybody smiled at her politely, nodding to give Aria an official greeting, but I was quick to continue. It was just a formality to introduce her—the same kind of thing I'd do for any other new hire. Jesus Christ. I disliked how much I had to examine all my actions when it came to her under this new lens.

"Now, let's move on," I said, trying to hide my annoyance, and diving into the schedule for the week ahead.

The full meeting only lasted just under an hour. Keeping things quick and concise, we covered a lot of ground in that time. Everybody was instructed to send me brief updates before their lunch breaks and before leaving at the end of the day. Dismissing everyone to get down to it, I was eager to get started on my own lengthy to-do list in the privacy of my office.

I wished it was a good time for me to move back into my office on the top floor, but of course, that would do nothing to stop my thoughts about Aria. I didn't want to hide—that would be stupid. No, she had access to the private elevator that reached the top floor and existed mainly for her father and brothers. I doubted she'd show up there, to continue her little game. My office had more privacy, for sure—well, aside from being nestled in so close to Miles, Oliver, and her father, Charles Henry. I cast aside any thoughts of just what we could do with all that *extra* privacy, or how dangerous it could be with them hanging around.

*B*y noon, I'd received check-ins from everybody on my team, except for Aria. It made me worry that something had gone off track and was holding her up—or was she just fucking with me? A few minutes later, I found myself venturing out into the mostly empty office to find her in the engineer room, kicking myself as I went in. What was I even doing here?

She barely turned as I tapped on the doorframe. "Everything going okay?" I asked and walked over to her desk.

"Yes, everything is fine. Thanks for asking." She sighed listlessly, still clicking away at the screen as she popped a piece of chocolate into her mouth. "I'll let you know if there's a problem."

Her casualness brought on an instant hot rise of anger. Why wasn't she intimidated by me the way the rest of my employees were? I glanced around the room, seeing that everybody else was gone for lunch, before leaning down next to her.

"Aria, typically I'm informed if there's going to be a delay with an update," I barked in a hushed tone.

My eyes fixed on the slow rise and fall of her chest as she tilted her head, putting her face inches away from mine. "Sorry about that, Mr. Copeland. I got distracted but I'm on it. Surely, you can understand."

"When can I expect it? After lunch?" I asked, trying to redirect the tone of our little talk before I blew my lid.

"I'll get back to it now and send you my progress report as soon as I can. Which is going to take that much longer if you keep distracting me." She winked and quirked a grin.

I knew exactly how to put her in her place if I could.

She needed another round of that good ole D. My mind kept racing with thoughts of spinning her chair around, lifting her up on the edge of her desk, and bending her to my will in other ways... with my glasses *on*.

"I look forward to that report then," I said, making no mistake of the discontentment in my voice.

Leaving her to work, I retreated into my office, letting out a frustrated breath as I went.

Ten minutes or so after I returned to my desk, a message popped up on the screen.

Aria: As you requested, Mr. Copeland, here is my update. As you will see, everything is on track. An impressive boss such as yourself must surely understand the importance and value of working until the job is done. Rather than sending an incomplete report so I could go to lunch, I decided to get this to you as soon as possible. I do hope this pleases you.

My finger clenched on my mousepad, calculating the perfect response. If she was going to push my buttons, I'd just have to push hers right back.

Damon: I understand the value of not leaving jobs unfinished, but surely you can understand my reservations given my first impression of you. You seemed to be perfectly content walking out on something before it was complete. I only want to ensure the same lack of good judgment doesn't happen again.

For a brief second, I wondered if she would catch the sexual innuendo, but smirked when I read her reply.

Aria: The way I remember it...

Aria: ...that job was finished more than once.

I smiled, shaking my head as I typed one final reply.

Damon: That job was far from finished as far as I was concerned. Maybe your standards are just a little low, based on your previous employers in that regard.

I pressed send.

My dick jerked against my fly as memories of our night together flashed in my mind. Now I was rocking a semi and had to adjust myself.

After raking my hands down my face, wishing the lustful hum pulsing through me would calm down, I grabbed the spare bag I kept in my office and decided to duck into the gym around the corner. Jesus. Soon I'd be the runner-up in a fucking Arnold Schwarzenegger contest. I may end up losing my mind before this whole thing with Aria was over. At least I'd be in better shape than ever with all the extra workouts I was getting in.

16

ARIA

*W*e were midway through the week when I decided I'd accomplished enough to earn a long lunch to meet up with my bestie, Zoe. She asked to meet me in the lobby of the building, which had an impressive buffet and coffee shop.

After going through the line with our trays of food with vegan Spicy Chinese Eggplant, Szechuan Sauce, and fruit, we sat down at one of the tables with a cute little bouquet of pink carnations in the middle. I couldn't resist bringing the vase to my nose as I settled into my seat.

"Hmmm, stopping to smell the roses and everything," she quipped. "Your time working *under* Mr. Sex-In-A-Suit here at your dad's company must really be going well." She laughed at her own joke, and I couldn't help but grin.

"They're not roses." I shrugged. "And don't put it like that. No one's getting underneath anybody. Except me getting under his skin...if you count that." I winced because I sort of felt bad for making him crazy. Well, not with my outfits. That part was fun.

And yeah, he'd gotten me good with his text. It'd caused me to stutter a bit. I'd laughed out loud to myself in an empty office like a lunatic.

"I should have known you'd use this situation for your entertainment," she said, shaking her head. "But come on. I saw Damon that night before you two hooked up. And I *might* have internet stalked him a little..."

I raised an eyebrow at her.

"Okay, I stalked the fuck out of him, but it's not what you think," she told me. "That guy is...beyond words. Too hot to handle. You can't sit here and tell me he's not getting under your skin right back."

Stalked him? I kept a discreet smile on my face and observed the other employees walking by. "Shush. I didn't come this far keeping this whole thing from my dad and brothers just to have somebody overhear our conversation." I smiled when one of my coworkers passed our table. "And, what do you mean you internet stalked him?"

"It was only to check him out for you—you know, like best friends are *supposed* to do? What if he was a serial killer or something? I needed to make sure he wasn't a bastard, like your ex, because with that dude I smelt BS the second I first saw him."

Zoe *did* warn me about Nate when I first started dating him. She'd never liked him and told me that something was fishy about him. I should have listened. Instead, I'd listened to Nate and all the bullshit he told me. He was so sweet in the beginning, and I was so in love.

"But, after I started," Zoe continued, "I went down the rabbit hole. And girl..." She fanned herself. "He is H.O.T. What's holding you back, anyway? You're into men with glasses. You already hit it. So what if he's your bo—"

"Shhhh!" I hissed. "You're *so* loud." I wanted to crawl under the table and hide. She was so embarrassing, but I loved her.

She leaned down, giggling to herself. "Doesn't that just make it even sexier though? It's so scandalous and secretive."

Well, Zoe *was* right about that. I shook off my mortification as I thought of just how damn sexy Damon was.

I brought a forkful of fruit to my lips with a smirk, rolling my shoulders as if I didn't have a care in the world. "Hell yes, girl." The added forbidden fruit aspect *did* make it more exciting. It also made it infuriatingly maddening.

We finished eating and strolled down to the nearby shopping strip, ducking in and out of a line of stores. I was perusing a shelf of perfumes, smelling each one to decide if it would aid me in my mission to drive Damon *wild*. Okay, "mission" sounded like a harsh word. Honestly, what it boiled down to was that I'd finally met somebody who excited me and wasn't unfazed by my actions. Like I said, the appeal of the forbidden made it much more exhilarating but I had the upper hand. I'd always been attracted to grumpy, broody, domineering types.

My ex was quieter and more laid back, and I'd always wanted somebody who could match my bold and expressive personality. Damon *certainly* did it for me. And it wasn't like I was punishing him—I knew he enjoyed my subtle seduction. I could feel it. Well, he didn't *dislike* it. At least not *all* of it.

"Perfume is definitely an important tool to have in your arsenal," she decided out loud as I inhaled the scent of a sprayed paper strip of amber musk.

"Couldn't this backfire, though?" I asked, crossing my arms and raising a brow. "I'm only at the company for this one project," I explained. "I don't want to work at my dad's company long-term. So..."

"Girl, the way to make a broody, dominant man fall in love with you is *not* with subtle hints."

"I don't want him to fall in love with me!" My eyes nearly bugged out of my head. "Didn't you hear me? He works for my dad." I lowered my voice because I realized I was almost shrieking. "It'll only make matters worse. I'm just trying to have a little fun with Damon."

Zoe stared at me pointedly. "But you wouldn't mind going for round two with him?"

"You might be shocked," I said with a shrug, "but it's not like I haven't thought about it."

She nodded. "Oh, I believe you."

"Also," I continued, "it's not like I can just walk up to him and tell him, 'Hey boss, let's have sex.' It could get me fired. Or him. Both of us. Hell, I don't know." I blew out a long breath. "It's wrong, I know. I'm such a chicken. I only know I want a repeat or four, even though I shouldn't."

"Does he know?" Zoe asked.

I sighed. "No. Well not exactly. He might suspect something, but he's a man, so you never know. It's not as if I gave it to him in writing."

Zoe tapped me on the nose and laughed. I swatted her hand. "Trust me, Aria. Men are like genies in little bottles. You need to make sure they know what you want, and then they'll make all your wishes come true. Ta da! But first, you need to rub them the right way. Just wearing something sexy won't cut it. You have to wear something really, *really* sexy. Two somethings, to be precise. A sexy number and a sexy scent. And then the trick is, you make him do all the work," she explained with a wave of her hand. "Time to let him out of the bottle."

"Zoe, I don't know."

"Don't be a chicken. If you succeed, I'll call you 'Queen Femme Fatale' for a month."

"Okay." I chuckled. Zoe was a nut job, but I'd go along with her advice. What could it hurt? "Queen Femme Fatale, huh? You got yourself a deal," I told her. "Now, help me choose a perfume."

"All right. Hit me."

I did.

"*Oww*. Ass. I didn't mean literally. I meant which perfume." She rubbed her arm, glaring at me. "You're lucky I love you."

"I know, and thank you, Zoe. I mean it. For listening." I was still laughing as I reached out and hugged her. "You're the best." After I'd composed myself, I squirted a rosy scent onto a sample strip and held it out to her. "What do you think of this one?"

She wrinkled her nose. "Too innocent. You need something more...devilish and seductive." Her eyes drifted to a far corner of the boutique. "And, one of *those*."

Turning around, I spotted the garter belts she was pointing to. I could see it now. Me going to work in a short enough skirt so when I sat next to Damon, the straps of the belt would show.

"That and an irresistible perfume should do the trick," Zoe said.

"Really? Don't you think that's a little too much? And isn't too much fragrance a turnoff? I heard it can give people migraines or even allergic react—"

"Of course not," she interrupted me. "If you don't step up your game, he'll *never* get it. The only other way is to speak to him and tell him what you want."

"That's not an option."

"Exactly. Then, this is fool-proof. Trust me. With men you need it to be foolproof. This way, there'll be no misunderstanding. It'll be crystal clear. Before you can blink, Mr. Genie will be putty in your hands, and fulfilling every one of your desires."

Every one of my desires? It sounded awesome—so much so my nipples started to tingle. Sign me up.

"Who's a genius?" she teased.

"You're a genius." I grinned, snatching up a bottle named "Hot Burn." There was a big black dragon with glowing black eyes and wildly spread wings on the bottle. Exquisite! It was a Wyvern, clearly—brutish, always aggressive and impatient—showing off its impressive black wings and a long tail equipped with a stinger capable of injecting a highly toxic venom. Wyverns weren't as big as ancient dragons, but they were fast, most likely making them fun to ride (wink wink). Exotic, sparkly, with perfect hints of cedar and vanilla, the perfume had just the right amount of kick and lingered with afternotes that were enough to turn anybody on. Anybody? That meant including controlling, short-tempered Mr. I.Q.

Zoe and I finished shopping and returned to our respective workplaces. I promised I would update her if anything happened. I may have been walking a fine line, but only because I knew I had enough self-control not to cross it. At least I thought I did. Okay, maybe self-control wasn't always my strongest suit, but I was positive I could keep a grip on everything this time around.

*T*he next day I marched right into the office with my new short, but still work-appropriate skirt—complete with the garter belt and stockings I'd bought. I spritzed on a healthy amount of "Hot Burn" and threw on my favorite pair of stilettos. My hair was pinned up into a sexy long ponytail, just to deviate from my usual style.

I looked and felt like a million bucks. It put an extra pep in my step all morning. But by noon, I was starting to worry it was all for nothing. Damon had been locked in his office with the door closed and his blinds shut. His secretary told everybody he was in hard-core do-not-disturb-mode. He didn't even respond to my midday progress report.

The late afternoon hours went on, and I was beginning to feel foolish. *Go figure.* But, I couldn't let all those carefully calculated touches to my outfit go to waste. I also didn't want to tell Zoe that our plan didn't work out.

When the last engineers and assistants from my team had finally filed out of the workroom, I decided to make my move.

Walking up to Bernadette's desk, she stopped me right away. "Mr. Copeland has asked for no one to disturb him," she reminded me.

"I'm aware of that, but as the head engineer for the upcoming project, there are things I need to consult with him on. He's been in there all day, and I'm sorry, but I really must insist."

She pursed her lips, and I got the feeling that she would have told anybody else to go to hell. But since I held the somewhat beneficial title of being the head boss's daughter, she let out a sigh and waved me forward. I cringed internally. It kind of made me feel like an asshole for pulling rank. "All right, fine. But don't say I didn't warn you. He's not in a good mood."

She grabbed a piece of paper and started fanning herself. Was it my *devilish and seductive* perfume? I thought most of it should have dissipated by now. Evidently, it had quite a long life span, or should I have said 'half-life' as I was feeling a nuclear hot pride in my appearance. Apparently, Bernadette wasn't feeling it, as she suddenly reached for her purse and grabbed an Advil, mumbling something about a headache. Oh no, it *was* my perfume. I comforted myself with the reasoning that Bernadette was a woman. It was only natural that she would have the opposite reaction to it. I sure hoped I wouldn't give Damon a migraine or an allergic reaction.

"Thank you, Bernadette." I smiled, innocently. "I appreciate it."

"Enter at your own risk."

Shrugging off her warning, I thought, *How bad could it really be?* I knew he was a grumpy grump. Old news. My "Hot Burn" would surely cheer him up! Also, the men in my family could be every bit as ruthless as anything Damon Copeland might have to dish out. I was immune to that kind of intimidating power, for the most part. I had to admit, it might even be a turn on, if dosed correctly. Damon knew how to dose it, no doubt.

I knocked lightly at first. No answer.

I knocked again, and when he still didn't answer, I stepped in anyway, ignoring his immediate gruff refusal.

"Not now," he grumbled, not looking up from his desk.

"Mr. Copeland, sorry to disturb you." I started. "Since it's nearing the end of the week, I wanted to make sure we touched base on everything in person."

He dropped his pen with a heavy sigh and finally lifted his gaze.

17

ARIA

The subtle twitch on his face was enough to make the entire thing worth it. His eyes drifted up and down my body, quickly taking in my outfit.

"Do you have a few minutes?" I asked.

"It's getting close to crunch time, Aria," he answered tightly. "I hired you because I expected you to be able to work confidently without a lot of input. I trust you to get the job done right, and if I have any concerns, I'll come to you. Got it?"

He looked worn down and stressed with deep grooves under his eyes. "And now, if you'll excuse me?"

"Are you sure you trust me?" I pressed on. "You look awfully anxious for someone who thinks it's all under control. Which it is, of course."

He ran his hands through his dark hair. He appeared annoyed. But God, the stretch of his suit across the wide expanse of his defined chest... I probably looked like I was off in space. I had to quickly clear my throat and lift my chin, reminding myself that *I* would be the one teasing *him*. Not the other way around.

"I'm just curious as to why you're so on edge?" I asked him, really wanting to know.

He leaned back in his chair, taking a few moments before he fixed me with his gaze. "Part of being a good leader is delegating and believing in your team to get the work done. I had to learn that the hard way when I first got into this business," he explained, revealing a surprising amount of open vulnerability. His tone switched from boss-mode to normal-guy-mode, just leveling with another adult. "I don't like loosening my grip on things. Especially things that are important to me. But it doesn't help anybody if I'm breathing down their necks and doubting their every move."

"So, you keep your distance when you get in these...moods?" I wondered aloud.

"When it comes down to tying up all the loose ends and finishing touches, I'll be back in the thick of it."

I felt my brain turning to mush at the thought of him not loosening his grip. I had a few things I wanted him to latch onto without letting go, but I, once again, swallowed that down and took the seat across from him. He seemed stunned at my boldness. Or was it my aura of hotness that was stunning him? Hang on—were his nostrils flaring? Like a wild, savage dragon? Would he spread and flutter his black wings?

"Would an in-person summary make you feel any better?" I proposed before he could protest. "It's just me. So, you can be as overbearing as you want."

"Fine, go ahead." He waved.

Oh my God, it's working. "Hot Burn" is the goods!

I proceeded to give a thorough update on how all the plans were coming together. I explained that we were planning on programming a software that would give the clients an in-depth three-dimensional rundown of the proposed design and could even show the construction timeline complete with dates, step by step.

But as I spoke, I made a point to shift my legs to the side, letting my skirt ride up just enough to reveal a hint of the garter belt I'd worn just for him. Sure, I wanted to give him some peace of mind. But I wasn't about to let Zoe and my whole glorious plan fly out the window. I could alleviate some tension while piling it on in other places.

His dark, stormy gaze lingered in all the right places but returned to my eyes. By the time I finished, his lips were slightly parted, but I couldn't tell what was going through his mind—my presentation or my clothing. I hoped his thoughts were far from anything having to do with work. I could be wrong. He had a poker face.

"I have written notes to give you as well," I told him, rising to approach his desk. I made a point to lean over, letting my perfume envelop him and giving him a spectacular view of my cleavage, as I slid the report across his desk. "You know...in case you had a hard time following any of that." I winked. Yes, I know. I was pushing it (this was fun!). "Anything else?" I asked.

"No, that will be all," he growled, standing to his feet, large and glorious.

"Have a good evening," I said as I headed toward the door.

Spinning around before reaching for the handle, I added, "You should really do something to blow off some steam, Damon. All this stress is bad for you. You need to lighten up. Maybe grab a few drinks at the bar on your way home? A place like...Talia's?"

I was feeling so smug with my perfect exit, I hadn't noticed him darting across the room behind me. By the time my palm grazed the handle of the door, I felt his strong hands on my shoulders, whipping me around to face him.

His eyes were filled with a primal hunger, burning into me.

He pinned my back to the door with his arms pressed against the wood behind me.

"You know, Aria," he growled in a low, sexy hum. "You can pretend all you want like that night didn't mean anything to you." His head dropped, moving in closer to my ear and caging me in even tighter. His lips brushed my earlobe as he whispered, "You can pretend like you don't get wet every time you think about me. Like you wouldn't moan my name over and over if I bent you over this desk and fucked you right now."

I gulped. Loudly.

His chin grazed my ear. "Is that what you want?" his deep baritone rumbled.

I was taken aback, my eyes sparking with need. If I wasn't wet thinking about it before, I sure as hell was now. Especially if the reward of pushing him to the edge were insanely hot moments like that.

"Do you want to be fucked?" he asked, pressing his body even closer to mine. "Is that what you need?"

I was trembling. *Yes, please.* The whole perfume-sexy-outfit setup was so working! Even I was a bit surprised, if I was honest. I was totally rubbing the genie out of his bottle! Except maybe, "genie" wasn't really the right expression. If we're staying in the fantasy realm, here, he still made me think of a dragon.

I was rubbing the *dragon* out of his *lair*.

I reached out slowly, wrapping my hand around his tie to pull his lips inches from mine—a closeness that, deep down, was killing me. I parted my mouth, and dropped my gaze to his delicious, kissable lips, hinting at a kiss that could come...

"Now what would your boss think of that, Mr. Copeland?" I murmured softly.

I swept my lips through the last tiny wedge of air between us before pulling back and touching my finger to his stubbled chin.

Riiiing. Riiiing.

It was his cell.

He ignored it.

But it snapped me back to reality. With my eyes locked on his, I reached for the handle and turned, forcing him to back up or fall over me, sending us both out onto the office floor.

He took a few steps back, letting me go.

I fully expected to run into my father. Or one of my brothers. Or all three of them.

Luckily, the floor was empty.

I felt super awkward about how I left it (so much for Queen Femme Fatale), that I had to immediately bolt into the engineer room and grab my things so I could escape to the elevator to go home.

*M*y nostrils were still filled with the scent of his cologne as my shaking hand pressed the button to go down. My heart was pounding, and my body was reeling from his forward display of dominance. I hadn't seen it coming, and it had me all out of sorts. My panties *might* have been drenched.

I full-on expected to meet my father in the elevator. Or one of the others. I was relieved nobody barged in on me this time.

I needed a few moments to compose myself before entering back into reality.

The current plan circling through my head?

Bed. I wanted a bed. With Damon. *No. Shut up, Aria.*

Dammit. Bed. Shower. Sex. *No. Fuuuuuuck...*

He broke my brain!

Try again.

My plan? Crawl into bed with my vibrator the moment I got home so I could banish some of the impossibly tight, yearning aches he had conjured up inside of me. Yes! That was it. Phew...

If his phone had not rung, what would have happened?

Oh, my gosh. Would I have caved in, kissing him, and letting him fulfill his promise of bending me over his desk? He said it like a dare and a warning all at once. I understood his message loud and clear. Lay off, or he'd stop playing nice. I could only tease the dragon so many times before he'd finally lash out and spit fire or acid. Was it wrong that it only made me want to entice him more?

I exited the elevator and stepped out into the brisk night air, hoping it would calm me down. But each piece of the puzzle amounted to something more enthralling than anything I had felt in a while. The cat and mouse game, with me in the lead. The fact that he was so incredibly off-limits and forbidden. The idea that I really wanted to be a femme fatale.

I could keep pushing. After all, it wasn't like he could fire me. Not with us sharing such a taboo secret. And he was so damn susceptible to all my little games, which only made it more fun. I loved seeing that wild look in his eyes every time I taunted him.

But it was so wrong, too. He'd warned me.

The walk home and up the stairs to my apartment did nothing to curb my appetite for him. Even after a healthy amount of "me time" and ice cream, I was still tossing and turning, just thinking about him.

Ordinarily, short-tempered, testy, straitlaced, uptight guys like

Damon weren't my type. Smart guys like Damon were. But his domineering side? That had always been a secret desire that unraveled me. And something I'd only ever really been able to fantasize about, since most of my exes usually took a quiet, laid-back approach to handling my unpredictable personality.

But Damon?

Suddenly I could see the potential for him matching my boldness in ways I never would have imagined in him. Now the game had flipped itself entirely, if I didn't get a grip on myself. Because I was the one dying for more. Much more.

18

DAMON

That woodsy musk mixed with peaches, berries, and vanilla lingered in my nose for hours. It was like a spell Aria cast on me. It'd been intoxicating from the moment it first wafted off of her, and now, it stuck with me.

I swore I could catch hints of it every so often when I turned my head.

It had taken everything in my power not to trail my hands up the satin straps of that damn garter belt she sauntered into my office wearing, especially when I cornered her against the door. Did she have any idea how much she was turning me on? I imagined her bending her knee, lifting her leg up so I could graze her thigh, while tormenting her with my words in her ear.

"You can pretend all you want like that night didn't mean anything to you. You can pretend like you don't get wet every time you think about me. Like you wouldn't moan my name over and over if I bent you over this desk and fucked you right now... Do you want to be fucked? Is that what you need?"

JOLIE DAY

"Now what would your boss think of that, Mr. Copeland?" she'd murmured softly.

It was eating away at me all weekend.

Truthfully, she was acting like a mischievous brat with nothing better to do than get on my nerves. And yet, she was still excelling in her work performance along the way. Which should have made me happy, but pissed me off more, because it left me with no excuse to reprimand her.

I wanted her. She had a special talent for getting under my skin, and she knew it. And to top it off, she had the upper hand. All it would take was for her to tell her brothers and Dad what'd happened between us, and I'd be fucked.

*A*ll this was still whirling around my mind when I called everybody into the conference room for a meeting first thing Monday morning. I made a point not to look at her as I walked in. The last thing I needed was to risk her throwing me off in front of everybody.

"Good morning, everyone. Hope you had a good weekend. We need to make sure we are all up and running in top gear for our upcoming trip to Maine. Also, we only have two weeks until we take this proposal to the client, which means we have one week to finish everything. I want next week to be devoted entirely to preparing for the pitch and fixing any last-minute glitches. Understood?"

Everyone nodded, except Aria, who lifted her pen in the air. "Excuse me, Mr. Copeland. Just to clarify...Who will be present for the pitch?"

"You as the lead engineer, the architect, and myself," I shot back briskly. "Any other questions? If not, let's get to it."

The room erupted in a shuffle of sliding chairs, and everybody gathered up their things to head back to their desks. Aria stayed put and called out again over the commotion.

"So, we'll be working closely together to prepare?"

Everybody stopped and stared at her before turning back to me.

I tensed up from the awkwardness of her question, which seemed to amuse her. But thankfully, nobody else seemed to pick up on anything odd about it. They were probably just eager to get the hell out of there, and so was I.

"Yes, of course. Any more questions?" I offered.

I groaned to myself when I noticed her staying put while the rest of my staff filed out one by one, until we were alone together again. After her heated departure from my office on Friday, this was not how I wanted to kick off the week. I'd hoped she would put her antics on hold for crunch time.

"What were you getting at?" I huffed, scanning the room again to make sure everybody had left.

"Nothing." She shrugged innocently. "I just like to know what to expect is all. It sounds like we'll be having a lot of long, late nights together."

"Yeah. Working. Your point?"

"No point," she chimed back with a smile, finally closing her binder and sliding it into her bag.

Of course, she was wearing another pair of her classic "come-fuck-me" heels, but this time with a pair of slacks that made her legs look...longer. But her blouse was no easier on me than her dresses were. It still plummeted down just enough to give me a hint of everything hidden underneath, inciting memories of what I'd already seen of her flooding my mind.

"I just look forward to working with you more directly," she said sweetly before spinning on her heels to leave.

I didn't buy her innocent act for a minute. But had anybody else been around—they would have.

"Oh! Oops!" she gasped suddenly before reaching the door. Her earring had fallen to the floor in what was so obviously an intentional cliché move. She bent over slowly to pick it up, giving me a full view of those long legs and her perfect, round ass. I heard her mutter, "Oh, *damn*," and scramble her fingers along the floor, ass still in the air, in search of one of her earrings. I'd seen it drop on the ground. With a fake cough, I had to fight to cover my grin, after she grumbled under her breath, "Awkward."

Wait. Maybe she didn't drop that earring intentionally? Her own reaction suggested she didn't. Was it a tactic, but it simply went wrong? I just could not tell. She was truly infuriating.

Aria glanced back over her shoulder as she stood up just as slowly as she'd bent over. I kept my face as blank as possible, but she knew damn well she was driving me crazy. That was the whole point.

"I'll have this morning's report to you by lunch," she added casually, clipping her earring back to her ear as if nothing had happened, before attempting to bounce out the door.

"Aria. Wait just a minute."

"Yes?" She turned to me with her hand still gripped on the door handle.

"About the day reports—did I not make myself clear during the meeting? For the sake of getting everyone more coordinated and to condense messages the following days, you and your team are to send everything to Josh so he can go through it and forward me the key updates at once."

"To Josh?" She frowned. "Why Josh?" Her question made it obvious. Clearly, she hadn't been listening.

"He's the manager," I said impatiently.

"Yes, but I'm the head engineer," she argued. "Wouldn't I be in a better position to filter through the information? I mean, if you really want them condensed. He might edit out something important."

"I don't need anything edited. The same reports. Just one email. I know how I want things done, Aria. It's my call. If I want your input, I'll ask for it."

She cut her eyes away with an incredulous smile. "Unbelievable."

"Unbelievable what? That I'm making a call as your boss and the head of this project?" I slid out from behind the desk and strode toward her. "I am your boss, Aria. No matter who your dad is, or who your brothers are, or what happened between us months ago, or whatever game you're trying to play with me now...I'm still your boss."

The way her eyes darkened over me as I spoke turned my tone deeper and more suggestive than I intended it to be. It was a low grumble, almost sounding like a threat, as I inched closer to her, feeling pulled in by the heat pulsating between us.

She stared straight into my eyes, unwavering. "I can't *believe* you'd make such a call based purely on trying to avoid direct messages with me. Especially since you were the one who derailed our last little DM chat."

"Don't fool yourself into thinking you know what my motivations are, sweetheart."

"Sweetheart?" she snarled, moving in front of the window overlooking the floor and crossing her arms. "Don't fool yourself into thinking you can call me pet names and that I won't slap you right across the face."

God, I loved seeing her get angry, the freckles on her face and chest were all red and spicy.

"Resorting to workplace assault?" I chuckled. "I think HR would have a few things to say about that."

"I think HR would have a *lot* to say about this whole thing between *us*," she retorted, getting more riled up by the second. At least I wasn't the only one, for once. "So would my father for that matter."

Closing the distance between us, I leaned my hand against the glass pane behind her, caging her in. She gasped, then stared up at me with timid defiance, daring me and recoiling all at once. We were right back where we left off Friday. "Maybe you *should* go talk to your father. Tell him all about his precious daughter running into strange men in bars and then going home with them, only to leave the next morning without ever seeing them again. He'd *love* that."

"You ran into me!"

"And *you* disappeared!"

"Men do it to women all the time," she defended. "You're just pissed because I did it to you before you did it to me."

"I think *you're* the one who's pissed here. Maybe because the real reason you left that morning was that you knew you'd be in just as much trouble if your dad and brothers knew what happened between us. Actually, more so than me. Because you knew the conflict and you still accepted this position."

"I was doing us both a favor."

"You were doing *yourself* a favor. You were bored out of your mind, just looking for a game to play. So here you are. And now you're mad because you know you want me, but you can't have me. You're just as stuck as I am."

19

DAMON

*H*er face softened as she batted those big thick lashes.

"I have no idea what you're talking about, Mr. Copeland. Now, if you'll excuse me, I have an awful lot of work to do. And apparently, I have to go pass the new messaging memo on to Josh."

She ducked under my arm and stormed out of my office, and I couldn't help but smile to myself.

I'd given her a run for her money instead of playing right into her hands. I'd noticed the way she looked at me and the way her breath quickened as I got near her. She was just as hopeless as I was, only better at using it to her advantage, but maybe that was finally about to change.

I glanced over the office floor through the large window Aria had been pinned against moments ago, just in time to catch Angie and Lulu staring right back at me. *Fuck.* Had they seen the entire exchange? Even without hearing what we were saying, our body language alone was enough to inspire a plethora of rumors. That was the *last* thing I needed piled on top of my already-mounting frustrations and stress. It was shaping up to be a less than ideal Monday morning.

*T*hings didn't get any better by noon when Aria's message chimed into my inbox. Going against everything we discussed, she sent in the team's midday updates paired with her own words.

Aria: You'll find the reports you requested attached, sweetheart.

I scowled at the message, fuming with anger.

Not only had she blatantly gone against my instructions, but she was also rubbing my nose in everything. I jerked my finger across the mousepad, firing the report off to the printer. I snatched it up on my way out the door, skimming over it as I walked, searching for any extra ammunition on what I was about to do.

A number of engineers were crowded around Aria when I walked into the workroom. They all jerked and turned with my moody entrance. I didn't even have to say anything to them.

With my eyes burning into Aria, I growled, "A word, Ms. Humphries."

They all scrambled out as quickly as they could, while she leaned back in her chair, crossing her legs as she looked up at me with a smug smile.

"Ms. Humphries?" she questioned once everybody had left. "I thought there were too many Humphries crawling around this office already."

"Apparently, we need to take extra measures to solidify the professionalism of our relationship," I snapped, waving the printed papers in front of her. "These were supposed to be sent in by Josh. And there are typos in the language on page three. That's part of the direct presentation for the client. Do you know how something like that could make us look? It could discolor their view of the entire pitch."

"Surely you're not so bent out of shape over one or two typos." She laughed. "You said yourself that next week would be dedicated entirely to ironing out all the tiny little imperfections. I thought the coding and functions of the software was much more important at this stage, and if you look, you'll see all of that is in perfect working order. No typos."

"Josh will be responsible for sending everything in from here on out, as I said earlier," I continued sternly, ignoring her feigned innocence. "And *Josh* will be double-checking all of your work. It's too late in the game for us to be so blasé about these kinds of errors. You'll report to me directly on coding software at the end of the day. Got it?"

Her eyes narrowed in defiance, but she quickly brushed it off with a breezy smile. "If you want to waste your time on the extra work, be my guest. I'll be sure to drop by your office before I leave tonight."

"Do that," I hissed, spinning on my heels to march back to my office.

As I went, I was still boiling with anger, but I knew I'd overreacted. Every ounce of traction I'd gained that morning was already lost, and she not only knew it, but she was *enjoying* it. She hadn't even done that much to set me off. Well, she *had* disregarded my orders. Just the sight of her name popping up on my screen unexpectedly, or that snide expression she always flashed at me—that was all it took.

Well, it was all of that and the allure of her deep-red lips and the wicked glint in her big blue eyes. Not to mention the glow of her tanned skin and the silkiness of her golden hair. The girly, fruity scents that wafted from her and the sway of her curves when she walked, or the way her skirt inched up her thighs every time she crossed her legs in front of me.

While one part of me was aching to lay her out in front of me and take all of my frustrations out on her body, ravaging her until she submitted to the pleasure, moaning and writhing in my arms. The other part of me was screeching with alarm bells that kept reminding me: *Hands. Off.*

*I*t was all spinning through my head and left me less than thrilled to see her appear at my door at five that evening with a printed report in her hands. I waved her in, and she plopped it down on my desk with spite.

"As you requested, Mr. Copeland."

"Good," I grumbled, snatching the pages up to read them over.

As I skimmed the words and coding, she sauntered over to my side and leaned down, propping her elbows on my desk next to me. I cut my eyes to her, ignoring the alertness that spread from the brush of her arm.

"Do you mind?" I cleared my throat, trying to turn my attention back to the report.

"I'm only ensuring I didn't miss anything myself," she defended with an annoying, yet adorable little pout.

And of course, as she perched next to me, she pressed her arms together against the bottom of her cleavage, allowing the hint of her breasts to push together and become more pronounced. No matter how hard I kept trying to focus, the sight of the little moon that formed between them kept pulling me right back in.

I attempted to shift away from her, pushing away my desire to rip the rest of that blouse open, sending the buttons scattering across the floor. I wanted to see her perfect breasts, set them free and suck each one into my mouth until she was a wet, shaking mess.

"That'll be all for today," I snapped, dropping the report to my desk. I swiveled my chair around to face the computer, turning my back to her.

"So, everything is in order then?" she asked, not budging an inch.

"I said that will be all today, Ms. Humphries." I hated the sound of that name rolling off my tongue. It was the worst time to have yet another reminder of who she was and one of the many reasons she was off-limits.

She sauntered back to the door, stopping to add, "I'll see you bright and early then. Have a good night. And, uh...sweet dreams, Mr. Copeland."

That look on her face nearly sent me lunging out of my chair after her.

Just two more weeks, I reminded myself. Less than that, actually. Then I could hire Cornelius's permanent replacement and put this whole fucking thing behind me.

20

ARIA

*T*he lead architect, Jonas, along with Josh, Damon, and I were hunkered down in the conference room. The table was littered with half-emptied boxes from our Chinese takeout dinner, along with a few empty water bottles and endless stacks of paper.

It was Thursday and past 7 p.m.

Our goal was to walk out that night with everything in a good spot for us to really kill it on Friday and move into our weekends with clear heads to rest and reset over the weekend.

A large brass clock with black Roman numerals hung on the back wall, and it seemed to be ticking louder by the second. I was hunched down in front of my laptop, squirming with restlessness. It wasn't that I was in any hurry to call it quits. It was more so that the scent of Damon in the air and his commanding presence, in combination with Josh and Jonas lurking around, left me feeling antsy.

Every so often I dared to drift my eyes over to Damon, only to catch him staring right back at me. Josh and Jonas seemed to be completely oblivious to my restlessness. Which was a good thing but left me feeling like a ball of pent-up lust and dissatisfaction—a feeling that had already been building enough over the past couple of weeks.

"Well, I'm going to call it a night," Jonas announced suddenly, eliciting an audible sigh of relief from me. "I've done all I can do until I can come back to this with fresh eyes in the morning."

"I'm packing up for the night, too," Josh said. "You two don't tire yourselves out too much tonight. Catch you tomorrow."

Josh slid his brown leather messenger bag over his shoulder and waved before walking out the door. Jonas slipped out right behind him. I watched them take their exit through the darkened office floor where even the janitors were wrapping up their nightly cleaning.

We were seconds away from being completely alone.

The only two souls left in the building would be myself and Damon.

Of course, there would be cleaning staff coming in later, and there was also security downstairs in the main lobby, but the guards made a point not to bother the higher-ups like Damon when they were working late.

I felt my body relax slightly. It wasn't just the freedom from having to be so careful about the obvious tension between me and Damon. There was a familiarity between us that allowed us to let go a little and breathe a little easier, even aside from all of our "drama."

Damon watched the men leave before walking over to a panel in the far corner of the room. He pressed his palm flat against it, pushing it in to reveal a hidden door that revolved around to release an entire minibar. "Now that they're gone, how about some fuel for working these kinds of hours."

He uncorked a bottle of expensive Scotch and held it up toward me. "Would you like a glass?"

"Dear God, yes," I groaned.

An awkward look washed over my face (I felt it!), and an amused one washed over his at the same time. We were both painfully aware of the memory from the last time I uttered that phrase to him—in an entirely *different* context.

But he played it off real smooth and continued pouring two glasses. I snatched it up from his hand, spilling a bit (Geez, girl, get a grip! You can't even hold on to your liquor now?), and I eagerly drew it to my lips. The bitter burn with a hint of black cherry rolled over my tongue, providing instant relief.

"You didn't trust the guys to know about your secret stash?" I asked him, staring down the amber liquid swirling in my glass. "I could've used this hours ago."

"All of the hidden bars are information that only your father, brothers, and I are privy to. But since you probably know all their other secrets—"

"Yes?"

"Why not bend the rules?" he finished.

Bending the rules... God, him saying that with his sex voice. *Oh, no. I'm screwed.*

He glided back over to his seat with that masculine charm he wore so well. The Scotch in his hand was paired perfectly with his expensive black suit and his slicked-back dark waves. I'd never seen such a perfect example of sophistication, just reeking of power and focus. A man with a mission who, despite all of his OCD quirks, worked well under pressure.

I couldn't say the same thing for myself. I felt like a hot mess with my hair that'd started to feel greasy from spearing my fingers through it all day, and I felt blazing heat trailing along my skin from all the surges of yearning Damon had inspired in me, only for it to fade again as I tried so desperately to focus on work instead of him.

But the warm burn of the Scotch was doing wonders to calm and relax me. I downed the first glass pretty quickly while we continued working in silence.

Then, I helped myself to another.

While focusing on work was easier with the alcohol as lubricant, it did nothing to keep me from repeatedly getting sucked back into my awareness of Damon's presence. It was like all the air in the room was crackling with an electric magnetism. Every move he made sent tingles through me.

Judging by his less-than-calm demeanor, I had a feeling I was *not* doing the same for him.

"What's your deal anyway? Outside of work?" I finally ventured to ask, breaking the tense silence.

"What do you mean?" he grumbled, barely looking up from his computer.

"You work constantly, and you work *out*. I know because I've seen you leaving with your gym bag. And you ride bikes with my brothers. Is that it? Is that all Damon Copeland has going on in his life? Aside from the occasional pick up at a bar, that is."

"I like routine." He sighed, adding with a frown. "Not that it's any of *your* business." He lifted a brow in challenge.

Well, *hell*. It just got hot in here again. Phew. I needed a fan. *Damn...*

Biting my lip, I felt like I was *dying* on the inside. Even his brisk attitude was turning me on, right down to the tightness of his grimacing lips as he squinted his eyes against the blue glow of his screen. Damon liked routine—I liked the opposite. Too much of the same thing set me off with an impulse to run or do something crazy to switch things up. And he'd already shown me a hint of just how well he could match that brazen urge when he cornered me in his office last week, and again in the meeting room on Monday. It was all boiling up inside of me, pushing me to the brink of exploding and doing something extreme.

I was tired of skirting around the issue. I was bored, exhausted, and hitting a brick wall with my work. *Forget all the flirting and subtle glances.*

I was ready to make a bold move.

I leapt up from my chair and marched straight for Damon.

He wouldn't know what hit him.

21

ARIA

*D*amon cut his eyes over to me but was making a point to try and ignore me. Until I pressed my palms against his shoulders, shoving his chair back, giving me enough space to slide into a seated position on the edge of the table in front of him. Then he couldn't ignore me anymore.

"What are you doing?" His voice was nearly a growl, but I cut him off, yanking him toward me with a tight grip on his tie.

His eyes burned into mine as he glared back at me with an expression I couldn't read.

"Careful what you wish for," he rumbled, his eyes dark. They slid down my face, dancing across my lips. "You might get burnt."

I didn't know what my plan was. Would I pull away? Drive the torment further by darting my tongue along his bottom lip?

Before I could make up my mind, he stood up and slid the chair backward several feet. "I'm fed up with all of your games," he growled, towering over me with a look that told me he was not taking any BS.

"Good. Because I'm done playing them," I shot back, panting a little from the rush of our momentary closeness.

I wanted more, and I was tired of denying myself.

Pulling his tie again, I stumbled over his shoe (because I was a *damn* sexy klutz!) and he plummeted toward me, sending his glasses flying to the floor and me falling back against the table with the weight of his exquisite body crashing over me. I was *so* freaking graceful—at least my arms hadn't gone flailing.

Quirking my lips into a grin, I shook off my clumsiness. "Are you going to stare at me all night or kiss me, Damon?"

We were in a standoff of fiery expressions when his lips parted to scold me more.

He shot a finger over my mouth. "Shut up, Aria."

The command set off an instant eruption of desire in me.

He leaned in and kissed my neck, my cheeks. Then his lips brushed mine, testing and teasing. His lips felt soft and warm, and the sensation sent a sting of excitement to my clit. When I gasped, he pulled back a mere breath's width and looked into my eyes, holding me there. Those stormy eyes! My heart was about to explode when he leaned back in and kissed me again, harder this time. My knees buckled, and I couldn't think straight. As he pressed closer—his sure, strong arms around me—the kiss became fierce, demanding, and passionate, and our tongues tangled for dominance. We kissed each other with every ounce of fury that had been building between us. The electricity was powerful enough to light up Manhattan, leaving me utterly breathless. We didn't stop kissing for what seemed like an eternity, and my body ignited past the point of return.

One small step over the line had been all it took.

His hands were rough as they restlessly kneaded into my body, moving from my thighs to my ass, then up to my breasts. Damon forced his hips between my legs, dangling me back against the table with his throbbing rock-hard erection pressing into me. He was moving against me rhythmically, struggling to go slow. I was on my elbows, craning up for his kiss like my life depended on it.

My lips were jolted from his. Damon squeezed my jaw between his thumb and forefinger, snapping my gaze to his. He was going to ravage my body with vengeance, and his eyes were giving me every warning to stop now if I couldn't handle it.

But I was more than up for the challenge.

I stared back at him, smiling and licking my bottom lip. I tried to snap my teeth toward him, but he shoved me back and drank in a long, slow, menacing look of me on the table in front of him.

"You've been flaunting every inch of this body in front of me since the first day you walked in here," he said with a growling rasp, eyeing me up and down.

"So? What are you going to do about it?" I taunted, intentionally aggravating him. I couldn't wait to see what provoking him further would do.

"You like teasing men?"

"I like teasing *you*," I quipped.

A faint, dark smile flashed across his face before he leaned over me, gliding his tongue along the shell of my ear. His head dropped to the side of my neck, and he sucked my flesh between his teeth. Every flick of his tongue and bite made me seize up with need.

"Is that what gets you off?" His voice was impossibly deep, vibrating through me, and his hand traveled further down my body, lighting me on fire from the inside out. "Trying to turn me into putty in your hands?"

"It doesn't get me off. But it's a start."

"Hmmm. You're such a bad girl," he hissed.

The clever reply on the tip of my tongue dissipated as he opened the front of my blouse and dropped his mouth between my breasts. To be honest here, my nipples were just begging to be played with. He licked and bit my breasts, taking them in by the handful, sparing my aroused nipples. I barely had time to catch my breath before he reached around to the clasp in the back and snapped it open. His hand snaked beneath the lacy fabric, sending a warm rush of desire straight to my core as he touched my bare skin, and his thumb brushed my hardened nipple.

"Damon," I whimpered, clasping my hands around his neck.

He pinched each nipple with his fingers, rolling them until I was writhing against him. My bra fell away as he inched his mouth around my breasts in a fiery trail of kisses, my little clit tingling with desire, all with one hand cupping my ass and his other one working its way between my legs.

"Ah, so I was right," he noted after his touch found its way to my pooling wetness. "You want me. And I bet you have this entire time."

I wanted to say something sassy, and to tell him that I hadn't, but once again he took the words from my mouth as he pushed the damp fabric aside and slid his fingers through my wet folds. I was tight and slick, and he effortlessly slid in and out, my legs already shaking.

Was I crazy for this gorgeous specimen of a man?

Yes.

Did this mean I would spread my legs for him?

Nnn...–Yes.

"I need you inside me, *now*," I demanded, yanking his mouth back to mine.

"Oh, I will be."

Our nostrils and mouths flared with hot, desperate breaths in between our urgently sweeping tongues. He hiked my skirt up to my hips and pulled off my panties. I busied myself with his belt and the zipper of his pants. He freed himself from his suit jacket, giving me the freedom to loosen the top buttons of his shirt so I could get another peek at that muscular chest I'd been dreaming about.

But the rest of it? We were too frantic for relief. He flattened his big, strong hand across my stomach, pressing me down to the table.

Panting, I watched as Damon pulled out his wallet and removed a condom. And holy *crap*. His dick.

Oh, *hell*. I'd forgotten how imposing he was.

"Mmm, whatcha got there?" I bit my lips. "Need any help?" I had grabby hands. I *wanted* what I saw.

Damon palmed his erection, giving it a few solid strokes before sliding the condom down the length of it.

"Lie back down," he demanded, tossing the wrapper to the side and shoving his wallet back in his pocket, as I lay back down.

He positioned himself at my opening, and I felt his crown pressing against me. I thought I might faint.

There was no escape now.

Inch by torturous inch, he thrusted inside of me. I closed my eyes as I took him in, getting used to his impressive size, moaning from the sensation of him finally filling me.

This was it.

The moment I'd dreamed about.

OMG, Damon was fucking me, my *boss* was fucking me.

I knew I wanted it.

I had been for a while.

But I didn't fully understand just how badly until it was happening.

"*Yes*," I hissed, bucking my hips to meet him as he pulled out and plunged back inside.

His first few thrusts were slow, he took his time, but then he broke into a steady, forceful rhythm. He growled each time his tip pushed into my core, with my muscles tightening around him. I was dizzy from the sensations of his scent, the commanding force of his hands moving over my body, and his manly sounds of pleasure falling from his lips.

He brought his thumb to my clit and began moving it in slow circles, setting off eruptions of a rising orgasm inside of me. Each time he pounded into me again, making no secret of his need for me, I felt myself getting closer.

"Yeah...oh God, yes..."

"Tell me when you're close?"

"That's it. *Please*, Damon. More...like that," I begged in a daze of building pleasure.

I could feel him twitching inside of me, scaling the same rise of climax quickly. "Oh, my...I'm...close."

"Don't come yet," he commanded, removing his hand from my clit.

"What?"

"Don't come yet," he repeated.

I was just about to lose myself completely but tried to relax. Bossy Damon was *so hot*. Aroused Damon, on the brink of orgasm, was even hotter. His hips stuttered against mine harder, and I felt warmth burst inside of me. Watching him come only made me more desperate to feel the same relief. My clit was swollen, and I was so incredibly close.

His finger returned to my clit. "Oh, yes, so good". His touch felt wonderful, and more intense than before. Only a few strokes, and I was sure I would come, I could feel it.

"Do that again," I moaned. His finger repeated the singular movement. Yes, that's the spot. Dead on. "Don't stop, please. Again." I encouraged, unable to concentrate. I started the countdown in my head. Three. The pressure rose. It felt so amazing. I felt another brush of his finger. Two, OMG. I would come so hard on his cock still buried inside me. I could barely think or concentrate on anything else. I was a moaning, wiggling mess. One more stroke, and I would explode.

And by explode I meant I would erupt like a freaking volcano.

I barely had time to register what was happening when everything between my legs suddenly felt bare and untouched. I opened my eyes to see he was zipping up his pants. *What the fuck?*

Sitting up, I stared him down with confusion. Damon knew what he was doing well enough to know I didn't have my...*Didn't he?*

I cleared my throat awkwardly. "Um...forgetting something?"

He arched a brow with an arrogant smirk. "Nope. I don't think so."

"You know I didn't...I wasn't..." I laughed under my breath.

He slid his big arms back into his tailored suit jacket. "I know."

"Huh?"

"You heard me."

I pulled myself the rest of the way up, my face now twisted with anger. "What the hell do you mean you know? You did that on purpose?"

He stepped forward, teasing his lips against mine. "Now you know how it feels to be teased relentlessly, pushed to the edge, then left unsatisfied—with blue balls. Which is exactly what you've been doing to me all this time."

Okay. So maybe I *did* deserve it, but I was so mad.

I could have screamed.

What a *dickface*.

He casually gathered up his things, swooped up his glasses from the floor, and walked to the door, leaving me there half-dressed, my hair messier than ever and still quivering with a need that was *so* close to being fulfilled.

He put on his glasses, stopped and looked me over on his way out, tormenting me with his body in my vulnerable state.

"This stops now. And if you keep pushing me—you'll never come with me again, *ever*. I can promise you that. You'll beg and beg, but I won't give you what you need. So, I suggest you put a stop to all these games." He straightened his tie. "Not only that, continue to push me, and you'll get a spanking." He nodded and left me sitting there.

"Bastard," I hissed in disbelief.

I forced myself up to throw my clothes back on in a huff. *The nerve! He blue-clitted me!* I closed the minibar back into its hidden compartment, even though I was tempted to leave it open in hopes of getting Damon in trouble. I was fuming as I snatched up my stuff and stormed off to the elevator to go home for the night.

White-hot anger surged through me the whole way home.

The only thing that soothed it was the lingering taste of him in my mouth and the buzz of my skin still reeling from his touch. But it was a vicious cycle. Those fleeting memories only made me more furious with dissatisfaction.

I didn't even want to take care of matters myself when I finally got home and plopped into bed. I was too pissed. I knew Damon was uptight and infuriatingly tedious and meticulous. Above all, he was extremely irritable. And the messed-up part was—I liked it! Who knew a man being so controlling could turn me on so much? I tossed and turned all night in a hot sweat of rage, lust, and relentless desire.

I should've hated him more than ever. Such a dick move should have completely extinguished any ounce of attraction I felt. So why did it seem to be doing the opposite and only making my need for him swell and encompass me completely?

22

DAMON

I'd been in one meeting after another as soon as I'd arrived at work. Josh hadn't been feeling well, and I had yet to see Aria, which kept my mind otherwise occupied on business and my hands busy. She hadn't liked getting a taste of her own medicine. I did. The look on her face was fucking hilarious. At least I'd got her attention. She finally forwarded her updates through Josh as I'd ordered her to do in the first place. I guess it'd taken a somewhat drastic move to get her to finally listen to me.

I should have been happy with that result. So, why was I still so tense and on edge? Not even the sun shining over the sprawling countryside landscape calmed me down as I drove past it on my motorcycle. A nice Saturday afternoon ride should have done the trick to shake it all from my mind, but it was no use.

Admiring the view as the landscape passed me by, I thought of how Aria's honey-colored hair had felt like silk slipping through my fingertips. The way her body moved beneath mine, matching me thrust for thrust, she'd been a stunning sight. I'd wanted to kiss every single one of her freckles. And her blue eyes boring into me as she begged for release, the release I refused to give her.

But I would.

I wanted her in my bed. On my desk. Anywhere. I didn't fucking care.

The more the thoughts spiraled through my mind, the more irritated I got.

Finally, I found myself pulling off the side of the road. I told myself it was just to enjoy the scenery, but who was I kidding? Deep down I knew it was all the building sexual tension frying my brain.

The roar of Miles and Oliver's engines came up behind me. I'd been keeping a good distance on them all morning, needing the space. But they caught up once I stopped, and their bikes slowed to a quiet purr before turning off completely.

"What gives?" Oliver asked impatiently. "Why did you stop?"

"It's just a nice view," I told him, staring out at the horizon.

I could see Oliver and Miles exchanging a sideways glance before Miles slowly approached me. "Hey? You feeling okay, buddy?"

He looked at me like I was a madman on the verge of a breakdown.

"Fine," I groaned. "Don't look at me like that. You're creeping me the fuck out."

"It's just that you never make unplanned stops." He shrugged. "Especially not for something like 'admiring the view.' What's up with you?"

Oliver removed his helmet and joined his brother's side. "Yeah. You okay? Is our little sister giving you a hard time at work?" He chuckled.

Miles shook his head, laughing. "We told you she could be a real brat. We gave you fair warning."

I nodded. "Yeah, you did. We've been busier than usual. Not sure where my head is these days." They'd prefer that admission than some of the other things I'd been thinking about her.

An awkward silence fell between us as Miles got distracted kicking sticks around in the ditch, then going for a piss. But Oliver focused in on me more intently. He was not so easily swayed by my vague explanation.

"Hey," he said. "Don't tell me you have a *thing* for her." He blew out a laugh, as if it was the most preposterous possibility. Not that I *would* catch feelings, but that I'd be so boldly stupid to allow it to happen.

"I don't have time for *things*. Chill," I answered with a forced chuckle.

We laughed together for a moment. It picked up when Miles joined in, "Oh, *yeah*," he joked. "Damon and Aria...Like *that* would ever work."

My laughter slowly faded, and against my better judgment, I couldn't resist wondering about what he'd just said. "What do you mean?"

Oliver's eyes stayed glued to me as Miles attempted to explain. "Come on, man. You two are like complete polar opposites. She's all spontaneous and carefree. You're calculated and serious. She'd drive you insane with her quirks. You couldn't make her happy. Not to mention, you know, bro-code. Do I really have to explain this shit again? You better not even think about laying a finger on her."

He said it passively, still convinced such a thing would never happen. But Oliver seemed much more concerned.

"Damon," Oliver said more sternly. "You don't...do you?"

I kicked a rock out into the open field in front of us. "Don't *what*?"

"Have a *thing* for our sister." His voice was dead serious this time, and unforgiving. Just like the tense expression on his face.

"Back off with your bullshit." I sighed. But he was still unmoved. "Jesus Christ, man. What's gotten into you? I've never seen you act like this before. Calm the fuck down."

Miles stepped between us, chuckling. "Oh, that's right. You haven't seen this side of Oliver before. He's always been protective of women that are close to his heart. I'd go a little nuts on you, too, *if* I thought you were messing around with our baby sister."

"So you don't?" Oliver stared at me.

"Of course he doesn't. Chill, bro," Miles said to him. "Damon wouldn't do us dirty."

"Answer," Oliver said.

"I hardly know her. Get out of my face. She's..." I racked my brain to find the words, "an irritating employee to have. Jesus, back off."

"I've never seen you all bent out of shape like this," Miles quipped. "I mean, sure, we always get the feeling you're all wound up and on the brink of having a nervous breakdown on the inside. But you're usually so good about keeping it down. She must *really* be getting to you."

An aggressive glint flickered in Oliver's eyes as he stepped closer. "Is that it? Is she *getting to you*?"

"For fuck's sake, man. Will you lay off already?" I shot back, trying to rethink my strategy. "I'd hate to have to beat your ass out here on the side of the road."

I meant it as a joke. Kind of. I thought it would lighten him up and break the rapidly rising tension between us. Miles certainly thought it was funny—about as funny as he thought the idea of something happening between Aria and me was. But he stopped laughing when he noticed the way Oliver's jaw tightened with anger.

"Seriously though, man. Do *not* fuck with her."

"I'm her boss," I defended.

"That could be fixed," he threatened.

Dead silence.

I knew he wasn't talking about letting Aria go.

"Really, Damon," Oliver continued, "I'd hate to have to argue for my closest buddy being fired. But I probably wouldn't have to provide much of an argument if our dad suspected anything between you two. You wouldn't want to have to answer to him in *that* situation."

I mustered up every ounce of restraint inside and faced him head-on, making no mistake of how adamant I was—a cost-benefit analysis was running in the back of my head, hammering out shit results. I could have cleared everything up here. Instead, I tried to cause a delay and push off my decision. "You have nothing to worry about," I said, feeling like an asshole. It wasn't that I enjoyed lying to my buddies. The whole point was to buy me—*us*—time. I'd worked too hard to let this go. It wasn't like I could undo what I'd done.

And now, she meant too much to risk anything.

"Yeah, we know, brother." Miles nodded and turned to climb on his bike.

"Good. Keep it that way," Oliver said, and his shoulders relaxed. "You can have any girl you want in New York. Do *not* touch our sister. Clear?"

"If you girls are done chatting, can we get back on the road already?" I asked, ignoring his question.

"Babs's Pie is calling my name," Miles called out. "And later, Roy and Joy's." He kicked down.

Oliver kept his eyes fixed on me as I pushed past him and got on my bike.

I was surging with even more uneasiness than before as we took off again. No fucking wonder Aria had disappeared that morning when she realized who I was. I figured her brothers wouldn't be too keen on the idea of me and their sister hooking up, and I couldn't fucking blame them, but I had no idea just how far they would take it.

Fuck.

Now not only did I have to keep my raging ache for her under wraps just to get my job done, but apparently, my job itself was on the line if I couldn't. Who knew how serious Oliver really was about getting me fired? I was in no hurry to find out.

I suddenly felt more understanding of Aria's position. She probably understood the gravity of this "thing" between us in terms of her family, even before I saw it firsthand. Maybe that's why she was being such a tease. I shook my head, cursing.

She finally decided to take the plunge and risk something else happening between us, while I came to realize all this had to stop.

No matter how I looked at it, and the longer I tried to come up with a solution, one thing became pretty clear—I was fucked.

23

ARIA

J tried to keep my head up when I headed into the office Monday morning. Damon and I hadn't interacted since our "special meeting", and I knew I was going to have to face him again with all these unsatisfied feelings inside of me like a clogged pipe waiting to burst.

My phone rang as I got off the elevator, and I glanced down to see Zoe's name scrolling across the screen. Perfect timing. She would give me the pep talk I needed to face the day.

"What's up?"

"Just calling for my weekly update on Mr. Hottie. Have you two killed each other yet? Or better yet, slept together? I'm not sure which one I should be placing bets on first."

"A little of both." I sighed.

"You don't say! Tell me *more.*" She giggled.

I pushed my way into the huddle of women around the coffee bar, holding the phone between my cheek and shoulder as I helped myself to a fresh steaming mug of much-needed Joe. The coffee maker looked shiny and new.

"I can't really talk right now," I said, "but let's just say...what did happen wasn't much to write home about. I mean, it was...it could have been, but he picked a terrible time to get revenge on me for teasing him so much," I explained as best I could without giving away too much to the eavesdropping secretaries.

"Uh-huh. Well, now I'm even more intrigued," Zoe said. "Can't you sneak off somewhere to spill *all* the tea? That's a terrible way to leave me hanging here, girl."

"I know, but I just walked into the office. I'll have to tell you more later. I'll call you when I get off." I winced at the irony of my words.

"Real quick before you hang up," she replied in a hurry. "Did the genie come out and play after our smart setup? Did he like the dragon-y perfume? Was it hot? Like the first-time kind of hot? All the mysterious problems aside."

"Until the unceremonious ending...You have no idea," I groaned, wishing I could relive those moments of his strong hands bending me whichever way he wanted. How good he'd felt inside me as he hiked my leg up over his shoulder. Ugh, just thinking about it had me every bit as turned on as I'd been in the moment. Like I was still suspended in time there, waiting for the job to be finished.

I ended the call with Zoe, leaving her just as hungry for more, just in a *vastly* different way. As I brought my cup of coffee to my lips, I was hit with the jolt of Lulu, Angie, and Bernadette's wide, expectant eyes burning into me.

"We heard that tone in your voice." Angie glared. "Who were you talking about?"

"No one," I shot back innocently.

I knew there was no way they could have known I was talking about *Mr. Copeland*, which was why I'd been so blasé about them lingering around. But I suddenly wished I'd waited to grab my coffee until after I hung up the phone. Leave it to me to get so caught up in gossiping that I carelessly blurted out so much right in front of them.

"Don't play coy with us," Lulu said.

"We heard your tone, and we see that look in your eyes. You already owe us an explanation as to what the hustle and bustle in the conference room, with Mr. Copeland, was all about. You stormed out like a class five hurricane. Anyhow...who have you been messing around with?" Angie interrogated.

"Come on. Tell us," Bernadette begged. "I'm married. And you have no idea how much I thrive on all the stories from you single girls. Come on! If it helps know that I made a complete tit of myself when I was younger, so I won't judge."

"There's nothing to tell," I insisted with a shrug. "Just a...a fling. Yeah. But it's over now. It was no big deal."

Oh, fuck. Just the situation I'd been afraid of—add Bernadette! Hound dogs, and I'd given them a freaking bone. *Great job, Aria. This is so my karmic payback. I can feel it.*

I was eager to escape, but Angie wasn't letting it go that easily. "At least tell us what he looks like."

Lulu's eyes flickered with mischief. "Or better yet...what *it* looked like. How big was the fella?"

"Yeah, how was *it*?" Bernadette stared at me, excited.

"Good morning, ladies." A deep, manly baritone sounded behind us.

The voice stopped me cold.

Shitshitshitshit!

I cringed and turned around slowly to see Damon had strolled in behind me. "Go ahead, Aria," he said. "Answer them. How was *it*? This fling of yours?"

Fuck. My. Life.

The universe was cruel. I wanted to die...

The girls looked shocked. It wasn't like he'd ever been known for jumping in on office gossip. In fact, he hated it. Especially the crasser conversations about our sex lives.

"I was just getting to work." I laughed nervously, trying to slide past them.

Please. If anybody's listening...let me pass. I'll be a good girl. Okay, I'll try my best. I promise!

"No, by all means. Don't let me interrupt," he said, blocking my path before driving me back to the others. "I'm here for the same reason the rest of you are, and then I'll be on my way. Pretend I'm not even here."

Thwarted again. Dammit.

Bernadette appeared tickled by her direct boss's request. I was sure it was a relief for her to see a more down to earth side of him. The other ladies shrugged, seeming pleased and eager to indulge him.

"I always wished I was the type who could have one-night stands," Bernadette confessed. "Instead, the one night turned into a lifetime, and that's how I ended up married to Bobby."

"Aria didn't say it was a one-night stand," Lulu argued. "She said *fling*. Which insinuates multiple offenses."

"Spill," Angie said to me.

Oh, crap!

I squirmed in place, noticing the way Damon's eyes made a subtle cut over to me, waiting for my reply. I bit my lip, trying to quickly plot some way out of this. But then I had a thought: Damon had picked the most inconvenient time possible to get his vengeance. This was the perfect opportunity to fire right back.

Score for Aria.

Zero points for Mr. Power-mad.

"It was decent while it lasted," I finally announced. "Which wasn't long. Some guys just don't have enough stamina for me, I guess. So, by the end…it was rather disappointing. *Underwhelming*, I would say."

I regretted the words as soon as they'd slipped out of my mouth. *OMG.* I was pushing it. *Will he punish me again? If there is another again. Which there won't be, of course.*

Damon put the coffee pot down to the burner, maybe a little too hard, then braced himself against the counter with one hand, taking a long sip of his coffee with the other. He was procrastinating on purpose, trying to stick around long enough to see what else I might be bold enough to divulge.

The ladies frowned.

"You poor thing," Angie answered. "Nothing's worse than a lousy lay. Stamina is super important."

"Where did you meet this guy anyway?" Lulu asked.

"Sounds like a loser," Bernadette said.

Angie nodded. "Totally. A lemon with a limp dick."

"Just at a bar," I answered breezily. "Talia's. Damon, have you heard of it?"

"Who hasn't?" he grunted before walking out of the room. Was there a spark of amusement on his face? Or was it irritation? He was hard to read.

Bernadette kept her eyes fixed on him as he left. The moment he was gone she huddled us all in closer. "Did you see that? That's the most he's ever said to us in here when he's been grabbing his coffee."

"That's not work-related anyway," Lulu added.

"He's jealous," Angie suggested.

"What? No," I said quickly. "He was probably just irritated that we were loitering around in here. We really should get to work..."

"I've seen the way you two look at each other." Angie grinned.

Lulu and Bernadette gasped, looking insatiable and impatient to hear more. Their eyes lit up, widening, as they leaned into me. "Is there something going on there? With you and *Damon*?"

"He's my boss. That's what's going on there," I hissed. "Shush."

It suddenly stopped being fun. And, that was my cue to get the hell out of Dodge.

A little harmless gossip, especially in the name of getting back at Damon, was one thing. But risking such a rumor getting back to my dad or brothers? Not the least bit amusing. Not even a little. God, my *brothers*? There would be blood. Unemployment. Murder. Maybe... Okay, not murder. Well, it would just suck. A lot!

"Ladies, it's been fun standing here and gossiping with you, but I have work to do."

I headed out the door, knowing the whole thing was my fault for indulging them as much as I did, and I was kicking myself for it the whole way back to my desk.

All my worries vanished for a moment when I pulled my chair back and saw a box sitting there, tucked away under the desk where no one else could see it.

It was black, tied up with a white satin bow.

I looked around the office with a puzzled expression before untying it slowly and lifting the lid.

Nestled inside folds of red tissue paper, there was a golden mini vibrator. *OMG. Really?*

I quickly slammed the lid back down and glanced around again to see if anybody was watching me. As I scanned the room, I caught sight of Damon in his office on the phone. Our eyes locked for a moment, and a smug grin flashed across his face.

Laughing and shaking my head, I peeked into the box again, this time noticing a small handwritten card.

I left the vibrator hidden in its box but pulled out the note to read it.

Might come in handy.
Keep it with you in case of emergencies.

I smirked to myself, then up at him.

He was back at work. He'd spun his chair around to face the giant window behind his desk, away from me. I was impressed. It was a bold move to leave this under my desk in the middle of the office. It was nice to know he would have had to arrange it before the break room incident minutes ago, which meant he must have been thinking about me over the weekend.

I liked he'd been smiling, even after what he overheard.

Tucking the note back into the box, I shoved it next to my purse —back into hiding under my desk. I was quick to log into my desktop and fire off a direct message to Damon.

Aria: Thanks. Definitely not the first time I've had to take matters into my own hands, so to speak.

I glanced over the screen, watching through Damon's office window as he turned to his computer and smirked at the message.

Damon: Maybe we can call a truce?

Aria: What kind of terms did you have in mind for this proposed truce?

Damon: I'm open to negotiations.

Damon: Maybe you should have a go with your gift first.

Damon: It might put you in a mood that's more open to compromise.

My cheeks burned hot as I read his reply. I'd bet he'd like to imagine me rushing home to pleasure myself, thinking of him the whole time. And I totally would. I couldn't help but smile, despite his usual arrogance.

I shook my head and continued typing.

Aria: Why the sudden rush to smooth things over?

Aria: You didn't seem to have a problem with me feeling rather...empty last week...

Damon: I thought with the trip to Maine for the pitch to the clients coming up this week, it might be good for us to be on better terms before going out of town together.

Damon: That's *one* of my motivations.

Damon: It seems Jonas is under the weather, so we're on our own with this one.

I sank back into my chair, filled with a rush of anticipation. A trip with the three of us was one thing. Just me and Damon? That was a whole other ball game—one that came with the promise of finishing what he started last week.

Shaking my head, I reminded myself nothing else could happen. That's what the vibrator was for, right? To get it all out of my system ahead of time.

*B*ut that didn't stop me from calling Zoe the moment I got off work later that day.

"Can you come over? There's been some changes with this work trip to pitch to the clients, and I'm in desperate need of cocktails and wardrobe advice while I start packing."

"Sure thing, girl," Zoe said. "Be over soon."

God, I loved her to death.

My head was spinning as I walked home. *It doesn't matter what you wear because nothing can happen on this trip. Every time you give into your cravings for him, you increase the risk of getting in over your head.*

He's your boss, Aria. Get a grip.

But he won't be my boss for much longer...Unless I end up staying.

But there was no way I'd stay at Humphries.

It was too weird working with my father and brothers...*and Damon.* That trumped any other good feelings I had about the job. Still, the endless stampede of thoughts, mixed in with my insatiable cravings for more of Damon, sent me into a frenzy as I started tossing clothes left and right out of my closet.

"What the hell is going on here?" Zoe appeared in my bedroom door, looking across the small mountains of hangers, garments, and shoes.

I popped out of my closet and rattled off an explanation for everything. All the details I couldn't regale her with earlier on our call. The vibrator. The trip. Jonas being sick and not being able to come. Damon and I...out of town together...*alone.* Then I rambled on to explain my system of organization with the clothes, which did exist—even though it just looked like a huge mess.

"Aria!" Zoe shouted, snapping me out of my rant. "Loungewear? Come on. If this guy ends up seeing you in your room, you're probably not going to be wearing anything for long."

"Don't say that!" I hissed.

"So, then it doesn't matter what you wear," she argued, taunting me.

"I still need to impress the clients!"

"Uh-hm." She held up a pink satin pajama set with black lace.

It walked a line between comfortable and seductive. I didn't want to look like I was trying too hard, after all.

"I'm sure they'll be really impressed with *this*." She scoffed, letting the top dangle from her pinky.

I rolled my eyes, snatching it back from her defensively.

"You're supposed to be helping me," I said. "Those two piles are options for day wear, and these are for evening wear. Also, what are you doing for lunch tomorrow? You have to help me shop. And I made us a salon appointment for Wednesday."

She laughed and shook her head. "Damn, girl. How long's the trip?"

"Uh, just one day."

"Just *one* day?

"Uh-huh."

"This guy has really done a number on you. I haven't seen your panties in this big of a bunch since college. Looks like you're preparing for a thirty-day Caribbean trip on a yacht. I thought you were indifferent to men and what they thought of you?"

"Uh-huh. I am."

"You're like one of the biggest ice queens I know. Could it be that Mr. Hottie is melting you a bit?" she asked.

Her suggestion sent me for an even bigger loop. "You're right. Which is exactly why I have to plan every part of this so carefully. I can't look too desperate, but I somehow have to look flawless and perfect without even trying. It has to be effortless, and I have to be aloof and—"

"Aria, you're spinning out again," she warned, cutting me off. "Just sit down. I'll help you, okay? But if I do all this and you don't get the best orgasm of your life or at least come back with some kind of juicy story, I'm going to be real salty about it."

I sat back and let her help, but not without a big gulp.

There was no way I could make it out of this trip without something majorly juicy happening. That was just the nature of my and Damon's chemistry. But whether or not that juice would flow in my favor? That was the question I was much more concerned with.

24

DAMON

*a*fter the ride with Miles and Oliver, I'd tried to stop my thoughts, but I couldn't. I fucking hated having to resist sleeping with her. The vibrator was a fun gift—there hadn't been a hidden message or anything. I'd known she'd get a smile out of it. Anything to make her laugh. The upcoming trip was a whole other matter, though. Normally, I'd be furious that my head architect was pulling out of a pitch at the last minute, especially when he was such a key player. Sick or not—you be there and finish what you started. Anything to land the deal. Those little unexpected surprises in life drove me nuts.

From a business perspective, it was fine. We could handle it. It left everything up to Aria and me, and even though I was constantly reminding myself that nothing else could happen between us—that didn't change the thrill I got from the thought of us spending a night dining together and staying in the same hotel, plus charming the clients and exploring the city. Was it despite *or* because of the forbidden element of it? Hell, I couldn't say.

Jonas and I were on a video call, making small talk, waiting for Aria to join in on the chat.

"You just rest up and get better," I told him. "You've been invaluable as always on this, and I'll need you well for the next one."

He seemed shocked at how easygoing I was being about it. I was shocked myself.

It was five minutes past when the chat was supposed to begin, but Aria still hadn't joined in from her own computer, so we went ahead and started without her.

I was surprised to see her appear in the doorway of my office, looking good in a tailored white pant suit, despite her red face. *Has she been running?* Her blonde hair was curlier than usual, resting just past her shoulders. She wore pearls and red lipstick.

"Hey, sorry for the delay," she said, trying to catch her breath. "I seem to be having some connectivity issues. Could I join in from your screen?"

"Of course." I nodded, getting up to pull an extra rolling chair next to mine.

With our chairs side by side, we tried to huddle in together for the chat. She was painfully close, and I kept catching traces of her strawberry-scented hair and the vanilla lotion on her glowing skin.

She cleared her throat and moved in close to the screen. We were shoulder to shoulder, with my hands accidentally grazing hers at her side. Had I wanted to seduce her, it would have been the perfect moment. I imagined carrying on with the meeting while caressing the palm of her hand, tracing the lines the same way I would across the rest of her body the moment we had privacy. Walking my fingertips up between her legs to tease her while she squirmed and tried not to give any hint of what was happening to Jonas.

If only. But I behaved myself and endured her closeness,

remaining professional, keeping my hands to myself. It was good practice for the resolve I would need to cling to over the duration of the trip.

Keeping to ourselves didn't mean it contained the tension or magnetic heat, however. The meeting continued, business as usual. But I was finding it hard to breathe at a normal pace and judging by the rise and fall of her gorgeous tits, coupled with the stolen glances out of the corner of her eyes, it was safe to bet she was struggling, too. Even more so than me.

She even seemed to breathe a sigh of relief as we wrapped things up and could retreat several feet apart again. My phone rang almost instantly—the attendant for our plane calling from the airstrip lobby to confirm the flight was ready whenever we were. Bernadette confirmed a car was waiting out front to pick us up, along with our luggage. Everything was on schedule.

"You ready?" I asked Aria.

"Ready." She nodded, sucking in a deep breath with a confident smile. I got a rush from the gleam of determination in her eye. She cared about this deal as much as I did. The work we had to do should have been a welcome distraction, it only seemed to make the lust crackling between us even hotter.

I hovered my hand above the small of her back, leading her out of the office. The workroom floor was scarce with employees as we passed through, and I couldn't resist taking the plunge to lower my hand to the cinched back of her suit.

Leaning into her ear while we walked, I rasped, "Did my gift prove to be useful?"

The corners of her lips took on a subtle, contained curl. "Some things are private, Damon. Even if you did supply the source."

"The source of your pleasure?" I grinned down at her. "I think the blush on your cheeks is the only answer I need."

"Oh, is it?" she asked, and her blush intensified. It was cute.

"Although, I'm dying to know," I said. "Did you bring it along in your bags? Your hotel suite could get awfully lonely at night."

"I should have, shouldn't I?" She spun on her heels to face me as we stopped at the elevator doors. "But I came fully prepared with everything I might need for this trip." She was enjoying our harmless flirtation, and so was I. Because that's all it was—a little innocent office banter. My gaze landed on the fullness of her breasts, and just as she tossed her shoulders back, I couldn't help but notice the way her pert nipples pressed against the fabric of her blouse.

Before I could react to her reply, my cock twitched with a craving, aching to be inside her. Just then, a voice called out to us in the lobby. A familiar one that was the last thing I wanted to hear in that moment.

"Damon! Aria! Glad I caught you." Mr. Humphries waved us down, speed walking to catch up to us. He smiled at his daughter, then directed his attention back to me. "I was hoping to send you off and wish you good luck."

"Dad." She laughed awkwardly, moving a few inches away from me. "I'm glad you caught us, too. And with such perfect timing."

In our weeks working together, I had managed to avoid this very moment. Aria, me, and her father—all together at once. And of course, it just had to happen in the middle of me teasing her over a vibrator that I gifted, balls tight and blood rushing into my dick. My stomach knotted, but I played it cool.

"You take good care of her while you're gone," Mr. Humphries addressed me. "I know you would with any associates accompanying you, but I trust you'll take extra care of this one. I'm a little biased." He winked at me and gave Aria a loving smile.

"Dad, I'll be fine," she said through clenched teeth.

"You have nothing to worry about, Mr. Humphries," I assured him, trying to ignore my inopportune semi.

"I know she's in good hands." He beamed, patting my shoulder.

He kissed Aria on the cheek and told her he loved her before finally setting us free for the elevator. What might have been a titillating ride down was now dampened with the unneeded reminder of our position. The haze of her father's presence seemed to linger in the air, keeping her several feet apart from me—even in the car ride to the landing strip.

I reached over and squeezed her hand, noting how tense she seemed.

"Relax, everything's going to be fine," I said.

She nodded, giving me a short look I couldn't read.

25

DAMON

*I*t wasn't until we settled into the company's luxurious private jet with champagne and bowls of fresh strawberries that Aria slowly started to unwind with the warm glow from her bubbly, golden drink.

"I've actually never been to Portland before," she confessed with a tinge of excitement. "We've stayed in a few resorts on the islands and along the coast, but never in Portland."

"Ah, you're in for a treat then," I said. "Not only is it full of culture, it's also a big hub in the tech world."

"So I've heard." She turned to look out the window, swirling her glass around in front of her tempting lips.

She looked beautiful, and with each passing minute, I realized this trip might prove to be even more trying than I anticipated, which seemed impossible.

I thought I'd realistically prepared.

Her eyes caught mine, and she admitted, "I'm glad Jonas isn't here. Only because...I'm more comfortable with you. I don't know him as well, I mean, personally. It makes it easier to relax and get in a good head space for the presentation."

My brows twitched for a brief moment. "You think you know me well personally?"

Her red lips spread into a pretty smile. "In some ways, yes. But... now that I think about it, I suppose there *is* a lot I don't know. And we have time to kill, don't we?"

"What do you want to know?" I asked.

"Well, why don't you tell me something about yourself I don't already know? In the name of business, of course."

"Of course."

"As I said, it will only help me perform better for the clients."

"Anything in the name of business," I replied, feeling comfortable. She was something else. "Hmm, well. I'm from Maine originally. The Cumberland Foreside, which is a mid-sized town. But the coastal neighborhood I grew up in was incredibly tight knit. It was very different from New York, that's for sure."

"When did you get your glasses?" she asked.

"Don't recall exactly. I've had them for as long as I can remember. So, since I was a kid."

"How much can you see without them?"

Ah, there it was—her theory. I didn't want to tell her that I'd overheard the rather gripping talk she'd had with our secretaries. But it was clear she wanted to know how "uninhibited" she could be around me naked and how much I could see. Women and their funny quirks.

"Just enough," I said truthfully.

"Oh good, okay." Her shoulders relaxed.

"So do you see everything really blurry?"

"Everything in the distance, yes. Up close I'm fine. I'm near-sighted, Aria." I said, watching her reaction. "I'm lucky I don't need them to read or to do things that require closer proximity." I kept my tone even, but I was smiling inwardly. She could take what she wanted from that straight up reply.

Her mouth dropped open, and she stared at me blankly. "Oh. So... if something or someone's right in front of you, you see—"

"—perfectly well." I finished her sentence.

"Oh." She swallowed.

Maybe I was an asshole, but it was amusing to see her putting the puzzle pieces together—her little theory was crumbling to dust. She looked flustered as hell.

"So when we were...you know..." she motioned between us, her voice now smaller, "you saw me, my freckles, everything—"

"—in crisply sharp definition." I paused, and then ventured to add, "Like in a nature program." I wondered how she'd react if I gave away the fact that I'd overheard her conversation and the women's talk of men's "primal natures." Apart from this, I'd seen her up close and naked, several times. She was drop-dead gorgeous, from head to toe, and she had no need to hide anything. "And I loved everything I saw," I added.

She looked up at me. Her cheeks were flushed, and redness was creeping down her neck. She gave me a "has he overheard our conversation" look, and then dropped it. My compliment had flown right past her. She shook her head, mumbling something like "I can't believe I didn't think of that. Duh."

Everything about her was fucking adorable.

"I had a fun childhood, it was good times," I said, trying to change the topic.

The look on her face told me she was more than happy to switch gears. Just when she opened her mouth to speak, my cell chimed. A message popped up.

Stella: Good luck with your presentation, banana muffin.

Stella: Hug emoji.

Stella: Kiss emoji.

Aria stared at the messages and stiffened a little. As she straightened herself, I saw something that resembled jealousy on her face.

"It's my sister," I told her.

Aria looked over at me. "Oh." She smiled. Was she relieved? "I didn't know you had a sister," she said. "Tell me about her. She calls you banana muffin?"

"Yeah, she calls me other things. She's six years younger, so I let it slide."

"What does she do?"

"She's studying architecture at Princeton."

"Wow! Is she involved in any groundbreaking new studies?"

"Like male anatomy and the position of certain organs?"

"Oh my God! You heard our conversation!" Aria shrieked.

"I did." I laughed.

"How much did you hear?"

"Everything. I was in the archive room by the elevator. I had no other choice but to become part of the *well of knowledge*."

At first, I thought she would be even more embarrassed. But then she waved her hand and laughed. "Ha, ha. How embarrassing."

"I know," I teased when my cell dinged again.

Stella: Text me when you're done. Don't f--k it up! Gotta run. Love you, dork.

I shook my head and shot her a reply.

Me: Thanks, pancake. Love you too.

Aria's eyes flicked back to mine, squinting slightly with amusement. "Okay, perfect cue to change the subject."

"Back to my childhood." I nodded, sliding my cell into my pocket.

"I can see it. Little Damon in his sweaters, walking along the coast in the winter with lighthouses in the distance. It must have driven you crazy to be thrown into the chaos of the city after that."

I tilted my head. "It wasn't my favorite thing, no. But it taught me to be adaptable, which I needed. And high school ended up going well for me."

"You were in the popular crowd with Miles and Oliver."

I could see her reeling with memories of different things she must have heard from them over the years. Her brothers, especially Miles, had always been like family. He and I shared a past that connected us on a deeper level, and we had the scars to prove it.

"Miles is like a little brother to me," I said. Always was, always will be. But both of them were cool jock types, smart and driven when they put their minds to it. They helped propel me into the world of real estate moguls through their father's company after college.

It stung to think of all that now, sitting next to Aria with such dangerous, dirty thoughts lurking around every corner of my mind. It was all overshadowed by the look in Oliver's eyes and the way he'd spoken to me on the side of the road the weekend before. Shit.

"Yes, and I'm grateful for them," I continued. "Without meeting them, I'd have likely never found my way to Humphries. I wouldn't have the life I do today, which I like."

"I'm glad to hear that. It makes me proud of my family."

There was a sparkle in her eyes, and I couldn't help but smile. "Now tell me something about you."

"What do you want to know?" she asked, taking a sip of her champagne.

"Something I don't know."

"Hmmm...I guess the thing people usually find most surprising about me is that I breezed through high school and college really fast."

"Why?" I had a suspicion of what she might say, but I wanted to hear her take.

"People always assume I'm a spoiled, reckless, wild child. Like I'm the black sheep of the family, even though that's *obviously* Miles. But actually...I really enjoyed my education, and I enjoy my career. Despite what my father wants people to believe."

"I can't say I'm all that surprised," I admitted. "For one, your father already told me about your educational background. And then, there's your age. You've accomplished much more than most women at this point in their lives."

"*Women*? How about most *people*?"

"Less than fifteen percent of the workforce in your field is taken up by women," I reminded her. "I guess age has less to do with it, but that just makes you all the more impressive."

"Tell that to Dad," she groaned playfully, rolling her eyes. "He's been his own boss ever since he took the reins from his father at our family's company. He doesn't know what it's like to toil away under a boss who doesn't challenge you or see your potential." She let out an apologetic laugh, touching my forearm. I enjoyed the feel of her soft fingers. "I don't mean *you*, obviously. Actually, I really love working for you. More than any employer I've had so far."

Did she really think so? Something in my chest stirred at her words. It hit me harder than I expected to. I stared off in thought for a moment. "Have you considered staying on after this project?" I asked. "You've been an invaluable asset to the team. And even once the papers are signed for this deal, there will be the construction and then the grand opening, alongside whatever else we set our sights on to tackle next."

Her face went blank, unreadable—but tight with concern. So was mine. Like a game of chicken to see who would cave in first.

She knew what this meant. I knew what this meant.

It was good for our careers.

Bad for everything between us.

A flirtatious affair amidst a temporary project was one thing. Continuing to work together put a whole new set of complications on our shoulders.

"Do you think that's a good idea?" she asked with uncertainty.

I'd always been one to put work and my career over everything else. That side of me wanted to believe we could make it work. For our jobs, which we both loved. And for the sake of her family, which she loved, and I respected.

But it was still hard to accept the idea of seeing her every single day, working side by side with her—and never really acting on my attraction. All the flirting and teasing would have to stop, on both of our accounts.

"Why not?" I decided out loud. I knew damn well why not.

She recoiled a little. "Oh. Okay. Well...I guess I'll think about it. This trip will give me a good chance to..." She shot me a sideways glance. "Consider all of the factors."

26

DAMON

$\mathcal{W}$e landed on a private runway near PWM an hour later and took a car to our hotel, wasting no time to proceed to the front desk to check in.

"Good afternoon. There should be a reservation under Damon Copeland."

The receptionist looked down and started typing as I turned to watch Aria spin around the middle of the lobby, taking it all in from floor to ceiling. The golden specks in the shiny flooring beneath her heels seemed to reflect in her eyes, even at a distance.

"Ah, yes, I have you in the Penthouse Suite with one king bed." The receptionist smiled.

I waited for more, but she simply blinked and stared back at me. "And?"

"And we'll have your bags taken right up. You're on the top floor, number seven."

"No, there must be some mistake. Are there two rooms in the suite?"

"It's a suite. There are multiple rooms."

"Two bedrooms, I mean. *Two beds.*" I gestured back to Aria. "There are two of us, so there should be two rooms." I attempted to explain, despite my growing impatience.

"No, sir. I'm sorry." The receptionist shook her head. "It looks like your assistant, Bernadette Brown, reserved the penthouse suite with one king bed."

"Is there a problem?" Aria appeared at my side.

"No, nothing," I mumbled, turning back to the receptionist. "There's been some kind of misunderstanding. We'll be requiring two separate rooms. Perhaps you can move us to a different suite, or we can book another—separate—room altogether."

The receptionist winced with a faint hiss. "Oh, I'm sorry, Mr. Copeland. We are completely booked. I'm afraid there is nothing we can do. Perhaps I could check with management about moving the furniture around? Maybe a bed could be fit into the living room area? I'm not sure about the logistics of that or fire codes, though. I could certainly have someone look into it for you, but it may take another hour or so to prepare the room if you don't mind waiting."

I glanced at my watch. It was already nearing five, and we were supposed to meet the clients for dinner at six thirty. I still needed to unpack, review my notes, and shower. I raked a hand down my face, then glanced at Aria who seemed far less concerned.

"Come on, Damon. What's the big deal? It's not like we planned this. It was a mistake, but we can roll with it. It won't kill us to share a room." She smiled, waving a hand dismissively.

Exactly. We didn't plan this. But hey, if she's cool with it, I'm cool with it. Just throws a major hitch in my plan to avoid any temptation and having to resist sleeping with her.

"Fine." I sighed, motioning to the staff that was standing near the pile of our luggage, waiting for instructions. They hopped-to and began transporting it up, while Aria followed me to the elevator.

I entered our suite with the hotel staff, our bags, and Aria followed behind. It was plenty of space, and the couch looked comfortable enough.

Problem solved.

Okay, it still wasn't ideal, but it could have been worse.

First, we had to get dressed for dinner and discuss our approach. Aria seemed to be buzzing with the rush of preparing for the big pitch. She was focused on work, and I enjoyed that we were united in how eager we were to "wow" them, which was a welcomed reprieve from all our other unsettled business.

We used separate rooms to get ready. I was sliding into my suit jacket when Aria appeared around the corner—a vision in her black cocktail dress. She moved with the confidence of someone who was obviously born into money, but her smile and the gleam in her eyes had a down to earth vibe. I was captivated. I could only assume the clients would find her just as charming.

"You look beautiful," I told her, studying her appearance. She was the perfect human touch to my stoic disposition.

She breezed over without a second thought, straightening my tie. "We've got this, Copeland. With your brains and with my natural charm, we're going to slay it."

"There's no doubt in my mind." I nodded.

Christopher Young, Mark Castell and his wife, Casey, along with Latoya Johnson and Camille Ortiz from Castell's team met us in the hotel restaurant—a reservation-only dining experience, sourcing from local farms across New England. I was looking forward to the oysters and other seafood dishes that I'd grown so accustomed to as a kid.

We hadn't been seated long before Aria took the spotlight. She pointed to Mark, Latoya, and Camille. "I have to say, I was incredibly inspired reading the mission of your nonprofit. Each of you started businesses of your own?"

They smiled and nodded, each telling us their unique tales of launching their own businesses from the ground up with next to no resources for starting out, working their way out of poverty.

"The three of us met at an entrepreneurs' networking luncheon, and it all fell into place from there," Latoya explained. "We agreed that if we could do it, anybody could. But it should be easier. The point of capitalism is for anybody to be able to be successful if they're driven and willing to work hard. Our hope for the center is that it will provide people with the resources they need to level the playing field for less fortunate individuals with big dreams."

"What an amazing idea," Aria marveled with the utmost sincerity. "And what about you, Mr. Young? If I may ask so bluntly, what is your stance on success? To what do you owe all your accomplishments?"

"I've been asked the very same question a million times." His loud voice was thick and raspy from the cigar he was smoking and all of its predecessors. He leaned back and stroked his chin. Mr. Young was a widower in his seventies, who still wore his wedding band on full display. "Young lady, do you know the quote made famous by Dan Peña?" There was challenge in his eyes.

"I'm afraid not," she said.

"Success is like being pregnant," he started, his expression bold and engaging. "Everybody says congratulations, but nobody knows how many times you got fucked."

I heard gasps at this bolt from the blue, but me, I had to laugh out loud. The man's analogy was vulgar, but on target. Aria looked at him as if she couldn't believe he'd actually said that. Camille, Latoya and Castell's wife looked down at their glasses.

Mr. Young turned to me. "Am I right, Mr. Copeland?"

"Personally, I try not to overthink it," I said truthfully. I'd get nothing done if I sat around worrying and let that little guy on my shoulder yell into my ear. He could move along. I didn't have the time or the mental space.

"A human being has three million pores in their body," Mr. Young continued. "I've been fucked in every one of them."

"In a bad way?" Aria asked, all innocently, giving him a charming smile.

I covered my grin, with a hand cupping my mouth and a fake cough. Her unsuspecting angel face was priceless. It was always on point.

"In a bad way," Mr. Young nodded, raising an eyebrow at her. He paused—for emphasis—then said, "At least twice."

"Oh. How very unfortunate," Aria replied. "Well, fortunately, Damon and I can't wait to show you our vision for the center, which will—I'm sure of it—stimulate you in a very good way. I was so in love with your cause that it was easy to come up with ideas."

"And we have some great ones for you," I said, liking the way Aria had charmingly shifted the talking point.

"We're looking forward to it as well," Mark replied, clapping my shoulder with a smile. "Should we—"

"And what about you, Aria?" Mr. Young interrupted, "I'm interested in the female perspective here. What was it about the mission that spoke to *you*?"

She considered it for a moment, finding her words. "Although I had many advantages as a Humphries, I still worked hard to put myself ahead of what was expected of me. And I guess I just always thought...anybody should be able to pursue their dreams in life, no matter what they were born into. Everyone should have a magical place they could go, like your center, to find all the answers in one place. Like building blocks to something better. It's up to them to use everything at their fingertips to its fullest potential, but it's like you're lighting their way. Showing them the path, if they choose to take it."

"I couldn't have said it better myself," Camille said, lifting a glass.

"Cheers to lighting the way!" Latoya added.

Mr. Young lifted his glass.

We all clinked our glasses in the center of the table and carried on with our meal. Just as I suspected, everybody was enthralled with Aria. The conversation flowed effortlessly. There was laughter mixed in with all the business talk and stories from our career ventures. She somehow made us all feel like we were just hanging out with old friends, rather than being at a business dinner, and I took pride in that.

"Good job," I said as we walked from the elevator back to our room at the end of the night.

"Good job?" She scrunched her nose with a pouty frown. "Come on. Is that all?"

"Okay, you were remarkable," I told her with a chuckle. "They liked you."

"Good. Because I think I *love* them." She looked happy. "It's not every day you get to work on a project you actually care about."

I stopped at the door with our card key suspended midair.

Looking down at her, with that light of accomplishment in her eyes, I realized more than ever that I couldn't let this thing between us hold her back in her career.

"It could be every day," I said. "If we keep working together."

Her smile faded. "Damon, I know. But..."

"You should really consider it," I pressed. "And by consider it, I mean you should stay with your father's company. You were born for this, Aria. Not just your engineering work, but everything you just proved at dinner. You're perfect for this kind of work."

"Thanks! Don't make me blush."

"All I'm saying is, don't let *anything* hold you back from that."

"That easy, huh?" Her gaze dropped to the floor.

"Don't let *me* hold you back from that," I added.

When she looked back up at me, we both knew why it wasn't that easy.

Betraying everything I just said, I sank into her blue eyes—sparkling under the shadow of her thick, heavy lashes. Her lips were so tempting and drawing me in like a moth to a flame.

"Maybe it's not so much you holding me back...as it is things left undone," she suggested, her voice low and provocative.

Our heads tilted in closer for the inevitable crash.

My mouth grazed hers.

Her lips were soft, inviting, and she was eager. I cupped her cheeks, enjoying the softness of her skin. She opened up to me, and when my tongue touched hers, a delicious moan escaped her. Aria was so responsive as she pressed her body closer to mine, tugging on the lapels of my suit jacket, pulling me closer. My hunger won out, and I dropped my hand to the curve of her ass, squeezing it between my fingers. Our kiss? Mind numbing. Explosive. Hot. The chemistry between us was at an all-time high.

Our kisses grew more demanding, and I felt her knees buckle when I lifted her skirt, pressing my hand flat against her heated and still-clothed mound—my fingers a mere breath away from her clit.

There were a million points to argue, but I had no interest in talking anymore.

27

ARIA

*D*amon's and my lips parted just long enough for him to unlock the door to our hotel room. When we checked in earlier and found out we'd be forced to share a room with only one bed (*oh, no*—how *unfortunate...Gasp*), I assumed it was something we'd worry about later in the evening. I'd sort out that temptation when the time came. But now the time was here, and we'd already set the course before we even walked in the door.

This was happening.

We'd already crossed the threshold and kissed, and now we both seemed to silently agree: There was no turning back. *This is happening.*

The room was quiet and empty, but the blank, dark space around me quickly filled with Damon's body and all the swirling intensities that came along with his closeness. He pressed himself into me, hard and fast, sending the door shut behind my back with a bang.

We smiled through the kiss...*Sweet relief, finally.* It was tender and adorable, and somehow, we got lost there for a moment—his muscular body pressing against mine, as we sank deeply into each other's mouths. They were inseparable like strong magnets, and the intensity of it was making me light-headed.

My hands ripped and pulled at his clothing as if I was clawing for dear life, admiring the naked and *extremely* defined planes of his chest. Damn. His extra workouts had really paid off.

As in our very first encounter, I removed his glasses and put them on the table next to us, and *not* because of my theory. So, I admit, I was totally off with my theory. Zoe had been right, *again*. Oh well. No need to dwell on it. He knew perfectly well what he was dealing with. In our intimate encounters he had made me feel sexy, desired, more than I've ever thought possible. When he took off the tank top beneath his dress shirt, his hair got that sexy, messy look I loved. The deep black sheen seemed almost blue, like the iridescence of a dragon's wing. I couldn't *wait* to run my fingers through it and tug the strands.

As soon as I reached up, he caged me with both arms against the wall.

I could feel his erection in his pants pressing against me, pinning me to the door. It was hot and throbbing, matching everything I felt between my legs. I was surging with a need that had been relentlessly building from the moment I stepped into his office for the interview. Our one-sided rendezvous in the conference room had done nothing to satisfy me, and judging by the hungry, determined look in his eyes—I had a feeling he was about to make up for that.

His attention moved to the pantyhose underneath my dress. He dropped to his knees, sliding the waistband down with him as he went. His hot breath hovered around the lace of my panties, followed by a soft press from his lips. I whimpered and squirmed against the hard surface behind me.

"You're torturing me." I laughed through a languid breath. "I'm not going to be able to stand it if you go so slow."

He stood up, pulling my dress over my head and kissing me again. "That's the point," he teased against my lips. "Don't worry. I won't stop."

I answered by digging my nails into the back of his hair, opening my mouth wide to let his tongue move over mine. "Don't you dare."

His hands smoothed down to my aching breasts, pulling my bra down just enough to let his thumbs graze my hardened nipples. It sent a hot pulse radiating through my body until I was writhing with a desperate need for more.

He quickly undid the clasp of my bra with my skin prickling under the brushes of his fingers along my bare back. His other hand dropped between us, teasing my delicate, wet folds. I almost moaned from the intense sensation he provoked. His arm spread my legs wider, and I felt the rising feeling of everything he'd neglected to give me the last time. He instantly rewarded me with several long, slow caresses.

I hissed as he tugged on my clit and fell back into a perfect rhythm of stroking and circling, tormenting me (in the most *delicious* way) until my legs were shaking.

"Damn." He pulled back with a frown. "I'm afraid that gift I sent you appears to have done next to nothing in satisfying you. I'll have to remedy this right away."

"How do you know I even used it? Or kept it?"

"Oh, I know you did." He rasped and continued his teasing as I gasped for breath. "But you won't be needing it tonight." He smirked with a deep growl, his lips still lingering close enough that every word, sound, or breath shuddered against me. Each time it was a promise of what was to come—and what wasn't being fulfilled nearly quick enough.

"Is that so?" I teased on a breathless sigh. "Last time you left me wanting."

"You really don't know what I'm capable of," he growled. "If I have my way with you, you'll be shot. You won't need to be touched again for at least a week."

I couldn't imagine not wanting his touch for that long—no matter what he did to me. He was like a drug and each time I used it, I only wanted more and more.

Our bodies collided together in a frantic push and pull until we managed to land on the bed with him crashing over me.

Kneeling between my legs, he undid his belt and tossed it aside, then unbuttoned his pants. He stripped them off, and I yanked at his boxer shorts until they were long gone—lost in the trail of shed garments leading from the door to us.

"Let me grab a condom."

He pulled back and locked his eyes on mine, smoothing his hands down the length of my body until they settled with a hard squeeze on my ass. I heard him work the condom over his erection just before his grip drew my hips up closer to him, so his hard shaft was teasing around the area I so desperately needed it to go.

"You're so fucking sexy," he rasped into my neck before gently sinking his teeth in.

I bucked against him at just the right angle so his tip landed at my opening—so close to sliding in.

"Then do something about it, Damon," I begged, wiggling my hips beneath him.

He didn't respond to my tease, just wrapped one hand around

my neck, staring back at me with a daring gaze. "Aria. That is no way to speak to your superior."

Smiling wide, I bit my bottom lip. "I guess you'll have to reprimand me then."

He lunged forward ever so slightly, guiding himself just an inch inside of me. "I'll have to think of a fitting punishment."

Gasping at his intrusion, I hoped, *wished* he'd continue, but he didn't. I grabbed his ass cheeks, indicating he thrust deeper, but still, he wouldn't budge.

I was just about to shoot back that if he teased me any longer, it would be punishment enough. I was so wet, open, and ready and teeming with a mounting pressure that felt humanly impossible to withstand.

But then he slid deeper, just an inch. "Do you like it?" he rumbled in a tone I liked too much, his gaze dark and hot.

"I do, I love it," I whisper-moaned. "Deeper, please, stop teasing..."

He slid deeper slowly, so much deeper, finally, finally, filling me completely.

It was beautiful and effortlessly, plunging deep into my core. I was in heaven—I was sure of it.

28

DAMON

"The things I want to do to you," I growled.

Inch by inch, I pushed into her, holding her gaze as she enveloped me, welcoming me into her body. I was stiff as fuck, filling her, owning her. It felt like coming home, and my arms quivered with the effort of holding myself up. She whimpered, dragging her nails down my back. Her legs tangled with mine, encouraging me with the soft rock of her hips up into mine.

I grunted and nodded my head, pressing my lips to her jaw as I began to move, taking what was mine.

Ah, she felt perfect. My movements started slowly, but soon picked up speed as my desperation for her increased. The sweat of our bodies mingled as they melted into one, her breasts pressed against my chest and her arms wrapped around my shoulders, hanging on for dear life.

"I love being in you, my Goddess," I rumbled into her ear, inducing a soft moan from her kissable lips.

"Oh, Damon," she whispered softly. "It feels wonderful..."

My fingers left indentations in her hips as I held her as close as I possibly could. Before she could so much as gasp, my fingers were stroking her little clit. I knew I could bring her to an orgasm within seconds.

The sensations and her delicious moans like sweet music under me made me feel as if the earth had suddenly shifted on its axis. The feeling of my hips pushing me deep inside of her made her breathless, and she moaned as she came around me. My hips stuttered against hers, and I followed seconds after, emptying myself. I collapsed over her, my weight falling atop her like a heavy blanket. She curled her arms around my shoulders, pressing sweet kisses up and down my neck as our sated bodies began to cool.

It was difficult for her to breathe like that, with my body resting on her, but when I moved to free her, she stopped me.

She was in no rush for me to move.

No rush at all.

29

ARIA

*T*riple *orgasm? OMG. I mean, double orgasm—okay. But triple?* That's never happened to me. *Ever.* When my bestie talked about it, I always thought, *Shut up.*

I'd thought there was no way in hell I could come again so soon after that intense of an orgasm.

I relished in the rush of just how well my body seemed to fit his like a glove, feeling another tidal wave of ecstasy slam through me —streaming from his mouth to the tips of my curling fingers and toes. I whimpered and cried, clawing into him. I could hardly breathe, let alone think. All I knew he had made up for the last time—and I wasn't complaining. The gushing sensation made mine even more intense, and all we could do was melt against each other and ride it to the shore.

My entire body went limp beneath him. I couldn't help but laugh.

"You weren't kidding. I *am* shot. I don't think I can do that again for a while." My voice sounded foreign and primal. *What was this man doing to me?*

His head perked up with a breathless smile. "That's what you think. But I'm sure I can surprise you again."

I stared up at the ceiling with my arm draped across my forehead. "Actually, I have no doubt you could."

He rolled to the side, disposed of the condom, and pulled my body against his before turning my chin toward him. He nipped at my lower lip and then slowly entangled his tongue with mine in a soft, savoring kiss. Just like that surprise third orgasm crept up on me, we melted into a long and slow make-out session. He continued kissing me like there was no tomorrow, and I loved every second of it. I couldn't remember ever doing that with a guy *after* sex before. When Nate and I were finished, we barely even cuddled. He hated cuddling, as much as he hated my freckles. Once the need was met, it was like he couldn't wait to get some space between our bodies. *Damn. Why am I thinking of my ex? Get outta here.* I chuckled slightly to myself. I'd barely thought of Nate even once since this job started. To think about him now, he seemed so insignificant. Like a tiny blip in my life that really didn't mean much. But Damon? I swallowed hard as I tried to imagine what I might think about him months or years down the road.

By the time we did pull apart with heavy lids and exhausted bodies and cleaned ourselves up, I was calm and contemplative. We laid there in the dark, still naked, with our foreheads pressed together as we searched each other's eyes.

Neither of us seemed to want to speak. It would only ruin the moment. After all, we both agreed I should stay on at Humphries. And that meant—no matter how intoxicating our time was together here in our hotel room, we would have to find some way to put it behind us and move on like nothing happened. Like we didn't want each other again and again and again.

I ran my hand down his chest. I noticed a few scars that I hadn't seen before, two on the side of his pec near his arm and one close to his belly button. Damon dismissed them with a wave of his hand when I raised my eyebrows in question. I was pretty sure I knew where the scars came from. That day in school. Typically, my brother Miles couldn't shut up about anything, but for some reason, I'd never found out what had happened when he and Damon were younger. I only know that Miles almost lost his life back then, and had ended up in hospital. I also discovered that Damon had been the only one who came to his help, without worrying about his own safety.

Funny how Damon never mentioned it once or seemed to see any point in bringing it up, not even now.

"It's not a big deal," he whisper-grumbled when I pushed for more answers. "Anybody would have done it. I already told you. Miles is my bro. He's family." He leaned forward and placed a soft kiss on my nose. "And now shhh."

"Why don't you want to talk about it?"

"No sense in reliving sad events from the past. Also, it's not my story to tell."

When I opened my mouth to say more, he placed his finger on my lips, followed by a soft kiss, indicating that this topic was done for him. Miles didn't want to talk about it, so it was obvious that Damon wouldn't break the trust.

Damon was a man with principles, and he was a brave hero who wouldn't even see himself that way.

What a man. At that moment, the whole conflicting situation with him, Miles, and my family became so much clearer to me. I understood how difficult it had to be for him to be caught in the middle, and still, here he was, brave enough to risk it all. Brave enough to be with me.

*M*aybe that's what made us so hell bent to make the most of it. We'd barely drifted off to sleep when I woke up, teeming with lust all over again. Like absolutely nothing had been done to satisfy me before. I was in a writhing hot sweat with his naked body sleeping next to mine, and I couldn't resist smoothing my hands along his chiseled muscles.

He barely stirred under my touch until I sat up and nibbled my way down to his cock. He must have been feeling the same way, because I found it at full attention. I gripped the base and gave it a gentle upward stroke.

He moaned and opened his eyes, lifting his head just enough to take in what was happening. "Good lord, woman. You're going to kill me."

"Please don't die." I smirked. "At least not yet. I need you for things."

"For things? What *things*?" he asked.

"Well, you know..."

"To fuck you?" He arched a sexy brow.

His dirty words sent electricity racing to my lady bits. I jutted out my tongue and ran circles around his tip until he was hissing through clenched teeth, tensing against the sheets. I rounded my lips around him, sliding him slowly into my mouth. I sucked it in, drawing him in and out.

"Fuck...yes..." He managed to grunt, twitching inside of me.

I loved how intense it seemed to be for him—how powerless he felt in my grip. I glided up onto my knees so I could use my hand against the motions of my mouth. The more it seemed to unravel him, the harder I worked.

"Aria... *fuck*...Your job performance tonight has...*fuck*... surpassed my expectations." He managed to say.

I let him pop out of my mouth just long enough to tease him with my tongue from top to bottom. I drew him in again, and then out, working him over until he was growling and clutching the sheets in his fists.

"Serves you right for underestimating me, Mr. Copeland," I said, playfully.

"It serves *me* right?" His voice cracked, trying to figure out if I was giving him sass. I totally was.

"Seems to me you're not as good a boss as you think you are," I continued to tease, giving his cock a squeeze. I loved poking the bear. It was such fun.

Right now, he wasn't the boss.

I was the *boss*.

Judging by his silence, he wasn't sure what to make of it, but only for a second. "Are you sure about that?" he growled, his eyes stormy.

"A hundred percent sure." I squeezed him again. "Just being honest here. Maybe *I* should be the one teaching yo—"

Before I realized what was happening, he'd got up onto his knees, grabbed me and turned me on all fours.

"Damon!" I shrieked in surprise. The next thing I felt was a good, hard slap on my bare ass. Oh my God! Was he spanking me? Honestly, I really shouldn't have been that surprised. He'd warned me often enough, and I *had* pushed him.

"Mr. Copeland!" I shrieked again.

"So you want to teach *me* a lesson?" he grumbled.

I paused. "Uh, maybe."

He let out a grumbly breath. "Bad girls need to be punished." He slapped my ass, again.

"Ouch!" Holy *crap*. It stung like a bitch! So, why did I like it? Why did it feel so hot? He caressed the pain away, with relish, and just when I thought he'd let me off the hook, I felt his hand smack my butt cheek, again. *Oh, my God!* This one really stung.

"Never disrespect your *boss*." He slipped a finger through my folds, his finger slightly brushing my clit. The way he stroked me... I was in heaven. "Have you learned your lesson?"

"Wh—wh—at?"

He nuzzled the sensitive skin, and I whimpered, attempting to wriggle out of his hold and away from the havoc he was currently wreaking on my body.

"Answer me," he demanded, retracting his hand.

Honestly, what was the question? I couldn't even say. He truly knew how to tease a girl *real* good.

"Have you learned your lesson?" he repeated.

"Umm—" I almost wanted to say no, because it was so crazy hot.

"I don't think you have," he grumbled behind me when I remained silent.

"I have, I have!"

A slap to my other ass cheek caused me to cry out, and I wiggled my ass against him, getting impossibly wet. He knew exactly what he was doing to me, and the pressure was becoming unbearable. I needed to feel him inside me. Now. I was aching. I wanted to be pounded so hard.

Somehow, I felt his smile, before a hand descended on me and, at long last, his finger swept through my folds. Once, twice...

If I was thinking more clearly, I might have been embarrassed by my desperate movements, but my mind was blissfully devoid of any thought other than the ecstasy Damon's hands sent coursing through my bloodstream. I felt as if I was suffocating and breathing simultaneously, for the first time in my life. It was *exhilarating*.

Then, Damon lifted me up and spun me around.

"First, I'm going to come in your mouth," he commanded, kneeling in front of me, "then I'll fuck you all over the room. Now, be a good girl and open wide."

A few moments later, I hummed around him, and my vibrations made it harder to keep his hips from pressing up into me. I could see his Adam's apple bobbing in his throat as I stared at his lips, which parted slightly under my heated gaze. When my eyes returned to look into his, I found them flickering down to my mouth, before returning to stare deeply into mine.

"There's my good girl...," he growled.

I felt a flush spread over my entire body. He went faster until he was exploding into me. My lips left him with a small sucking sound, and I watched his breathing calm as he moved back and stared at me, his eyes dark. His gaze scanned the entirety of my body, taking in my bare, heaving chest and all the freckles that stood out against my pink skin.

Damon's fingers tightened in my hair, and he tugged, pulling me up until the length of my body was pressed against his. He caressed my cheek and hair and then leaned in to kiss my lips, before pushing me back down to the bed.

Just as I was attempting to crawl back to him like a cat, wanting to curl against his side, he rolled over on top of me, biting and kissing my neck down to my breasts. A huge smile spread across my face as I realized after what happened before, he was not about to let himself come a single time without returning the favor several times over. I certainly wasn't complaining.

I leaned back and relaxed, eager to learn what else he could do to my body.

I glanced down my body, at where his head, with its strong jawbones, was nestled between my thighs, his mouth open over me. I met his gaze, and his dark eyes settled on my face. My breath halted in my lungs. It felt as if he was looking straight into my soul, while his tongue swiped over my clit, sending a flood of mad sensations through my veins.

"Are you ready to come, baby?" he rumbled.

"Please...yes," I whimpered.

I was rewarded with another long swipe of his tongue through my folds. I threw my head back, calling out his name as my eyes shut tight, and I gripped his dark hair. His tongue stroked me through it, maximizing my pleasure.

My mind drifted back to that night we'd spent together after leaving the bar. No wonder it was so devastating to learn who he was. This night was a reminder of just how good it was. How good *he* was. How sexy and wonderful and *savage* he made me feel.

If it weren't for that one, extremely unfortunate tie between him and my family, nothing would have stopped me from trying to keep him and all of his mind-blowing sex around for good.

In fact, it was almost scary to think about where things might have gone if I hadn't stumbled out to see that picture of him and my brothers in his living room. Or if I had never come to work at Humphries. What then? The universe seemed perfectly content repeatedly putting us in each other's paths—just never coupled with a solution for how we might actually make it mean something more than secret sex.

Although, what we did to each other for the rest of the night certainly felt like far more than just secret sex. It was intense, passionate, and addictive.

We couldn't get enough of each other—until a long while after the sun came up.

30

DAMON

*I*t must have been the twentieth time I stirred awake that morning, which was odd. After Aria and I stayed up all night having sex until our bodies gave out, I was exhausted and expected to sleep like a rock for the last few hours we had in the hotel room before we needed to check out. But it felt like I hadn't stayed asleep longer than fifteen or twenty minutes at a time.

Each time I came to, I was hit with all the sensations of having her curled up next to me or draped over my chest. My nose was flooded with her sweet scent, and my whole body was lulled by the warmth of her naked skin against mine. I watched her sleep and stroked her hair, trying my best to enjoy it. But my gut was too twisted in knots with worry.

After a while, I gave up and slid out from under her, grabbed my glasses, and retreated to the bathroom for some water and aspirin. The longer I was awake, the more it became clear that my nerves were less about our client's decision on the pitch, and more about Aria.

I returned to the bedroom, still sipping my water, and stood there for a moment, watching her in bed. She was lying flat on her stomach with just a hint of her breasts bulging from the side. Her back was exposed, with the sheet draped over her, just above the luscious curves of her butt. She moaned and turned her head to the other side, bringing the peaceful, resting look on her face into my view.

Damn. She was fucking beautiful. I could get used to seeing a sight like that more often.

I wasn't a fucking Romeo. Romance and love weren't my forte. It wasn't like I'd ever devoted much time to that area of my life, that was, beyond the art of getting a woman into my bed. But it didn't take an expert to know I was falling for her. This was starting to be about much more than just sex.

That would have been a terrifying thing for me to admit about any woman. Falling in love was not on my radar and definitely wasn't a part of my plan for my life. But it was especially troublesome to be feeling that way about *her* of all people.

For one, I had no fucking idea if she felt the same way. I could just be some office fling to her. Maybe she hadn't been laid in a while. Or she just enjoyed sex. Who knew? Maybe it was all about the thrill of the forbidden fruit—fucking her boss. She didn't seem like the type to purely be motivated by something like that, but what did I know?

Then there was the second, *very* fucking huge problem: Her brothers.

The third, even fucking bigger problem: Her father.

Even if she did feel the same way about me—what the hell would we do about *them*? It was giving me a headache that was too bad for any number of aspirin to fix.

I turned for the balcony, thinking the fresh air might do me good, but her sweet voice caught me halfway.

"You're awake," she murmured with a smile and a stretch.

"Couldn't sleep," I grumbled.

"I slept so hard I forgot where I was for a moment." She smirked, sitting up to observe the room. "And I feel like I could sleep for another nine or ten hours."

I tipped my glass of water in the air. "Ditto."

As I checked my emails on my phone, I heard Aria get up and go to the bathroom. It sounded like she was brushing her teeth. When she came out, she jumped back in bed and pulled the sheet up to her chest. I only saw a blur practically leap across the room. I shook my head and let out a slight chuckle.

"Should I order some room service for breakfast? And coffee?" she asked through a yawn.

"Sounds great." I shuffled toward the balcony doors, but she stopped me.

"Hey, you." She snickered, climbing to the edge of the bed on her knees. "Come back here. Where are you running off to?"

The sheet fell, revealing her gorgeous body, which was more than enough to stop me in my tracks and derail my plan of escaping outside. She held out her hands and pulled me closer, stretching to give me a kiss. I couldn't resist her.

"Even though we did everything I swore we shouldn't or wouldn't do." She smiled against my mouth in between a string of kisses. "This trip turned out to be the most rewarding work trip I've ever been on."

"I'd have to say the same," I said, trying to give her a smile.

Her brows wrinkled as she stared back at me, searching my eyes. She was too sharp to miss the uneasiness that had fallen over me.

"Everything okay?" she asked.

I sighed, wondering if I should go out on a limb and tell her how I was fucking feeling. But there was an easier option, which quickly overshadowed all my other noisy thoughts. I ran my palms down to the perfect round curves of her ass and squeezed, teasing along the edges of everything between her legs. She hissed and kissed me deeper, setting me on fire with need all over again.

I never made it to the balcony.

Instead, I sank onto the bed with Aria. I guessed if we were going to give ourselves a pass to sleep together on that trip, we might as well make the most of the time we had before we returned home, and things got more complicated.

I couldn't un-fuck her, so I might as well go full-in while we were here.

All those naked curves pressed against me inspired an instant hard-on that was so erect you'd never guess we'd had sex countless times throughout the night. I pinned her arms above her head and told her to grab the headboard. When she complied, I kissed down her body and drew my tongue along the sweet folds between her legs, sucking them in as she shuddered and moaned. I buried my face into her, teasing her.

When we got back, I'd have to sort through my feelings for her. Find some way to keep this thing between us alive, because giving her up now seemed impossible.

But who was I kidding?

Sooner or later, I'd have to face the fact we wouldn't be able to keep it a secret forever.

But none of that mattered as she bucked against my face, urging my tongue to play with her.

he sun was shining down on us as we boarded the jet, letting me know we could expect a smooth and speedy flight. Why wasn't I happy about it? Those last few precious moments on the plane with her would be all I'd get before we landed back in our day-to-day lives, into hiding. I was in no rush to return to any of that. I made sure to grab a drink on the plane first thing—something to calm my fucking nerves.

As we settled in to return to New York, Aria sank down into her seat with a sleepy, contented smile.

"You look like you could use a nap," I teased her, noting her heavy eyelids.

"And whose fault is that?"

"I don't know," I said.

"You're not looking in much better shape, you know."

Before I could shoot back a clever reply, my phone rang. I glanced at the screen and saw Mark Castell's name scrolling across. That was quicker than expected. They must have made their decision. I didn't anticipate knowing the result of our meeting before tomorrow, but I appreciated not having to wait. I thought it was a good sign. *Or,* it could be incredibly bad. I held up a "give me a second" finger to Aria and quickly answered, then moved to the back of the plane to make sure I could hear him.

A few minutes later, I felt the opposite of tired. I was pumping with adrenaline as I walked back to Aria.

"Everything okay?" she asked, seeming alarmed.

I hung my head and answered with a grim tone. "That was Mark."

"Oh." Her face drooped. "Is it...not good?"

All I could do was shake my head "no" in response.

"You're kidding me!" She held a hand to her mouth in shock. "They didn't go for it? I thought we had it in the bag!"

"We would have." I sighed, dragging my hands down my face. "But there was one problem."

"What is it?" she shot back eagerly. "Is it something we can fix?"

"I'm afraid not." I frowned, leaning down to her. "The problem is," I whispered, "Mr. Young didn't like our pitch. Looks like he and Mark Castell didn't appreciate any of your natural charm, and none of my smartness. They don't want us on the team."

Her face scrunched up, and her mouth dropped. "What. The. Hell," she murmured.

I couldn't contain my smile any longer. It spread across my face, prompting her eyes to grow wide with realization just before she started playfully smacking me on the arm.

"You jerk!" She laughed. "I can't *believe* you pulled that. So, does this mean we got it?"

"We sure did," I told her. "They liked everything we proposed, and they want to start the next phase as soon as possible."

She finally stopped trying to beat me up long enough to unbuckle and leap to her feet. I stood and watched as she jumped in circles and squealed, all leading up to her throwing her arms around my neck and squeezing tight.

"We did it, Damon!"

No sooner than she pulled back and our eyes met, the plane hit a brief patch of bumpiness and sent me flying backward into my seat with her landing on top of me, her soft tits crushing into my pecs. She stared me down with an intense longing, but then her smile faded.

I knew exactly what just happened. We were well on our way back to New York by then, and something about being that much closer to Humphries Properties headquarters—complete with her dad, her brothers, and all the shitty complications, made our close-ness seem taboo all over again. The reservations that had melted away in the privacy of our room were all back in full force, and she felt it. I fucking felt it. We had to be careful.

Nonetheless, I stopped her from instinctively pulling back and held her close, caressing her sweet freckled cheeks. I kissed one that I especially adored, a big one next to her nose. There was a beautiful spark in her big blues.

"Damon," she whispered, tenderly.

"I know, baby," I whispered back, resting my forehead against hers.

Her eyes closed when my lips melted against hers like warm butter, filling me with the scent of her fruity Chapstick.

My lips lingered longer than they should have.

When she pulled back again, the affection in her eyes was over-whelming—enough to make me think I didn't have to worry if she felt the same way or not. It was written all over her face. And if it was that obvious coming from her, I had to assume it was just as apparent to her how I was feeling.

She cleared her throat as she slowly moved back to her own seat, straightening her clothes. The pilot came over the intercom to let us know we were nearing our landing with perfect, or not-so-perfect timing. I had little time to get myself under control. Aria was like a drug—never failing to inspire a new flood of arousal in me, even when I felt like I should have nothing left.

"I take it you'll be reporting back to the ladies at the office that your 'fling' proved to be more satisfactory after all?" I joked, trying to ease the heaviness between us.

She cut her eyes to me. "I don't think that'd be the smartest thing to say first thing after returning from a trip with you. They think you're jealous of whoever my mystery man is. Let's keep it that way."

"Works out well for you and your image. Not so much for mine."

"It's better than the alternatives." She shrugged.

"Such as?"

"Me being your dirty little secret." She flashed a suggestive smile—one that made me want to pull her into the back room of the plane and tell the flight attendants to leave us alone in there after we landed.

But I did my best to get myself back under control and to steer the topic to the reason we'd been on this business trip in the first place.

To land the account—which we did.

I tried to raise the mood by emphasizing the favorable outcome and to distract her by planning the upcoming steps we would have to take over the next few days. I went on, until I felt her relax and saw the excitement return to her eyes.

*S*oon, we pulled onto the landing strip and the stairs ascended.

Aria was giddy with our success as we made our way off the plane. Despite the lingering worry, we were in a good mood and high on our work accomplishment. Our hands brushed, almost interlocking together, as we went down the steps to exit.

She stopped suddenly, once our feet were back on the ground, and faced me, lightly tugging on my tie with her other hand spread across my chest. "We did great, Damon. Thank you for everything. We wouldn't have landed these guys without you leading the whole thing."

"We definitely couldn't have done it without you."

Something caught the corner of my eye. I looked over and felt a chill wash over me when I noticed Charles Henry Humphries himself standing there, waiting for us at the limo. He had a strange expression on his face. One that made it clear he wasn't oblivious to the energy crackling between us.

"Mr. Humphries." I breezed over quickly, reaching out to shake his hand.

"Dad. What are you doing here?" Aria gawked, fidgeting with her clothes like they still might be disheveled from our embrace on the plane.

"Hello, you two." He scanned us from head to toe, skeptically. "I just got off the phone with Mr. Young. He called me right after Mark called you and shared the good news. He wouldn't stop singing your praises. Especially you, Aria. They were extremely impressed."

"We're very happy with the results." She smiled tightly.

"Yes, well, I thought I might take you two out to celebrate, but, now I'm not so sure. You both look exhausted. Like you haven't slept a wink." He narrowed his eyes at us—especially me, seeming displeased.

"Nerves." She shrugged. "We were on edge over the outcome and had trouble resting. Nothing a little nap won't fix. But I'm down for a celebratory glass of champagne first."

I swallowed hard. Hanging out with Mr. Humphries and his daughter after the night we'd just spent together sounded awful. I could still hear her delicious moans.

"Let's go then." He finally nodded, opening the limo door and waving us in.

Aria climbed in first, but when I stepped up to follow, he quickly inserted himself between us. "Excuse me."

Thankfully, the tension eased up somewhat by the time we got to the restaurant. Before long, we were all toasting to landing the deal. If Mr. Humphries did suspect anything, he wasn't showing it anymore.

Him being around did put a damper on any proper goodbye Aria and I might have shared, and I wondered if he'd stuck around for that very reason. It was probably for the best. It wasn't like we could keep this thing up forever.

We all said casual farewells and parted ways, freeing me up to finally go home and get some sleep.

31

DAMON

By Monday morning, I'd decided to try not to read too much into the awkwardness with Mr. Humphries upon our return. It was a little strange for him to call me into his office first thing, but I made an effort to assume it had to do with the project.

That was until I walked in and saw the look on his face. It was not the expression you'd expect to see on a man who was pleased with his staff just landing a huge account.

"Sit down," he said briskly.

I unbuttoned my suit jacket and lowered into the chair, doing my best to act casual.

I wasn't about to be the kind of player who gave himself away by just presuming he'd been caught—until Mr. Humphries actually hinted at knowing anything. By "hinted at," I mean told me directly that he knew I slept with her *and* showed me actual physical evidence. There was no way in *hell* he could know *or* give proof of anything.

This had to be about something else entirely, but either way, I was putting on my best poker face.

"Sure. What's up?" I asked.

His eyes were locked on me, and his face didn't soften the least bit. "The hotel called, Damon. There was an issue with the bill. There was an error with the card number your assistant gave and then some confusion about the amount of the bill..." He paused.

"Yes?" I asked. Where was he going with this?

"Long story short, they dragged me into it, because clearly, I don't have more important things to do, and I ended up on the phone with them and was enlightened to the fact that you and Aria stayed in the same room."

Fuck.

He stood from behind his desk and circled around to the front of it, leaning against the edge and towering over me with his arms crossed. Classic intimidation tactic.

"Yes. We ended up with only one suite," I answered plainly. "There was a mix up with the reservations."

His darkened expression told me that *that* explanation was not going to be enough for him. "So, you slept on the couch?" His eyes bored into mine.

"The suite had separate rooms, of course," I offered with a dismissive shrug, wrinkling my brow. I didn't want to flat-out lie to him—let's just say, wiggle around the truth instead. *Jesus.* It seemed to be becoming a daily practice.

"So you're trying to tell me that absolutely nothing is going on with you and Aria?" he asked, focusing on me. I didn't budge. Déjà vu hit me. The interrogation with Aria's brothers had left a bad taste in my mouth, and I felt as if I was reliving the same fucking situation. I decided to remain silent, for now. "I might have been stupid enough to believe that," he continued, with a slight nod of his head, "had I not caught you two in that little moment coming off the plane. I didn't want to say anything to upset Aria when we went out, but give it up, Damon. I've been around the block a few times. I know something happened between you two."

For a brief moment, I considered telling him the truth.

But it wouldn't be a fair move toward Aria. She and I had agreed to keep our "dirty little secret" confidential. At least, we hadn't agreed to share the news. I couldn't just go behind her back and tell her father what had happened. That would result in a shitstorm. Not just for me, but for her as well.

"Mr. Humphries, I assure you." I sat up straight and serious. "You have nothing to worry about. We're professionals."

He shook his head, unconvinced. "You'd better think long and hard about this before you ruin your career by messing around with my daughter." He lowered his voice. "It wouldn't just be your job *here* you'd have to be concerned about, you know. I'm a powerful man with a lot of friends who wouldn't hesitate to black-list you at their companies with just one phone call from me. What has gotten into you?" He sighed. "This is an inescapable loss-loss situation. Don't make my daughter unhappy by putting her into a dead-end affair. Damon, I know you better than that. Have you ever thought about her?"

"Mr. Humphries..." I hesitated, hating that I'd made a man I'd looked up to for so many years look at me and talk to me that way. "I appreciate your concerns, but as I said before: you don't need to worry."

"I'm not an idiot, Damon. And I don't like being treated like one. I'm not blind, either. Whatever you claim hasn't been happening— put a stop to it. Now."

He returned to his seat behind the desk and immediately got on his computer, making it clear that the conversation was over. Any feelings I had for Aria were sucked into a vacuum in that moment, shoved off into another distant part of my mind. Any thoughts I had of telling her how I felt, or even daring to ponder how we might handle her family and our jobs—they all fucking dissipated.

Mr. Humphries made his stance clear. Oliver and Miles had done the same. Lay a finger on Aria, and I would not only be losing Aria by "making her unhappy", but I'd also lose them as close friends. Not to mention that my entire career would go down the fucking toilet right along with them.

I finally stood up, preparing to take my leave from his office. "Good day, Mr. Humphries," I said before walking out.

*M*y heart was pounding as I headed back to my office, ignoring anybody who attempted to speak to me as I passed.

"Bernadette. My office. Now," I boomed as I darted past her desk through my door.

She leapt up immediately and followed behind. "Yes, Mr. Copeland?"

"Get as many candidates for the head engineer position as you can lined up for me ASAP."

She hesitated for a moment. "You mean...Aria's position?"

"I mean exactly what I said, Bernadette," I grumbled. "Can you get to it?"

"Yes, sir. Of course." She bounded out just as quickly as she had come in.

"And shut my door behind you. Please."

She nodded and pulled the door to, finally giving me some privacy. I ran my hands down my face. This was not how I expected my Monday morning to go.

I was kicking myself. What had I been thinking? I knew this would happen, but I let my dick think louder than my brain, and now everything that was important to me was hanging by a thread.

But the scarier thing to admit, the thing I fully realized the morning we woke up in the hotel after having sex all night—was that I hadn't just been thinking with my dick. It was more than that. Aria stirred up parts of me I didn't even know I had. She inspired me to be calmer, more relaxed—except when she was being a pain in my ass and irritating the shit out of me for not following direct orders. Other than that, I found myself trusting enough to just go with the flow when she was around. Because with her, it didn't really matter if things went according to plan or not. Everything seemed easy. Felt easy. I was just happy to be near her.

But none of that changed the position I was in now.

Telling Aria about my talk with her father would only make things worse. *Fuck. Fuck. Fuck.* I knew I needed to cut things off before it all ended in disaster for both of us. I didn't want to see her hurt. I didn't want to make her unhappy. I didn't want to see her suffer. Not her. This was for the best. She was only supposed to stay on for the pitch anyway, and it was over.

Which meant—her time here and everything between us officially needed to be over, too.

Now.

32

ARIA

*D*espite not seeing much of Damon on Monday, I knew with the new account, he'd be busier than ever, and I didn't want to smother him. I was still buzzing with a high from everything and in a great mood on Tuesday. Even Dad seemed more affectionate toward me than ever. I loved making him proud. Of course, everything between us had me on cloud nine, even with all its uncertainties. But I was also getting more and more excited about the prospect of staying on at Humphries. *Yes! I've changed my mind. Or better, I've made up my mind,* inspired by what Damon had said.

I knew it was a perfect decision, and I was ready.

I'd avoided committing to my family's company, because I wanted to go out into the world and make a name for myself in my own right—without my father's help. I'd done that and gained plenty of experience. But for the first time, I had a job I was excited about going to every day. It challenged me and utilized all of my skills. It felt like everything I had to bring to the table was truly valued and put to good use. The more I thought about it, I'd be crazy to walk away from it and how good it felt.

Even without the added bonus of seeing Damon's blazing-hot body and utterly handsome face every day, my time at the company so far had been everything I'd been looking for and then some. But of course, his encouragement helped. As far as our "dirty secret" went, we would wait some time, and then wait some more, and then slowly drop the bomb on them. By that time, they would see how excellently we worked together and how much we felt for each other.

Was I being naïve? Yes, but I couldn't walk away. I didn't want to walk away. They would understand—I'd make them understand. Maybe it was best to start with Dad, but with Mom's help. Mom was a hopeless romantic.

I spent all of Tuesday and yesterday morning preparing to move on into the next phase of initiating construction. This was where my role became especially vital. Putting together an impressive pitch was one thing. Now it was time to buckle down with the architect and contracting team to ensure everything was brought into reality just as we'd promised.

Sitting at my desk, I looked over my initial proposal for moving forward with a smile on my face. I wasn't too modest to admit that it was an impressive jumping off point, and I couldn't wait to share it with Damon.

I gathered everything up and inspected my dress, brushing off the crumbs from that morning's everything bagel. They were a good reminder to pop a mint in my mouth to chase away the coffee breath. I also made sure I had no lipstick on my teeth. God. I could see it now. *Standing in front of everyone, thinking I'm rocking the presentation, when Damon clears his throat.* I'd be like, "Yes, Mr. Copeland?" He'd shake his head and run his finger across his teeth.

But everybody would see him trying to be discreet. My face would pale, and my clumsy ass would furiously wipe at my lips only to end up looking like The Joker with lipstick smeared over half my face (seriously, that could *so* happen!). It would be priceless. So, yeah. I checked my damn lipstick. We did *not* need a case of "Aria" happening. Not only could it potentially put a damper on everything I had to present, but it would definitely prohibit the likelihood of me stealing a secret kiss in the privacy of his office.

Reeling with hope for that very thing, and excitement over the project in general, I set off for Damon's office, just after making sure that my boobs were on point. Before making the walk across the workroom floor, I clutched the report in my hands, smiling down at it. Maybe it worked out for the best that I hadn't seen Damon all day. Having time to put this thing together gave me the perfect opportunity to surprise him and tell him that I thought about everything he said on the trip, and that I'd decided I was going to stay on at Humphries for good. And the job wasn't the only thing I wanted to keep. Whatever was happening between us, I was determined to keep that going as well.

We'd find a way.

I was so happy.

"Good morning, Bernadette. Is Mr. Copeland in? I have some important information to go over with him."

She was gathering up a handful of folders from her desk and barely glanced at me. "Mr. Copeland has returned to his office upstairs. I'm just about to join him up there myself."

"Oh...I see," I puzzled, watching her struggle to collect her things. "Well, here. Let me help you with those, and I'll just follow you up to see him."

"I'm afraid that won't be possible today, Aria. He's booked with interviews and asked me not to disturb him with anything else."

"Interviews?" I was hit with a strange feeling and tried not to get carried away with it. But my uneasiness seeped through my smile. "Oh. Okay. Uh, which position?"

"The one you've been temporarily filling," she stated, standing up straight with her arms full. "Now if you'll excuse me. I really must get up there."

I was frozen.

I stood there, unable to move, watching her scurry off with my mouth hanging wide open. It felt like I had just been punched in the gut, and I was finding it hard to breathe.

Huh? My position? I didn't understand.

He was the one who tried to convince me on the trip to stay on at the company. I was pretty sure I'd have *never* even entertained the idea long enough to decide it was what I wanted had he not suggested it. What the heck? Now not only was he interviewing for my replacement, practically as soon as we landed, but he hadn't even discussed it with me. I felt stupid. Really, really stupid.

I finally managed to close my gaping mouth and started back toward my desk. But by the time I got back and sank down into my chair, I felt lost and clueless over what to do next. The presentation I had been working so hard on seemed useless now. I tossed the paperwork onto my desk and felt tears welling up in my eyes as I stared at it.

What the hell happened? We'd been working so well together. We nailed the clients down, and even though I didn't like to toot my own horn, a lot was thanks to my help. I'd exceeded the expectations for my role there—and last I heard, he was pleased with my performance. Maybe even more than just pleased, although Mr. Wonderbrain would never say so.

It wasn't just my position that felt like it was being pried out of my hands.

I was losing Damon, too—at least what I thought I had.

I couldn't very well keep sleeping with him after he pulled something like this. Even *if* he was operating from the delusion that this might somehow afford us a better chance at being together (I *highly* doubted it), he should have talked to me first. I had a sinking feeling his intentions behind this weren't nearly so pure or romantic.

How could I have misread everything? I thought I meant something to him. I thought our night had changed something in him, too.

I reached for my mug and spilled coffee on my desk. Great. When I cleaned up the mess, I reminded myself that I shouldn't jump to conclusions. I reminded myself that, according to Zoe, even *really* smart men had very basic thought patterns. But I kept coming to the same conclusion: No, this wasn't a simple misunderstanding. But apparently, I couldn't even talk to him, and I wasn't sure how long I could wait for that to happen.

My eyes started to sting, and my chest kept getting tighter.

I had to get out of there, and judging by Damon's behavior, it seemed I wouldn't be missed. Hell, he apparently couldn't wait for me to leave. He was practically kicking me out the door with no warning.

What a jerk.

To save myself from the embarrassment of bursting into tears right there in front of everybody, I quickly snatched up my purse and bolted for the elevator.

I ran smack-dab into Angie halfway there.

"Oh, Aria! Good to have you back. How was your trip? Must have been hard to focus with that tall drink of water—Mr. Copeland—around."

I stopped and gaped at her, feeling like my heart was being

snipped in two. "It was fine. I'm sorry, Angie. Please excuse me." I knew she was only being friendly and wanting to joke around, but I didn't have it in me to do so. I couldn't. Not then. Likely not ever. I had to get away from everyone, away from anything that was a reminder of Damon and our time together.

She appeared alarmed as I pushed past her and practically ran to the elevator doors. I held my breath as I waited for them to close, praying that no one else would get on. Once I was finally ensured privacy for the ride down, I closed my eyes and sank against the wall. I hadn't felt that heartbroken since Nate. But who was I kidding? Nate had meant nothing to me in comparison to the sparks I'd felt with Damon. Or with this job, for that matter. Now it was all being ripped out from under me.

I didn't bother telling Damon or anyone else that I decided to be out for the rest of the day. Why would I? No one bothered calling or texting to see where I was, which only poured salt into my wounds. I spent all afternoon and evening feeling like I was suffocating in all my confusion and hurt. It was the worst, and I wanted more than anything to confront Damon. But I knew if I even attempted it before I had a chance to calm down, I would break in front of him. I already felt humiliated enough. I didn't need to pile that embarrassment on top of everything else.

～

*B*y the next evening, I finally felt strong enough to face him. I waited until most everyone had cleared out, including Bernadette. Not bothering to make a stop in front of the mirror this time—*because why?*—I hopped onto the private elevator going up to the top floor where Damon's main office was. I was the only employee outside of him, my father, and brothers who knew the code. It was only given to me so I could visit my family for lunch or other things long before I ever started working there.

But desperate times called for desperate measures.

I wanted answers.

Damon was clearly avoiding me, and I wasn't about to give him the chance to blow me off or make excuses.

The top floor of Humphries headquarters was decked to the nines with black-and-white marble flooring, speckled with flakes of gold to match the ornate crown molding that bordered the painted ceilings. An elaborate view of the city had been done as a mural up above with a large chandelier hanging from the center. It was dark and empty, and my heels echoed along the floor of the empty lobby. All of the office doors were closed, the windows dark and void of any movement behind them. All of them except one.

Just as I had hoped, everybody was gone for the day. But his door was open, and the light was on. I marched right in and slammed the door behind me. A perfect Queen Bitch entrance if I may say so myself. I was done being polite or professional. He certainly hadn't been *either* of those when he started interviewing behind my back.

"Aria?" He glanced up, surprised at my hasty, unannounced entrance. "Good evening."

"Hello, Damon."

"You should have set up an appointment with my secretary. Or at least knocked. You're not even supposed to be on this floor," he said calmly, sitting behind his desk.

I should have set up an appointment? Or knocked? What the hell? Was he serious?

"Oh, I'm sorry," I shot back sarcastically. "I just figured if you were going to be unprofessional enough to replace me behind my back, I could take the liberty of being a little unprofessional myself."

"You were only supposed to be a temporary fill-in until we found someone else." He sighed, not looking the *least* bit apologetic.

My hurt was rapidly turning to white-hot rage. "You know damn well we discussed me staying on permanently. It was *your* idea, Damon!"

"I have to make decisions based on what's best for the company as a whole, including you and me."

"What the hell is that supposed to mean?" I shrieked.

"Keep your voice down. Look," he groaned and speared his fingers through his hair. "It's late. I'm tired. Can we discuss this tomorrow?"

"Do I even still have a job tomorrow?" I shot back. "I wasn't sure if you'd even bother to notify me before my replacement showed up."

"Stop it."

Ugh. Thoughts were tearing through my brain in rapid fire, faster than my mouth could even process them. But the look on his face, his whole demeanor—that's what was making it impossible to get anything out right. Every time the startling indifference in his expression caught in my eyes, I felt my throat catch right along with it. It felt like I was choking. Who was this man all of a sudden? He didn't seem to care about *anything* that had happened between us. Had I been wrong about where this was going? I assumed it was more than just sex. Was it not? It was for me, and I thought he felt the same. But now he didn't even have the promise of a future between us to offer in place of the job offer he was revoking so carelessly.

"*You* stop it," I yelled back.

"Aria, calm the fuck down—"

"*Don't* tell me to calm down, *Damon*. Why are you acting so cavalier? Like I don't have a right to be upset." I was getting angrier by the second, watching him just sit there and stare at his desk without a word to say to me. "So, that's it then. You got what you wanted out of me, and now you're through? You got a good lay, and you won, because I finally gave into you. And you got the account on top of that. Now you're just done with me and hiring someone else?"

"Aria, no. Please. It's not like that."

"Then tell me what it's like!" My voice grew shrill, and despite all my efforts, I felt my chin start to quiver. I wouldn't completely break down in front of him, but I didn't know how much longer I could keep my tears at bay.

"We shouldn't talk about this here," he insisted, looking out the windows to see if anybody was around. If they had been, I was more than loud enough for them to hear everything I'd said.

"Fine," I said. "Come with me back to my place, and we'll talk there." I knew it was a bold move. I could have just asked for a cup of coffee in a private bar, but it was go big or go home, right?

He shook his head. "That's not a good idea."

"What the hell do you mean it's not a good idea? Just a couple of days ago, we were—"

"Enough," he growled, shooting up from his seat. "I said we can't talk about this here at work. And it's not a good idea for us to be alone together at your place."

"Why? Scared of what might happen? That it might end up being a repeat of what happened on the trip? Or, let's see...the conference room. Your apartment after we first met."

He snatched up his coat from the back of his chair and stormed over to the door. "Out," he thundered, pointing a stern finger. "We'll talk. But not here. Not like this. And I'm not going to have us leaving together on the cameras. Not with you—"

"Acting *rightfully* angry? Just forget it, Damon," I hissed. "You don't need to explain anything. I can see exactly what's happening here. I know lying asshole men who will do and say whatever it takes to get what they want all too well. Only to turn cold and lose interest the minute they get their rocks off. No, thank you."

"Aria, for fuck's sake—"

"I just didn't think you were one of them."

I spun on my heels and wiped my cheeks and nose, sniffling the whole way back to the elevator. I kept my back turned in case Damon was standing there watching me get on, so he wouldn't see just how deep he'd gotten to me.

I'd never been so desperate to get the hell away from someone. As anxious as I was to hear how he would run after me (he wasn't) or might even try to explain himself (yeah, right), I had been able to tell by the look on his face that he was only going to feed me a bunch of bullshit lies and excuses.

I was beginning to realize just how likely it was that he'd been doing exactly that the entire time. *Men.*

The only thing worse than it not working out with a job you really wanted, was heartbreak over a guy. And if you had to feel stupid for being too blind to see it all coming, you had the massive blow to your ego to boot.

I wasn't surprised to see it was raining by the time I made it out of the building. Of course I didn't have an umbrella with me. Geez, thanks. Just the last little kick I needed from the universe when I was already feeling lower than ever. And then my heel broke.

33

DAMON

uck. I muttered a string of curses to myself as I chased Aria down the street. It took everything in me not to run after her as soon as she stormed out, but with Mr. Humphries being on high alert over fucking everything he suspected between us, I couldn't risk him seeing too much of a scene on the security cameras, if he went so far as to check.

I hung back for a few minutes with my jaw tight and my fists clenched, then when I thought it was safe—I took off after her.

When I spotted her down the sidewalk, hobbling around a corner, I ran faster. "Aria, God dammit. Stop for a fucking minute and talk to me!" I called out over the rain, catching up to her to put an umbrella over both of our heads.

"Oh, now you want to talk?" She turned her head and scoffed.

The hurt expression on her face caused me more pain than I could ever let on, especially knowing I was the one responsible for it. I inclined my head to the café entrance nearby. "Come on. Let's get in out of the rain."

"I can't be out in public right now," she said, looking away and fighting back tears. "I want to go home. My heel is broken, and my feet are cold and wet."

"Okay, I'll call my car around to pick us up. I had one waiting to take me home from the office anyway."

She didn't seem thrilled about the idea, but she didn't stop me either as I pulled my phone from my pocket and called the driver.

We were stuck there under the umbrella. She was shivering from the cold, and I wanted to pull her into my arms and hold her until all this was over. No, more than that. I wanted to kiss her, promise her everything would be all right. But it would've been a lie. Nothing was okay. I'd fucked up by not admitting it sooner. I couldn't keep on making that same mistake, avoiding the inevitable end between us.

A few minutes later, the black SUV pulled up to the curb.

We climbed in, and I instructed the driver to head to Aria's. I knew she wouldn't invite me in, but being in the car would at least give us a chance to talk somewhere dry and private that wasn't the office.

"I know you're upset," I started, even though she refused to look at me and kept her arms crossed tight, staring out her window. "I'm a man," I continued. "I hate more than anything admitting when I'm in over my head, but let's face it. This whole situation is too risky. We can't throw our whole lives and careers away just because we're good in bed together."

She whipped around, and suddenly I wished she would go back to avoiding eye contact. The anger on her face was gut-wrenching.

"So that's *all* I was to you? Just a good fuck?"

My mouth opened, but nothing came out. Nothing I wanted to anyway.

Maybe things would have been different if I told her how I felt on the plane or at any point on the trip. I wished I could say it meant so much more than that. Because it fucking did. If I'd confessed my feelings before, this might make more sense to her. But it was likely for the best that she didn't know, given the circumstances.

It would only make things harder.

"I'm sorry," I said, feeling like shit. "I truly am. But…I can't sleep with my employees."

"Ha. Too late for that." She huffed.

Every word she said was another blow to my chest, like being punched. But I knew I had to stick to my guns about this.

"This whole thing was a mistake," I continued, hating my words, hating myself for saying them.

Hurt flashed across her face. "How convenient that you didn't decide that until *after* you seduced me at the hotel."

"Hey, it took two of us to make that happen," I defended, asshole that I was. "Whether you want to believe it or not, I'm looking out for both of us here. It's your life and career on the line, too."

"*Really*? Because it doesn't feel like I'm getting looked out for at all. You got *everything* you wanted! You got me into bed. You got my help with the project. And now I'm just getting tossed aside like a piece of garbage. You used me in and out of the office, Damon."

My mouth tightened, fighting to keep all the wrong words in.

"Forgive me," she added, her eyes cold, "for not seeing how this has helped me in any way—besides being a waste of my time."

Fuck. If I told her about what her father said, or even her brothers' suspicions from before, she might react irrationally and go off to try and talk to them. It would only make things worse. If she admitted to everything that had happened between us, she was done for—I was done for. Was I a fucking coward? Probably. Was I willing to risk it? No. She already hated my guts. What good would I be to her or anybody, if I told her how I truly felt? She would hate me no matter what. At least I wouldn't drag her into the whole mess.

I hated for her to think I just didn't care, but it was better for her to despise me and leave rather than me coming between her and her whole family.

"I should have told you I decided to move forward with finding a different permanent replacement," I admitted. "I'm sorry, Aria. But this is for the best. Trust me."

"Trust you?" She sneered. "You don't have to worry about replacing me, Damon. Or should I say, Mr. Copeland. Since we're being *so* professional all of a sudden."

The car pulled up in front of her building and rolled to a stop so slowly it felt like an eternity. It'd barely finished parking when she reached for the door handle.

"None of that matters now," she spat, "because I quit."

"Aria," I said, reaching out to stop her.

She paused and faced me. Her eyes searched for something, anything that would make this go away. But I couldn't give that to her. When all I had to offer was silence, she shook her head and lurched out of the car.

I sat and watched as she stormed barefoot through the front doors and disappeared inside.

"Sir?" the driver called out to me for his next instructions, which meant we'd been sitting there even longer than I realized.

"Home."

The rain came down even harder as we drove away.

I felt like shit.

For a moment, I found myself wondering if I was losing more than I was getting out of this fucking deal. There was a sudden gap in my life that I hadn't noticed before. It was massive. Fucking huge. I'm talking the size of fucking Jupiter or some shit dimension. Jupiter is two and a half times more massive than the rest of the planets in the solar system combined. Jupiter is so big that over 1,300 Earths could fit inside of it. Aria was my Jupiter, and I hadn't realized how much space she had been taking up in my mind until she was gone.

And all that was left were regrets.

I wished I could go back to the night we'd run into each other at the bar and just avoided her altogether. Then she could have come on at Humphries, no problem. We would have met as professionals and remained such. Neither of us would have had to worry about our lives and futures. Neither of us would have been hurt.

But there was still a big fucking part of me that thought the time we'd spent together was worth it—that I wouldn't trade it in for anything.

Looked like I wasn't just a fucking coward but a fucking masochist as well. Shit. All this was killing me inside. But no matter how much I racked my brain to find a way out of this mayhem, the best thing for both of us to do now was go our separate ways and forget our time together ever happened.

34

DAMON

*I*t felt like it hadn't stopped fucking pouring since Aria quit. I sat in my office, staring out the window as sheets of rain blanketed the gray sky. Raking my hands down my face, I stood and stretched. I needed to get my shit together and stop thinking about what'd happened with Aria. I made my bed and now I had to deal with the fallout. More importantly, I needed to focus on work. Sinking back into my seat, I got started on the days' tasks.

A knock came to my door, interrupting my concentration.

Dana, the new chief engineer, came in to go over the daily reports. It had been perfect timing that she'd become available and was looking for a new position in NY. According to Bernadette, we could count ourselves lucky that Dana wasn't snatched up by the competition. She was incredibly experienced. Competent. Detail-oriented. An A-type, no-nonsense kind of person. *Not Aria.*

I listened to her daily report, thanked her, and tried to send her back to work. But she was hesitant to leave.

"Was there something else?" I asked.

"No, sir. Well, actually...just one thing. I was wondering if you were happy with my performance so far."

I stopped myself from saying I'd be happier with it if she'd get out of my office and leave me alone. "Yes, you've exceeded expectations," I said, and I meant it. "Now, if you'll excuse me, I—"

"It's just that, it's kind of hard to tell. You always seem so indifferent."

Holding back a groan, I mustered my best polite smile. "I'll try to be more enthusiastic with your performance reviews. And as we get into later stages of the projects, you'll hear more from me. Is that all?"

She didn't look pleased but took my answer as the best she was going to get. "Yes, sir. Okay then. I'll let you get back to it. Thank you."

The moment she was gone, I poured myself a drink and sank down onto the couch in the corner of my office. I remembered when Aria was around here, along with my naughty thoughts of her, how I'd sometimes fantasize about laying her down on that couch and doing all kinds of kinky things to her. Or maybe even just having dinner together, like people who cared about each other outside of the bedroom, too—and they were the kinds of things that could have never really happened without both of us risking the loss of our jobs. I supposed they were the kinds of things I never should have been thinking about in the first place.

The time passed too slowly the rest of the day, and I barely got anything done on my to-do list. But I left at a decent hour and hit the gym. The treadmill seemed to be my only dependable tool for getting my mind off shitty thoughts. But after a while, my legs started to ache.

I said "fuck it" and went home.

. . .

*I*t was Friday night, but I had no interest in doing anything. The rain was supposed to clear up over the weekend, so I decided to go to bed early and get up at sunrise to take a long ride on my motorcycle. But first, it was the same old beer and take-out dinner I'd gotten used to in the past few weeks.

I sucked down the last few gulps from my bottle, and just before turning in, I found myself just sitting there and staring at my phone. Every night it was the same thing. I'd scroll to Aria's name and think about all the texts I wanted to send but knew I shouldn't. When I talked myself out of texting or calling, I'd have to keep myself from jumping in my car and heading to her place.

I wanted to show up at her door and tell her how I'd fucked everything up for both of us. How I'd said the wrong things. That whatever we had, meant much more to me than a random fling or office affair. I was in love with her. I knew that now more than ever. I would throw everything away for her, given a second chance. But I couldn't bring myself to do something that would result in a bigger shitstorm. And even though it might sound lame as fuck, I was concerned about ruining her relationship with her family, and as a result, her hating me even more than she did now.

The notion of "Us against the world" sounded great in the movies, but this was reality. What good could come from starting a relationship on a fucked up base like this? Sooner or later, she'd regret having to put up with the BS all this would cause her. Miles, Oliver, and Mr. Humphries would never change their minds, no matter what approach we took.

I'd racked my brain for solutions.

The only one that was fair toward her was to let her go.

I could only hope things would get easier with time. After

resigning myself to the facts yet again, I pulled myself up from the couch and crawled into bed.

*T*he only thing better than the treadmill was a long, quiet ride on my bike. And the weather the next morning was perfect for it. I had taken to going out on my own since I was disciplined enough to leave early when everything was peaceful and still. When I used to go along with Miles and Oliver, we'd always have to leave later in the morning. But I had a hard time being around them after that talk with Mr. Humphries. I didn't know if he had said anything to them or if Aria might have hinted at something. Not knowing what to expect from them made me think it was better to just stay the fuck away. I wasn't good company to be around these days anyway. I'd even tried to reach out my old buddy, Ace, to ask for advice. Ace was a relationship guy, a Romeo if you will, who'd moved to San Fran for his girl. If anybody knew what to do, it was him. We generally spoke once or twice every other month. When I called his cell, his girlfriend picked up, and she told me that Ace was out, getting a U-Haul. They were busy moving to a new apartment. I told her to say hi and that it wasn't important. I didn't want to bother him with my shit.

I made it to Roy and Joy's around noon but settled into a smaller corner table rather than our usual spot—since I was planning to dine alone.

"Well, aren't you a sight for sore eyes," Marleigh gushed when she came over to take my order. "I've been asking your friends what happened to you."

"I've been exploring some different routes on my bike."

She narrowed her eyes at me but kept whatever she was thinking to herself for the moment. "Whatever you say, hon. I think your boys miss you. They've been looking about as bummed out as you are. But I guess it's none of my business. What'll you have today?"

"Just more coffee," I requested as I sipped down the last few dregs from my mug.

"Oh, come on. Let me at least feed you. You need fuel for those long rides back into the city."

"I'm not hungry." I smiled tightly.

That skeptical expression washed over her face again. "If I didn't know any better, I'd say you're having woman troubles. I always took you as a player type, but I'd swear some lucky gal must have managed to get under your skin."

"Nothing like that," I said, because I didn't want to go into my love life (or lack thereof) in a diner.

She shook her head, unconvinced, and turned around just as the door dinged with more customers entering. "Oh, well, lookie here. There'll be a reunion after all."

I knew exactly what she meant. My suspicion was spot-on when she headed for the kitchen, moving out of the way to reveal Miles and Oliver standing at the front of the place, looking straight at me.

I was at a table for one, but that didn't stop them from squeezing over two extra chairs anyway and inviting themselves to sit down. Part of me was glad to see them. Timing was a bitch, but I'd have to face them eventually.

Miles held out his hand for a fist-bump, and I returned the gesture.

"No wonder you haven't been answering our calls or texts all morning," Oliver said, clapping me on the shoulder. "You beat us to it. And here I thought we got out on the road early this morning."

"You must have to catch me here. I left at dawn."

They both nodded and shot a look at each other before Miles

leaned across the table. "If I didn't know any better, I'd say you were trying to avoid us."

"You think?"

"What's with all this solo riding lately?" Oliver asked.

I sipped down more of my coffee and shrugged. "Just haven't felt very social lately."

He twisted his mouth and kept pressing. "Remember when you and I had that little chat on the side of the road a while back?"

"Sure do."

"You seemed like you had something on your mind then, and now, you're like that, only ten times worse. It seems strange that all of this has lined up with our sister coming on to work with us and then quitting."

"You can't take that personally," Miles insisted. "Aria quits jobs all the time. Our father even considered offering some kind of financial incentive if she'd stay in one place for longer than a year or two. Even though she'd never take it."

I cringed inwardly to hear the sound of her name out loud. "I'm stressed about work," I offered. "I'm not ready to talk about anything else going on in my life right now. Sorry, guys."

At least the way they were talking made it sound like Mr. Humphries had kept our little chat to himself. And Aria must not have let on that her leaving was anything more than her usual impulsivity. That only made me feel worse. She'd finally found something she wanted to stick with, and I ruined it for her.

"I should get going," I decided, gathering my things from the table and tossing down some cash for my bill along with a hefty tip for the waitress.

"What?" Oliver gaped. "Leaving already? We just got here. Come on, man. You avoided us on our ride in. The least you could do is stay and have lunch and then ride back to the city with us."

"Yeah, man. It's not the same without you," Miles added.

"It's not like we can talk to each other on the ride back." I shrugged. "You won't miss me. I'll catch up with you guys later."

They didn't look happy, but I kept walking anyway.

All that talk about Aria and work—it made me feel claustrophobic. I was just as desperate for another long ride, almost as I had been that morning, as if I hadn't already been out on the open road for hours.

I took my time riding back, and it was just past sunset by the time I got into the city. I found myself riding aimlessly down random streets just to kill time until somehow, I found myself pulling to the curb in front of Talia's. Don't ask me why. Because I fucking wanted to see her, that's why.

I stared at the brick wall next to the entrance where Aria and I had made out just before I took her back to my place. It stung to look at, so I strapped my helmet to the back of my bike and headed in for a drink to wash it down.

Walking in, I couldn't help but scan the crowd for any trace of her. Every blonde in the joint made me do a double take, but none of them were her.

After grabbing a whiskey on the rocks from the bartender, I settled into the same table where she and I had sat that night we met. I laughed at myself, marveling at what a masochist I was being after all. But I wasn't so much trying to pour more salt into my wounds as I was hoping she might be doing the same thing. That she fucking might be there, too. Retracing our steps, hoping to run into me.

I didn't even know what I'd say if I saw her. God, I was fucking pathetic. Everything I wanted to say, I knew I shouldn't. Or else I would have been knocking on her door that very moment instead of sulking in the damn bar. It was the same dance I had been doing for weeks. The thing I wanted to do most was the very thing I couldn't.

"Hey, you." A woman's voice cut into my circling thoughts. "Want some company?"

I looked up to see a pretty, young brunette standing there. She was hot, sure, with long tan legs. But she wasn't Aria.

"I'm Lexie."

"No thanks, Lexie. I think I'd like to be alone."

"Damn. I was hoping you'd buy me a drink," she quipped. "But the way you're looking, maybe *I'm* the one who needs to buy *you* a drink."

"You're not the first person today to insinuate that I look like shit," I said.

"All the more reason to share a drink with me." She smiled.

I considered it for a moment, eyeing her full lips. If I did have a few drinks with her, I knew she'd convince me to bring her home with me. It'd be better than going home alone, and it might help take my mind off things. Maybe it'd even be a little easier to get Aria off my mind the next day.

But I couldn't bring myself to say yes. I wasn't interested. I was exhausted and crawling into bed alone sounded like a much better alternative. I politely declined the young woman, yet again, and headed for the door. I stopped one last time to see if I might spot Aria, but no luck. *Yeah, right. Stop dreaming.* The only thing that'd be better than going home alone would be to find her and take her home with me. *Right, idiot. Like she'd come with you.*

Just as I was reaching for the door, I saw a familiar face. The bouncer who'd almost kicked Aria out.

"Hey," I nodded toward him. Surprised, he nodded back and approached me with a happy sparkle in his eyes. "Quick question,"

I said immediately, before he got any ideas. "Have you seen my sister?"

"Your sister?"

"The gal who helped me out with the TP a few weeks back? Remember? Men's bathroom?"

"Oh. Yeah. I remember. The girl with the freckles!"

"Yep. That's the one." I nodded.

"She really your sister?" He gave me a suggestive smirk, then glanced toward my dick. Jesus. I needed to get out of here.

"Dude, just answer," I said.

"Nope, haven't seen her again, and I never forget a face." He looked back up at me, winking. "Leave me your number, and I'll call you if I see her."

Fuck. I took the last few steps out the door and jumped back on my bike, calling it quits on another day without her in my life.

35

ARIA

*K*nock. *Knock.*

I woke up to a distant, incessant rapping tap against the door.

Knock. Knock. Knock.

Ugh. *Nope, keep knocking. Or better yet, get lost. Not getting up.*

Knock! Knock! Knock!

The longer I kept my eyes closed, the more persistent it became, until finally, it turned to the sound of footsteps. For a moment, I thought I should panic. Was somebody in my room? I raised my head into the darkness, opening my eyes. Zoe appeared over my bed with one hand on her hip, staring down at me with disapproval.

I let my head fall back onto the pillow.

"Oh, hey," I murmured, my voice cracking with sleepy hoarseness. "What are you doing here? What time is it?"

"Time to drag you out of bed."

"No, thank you," I said politely, promptly pulling the comforter back over my head.

Just as soon as I did, she yanked it back, exposing my whole body to the cold air in my room. She didn't stop there. After throwing my covers into the corner so I couldn't snatch them back up, she worked her way around the room—turning on all the lights. By the time I resentfully pushed myself to the edge of the bed and rubbed my eyes the rest of the way open, she'd returned with a trash bag and was gathering up all the trash around my bed. A pizza box. A donut box (half-empty). Hershey kiss's wrappers (multiple). Peanut butter cup wrappers (more than multiple). A pint of Ben & Jerry's, Mint Chocolate Cookie, if we were being specific here. A bottle of wine from the night before. Okay, fine—two.

"You're the devil," I quipped, stretching my aching legs out in front of me.

"Well, the devil is about to turn on the hot water for you. And then you're going to take a shower."

"It's Saturday," I groaned. "I don't need to take a shower, and I don't see why I need to get out of bed. That's for Monday morning."

"You can't spend another day and a half in bed," she argued. "I'm not going to let you. Your brother texted me."

"Which one?" I asked.

"The hot one."

"Which one's that?"

Zoe whipped back around, putting her hand on her hip again like an angry mom. "You know which one. *Hello?* Wake up. Miles, duh. He says you're supposed to go out for drinks with him and that Rose chick tonight, in exactly two hours, but you stopped answering his texts."

"Geez, why is everybody being so dramatic?" I plopped back on the mattress, crawling underneath what was left of my sheets and blankets. "You all know I'm not dead. I just quit another job. I'm depressed. Leave me alone."

"Do I need to strip those off the bed, too?" she snapped. "You've had enough time moping around. You're getting up and taking a shower. Then you're going to put on real clothes and come out with me. I'm taking you to have drinks with your brother because you told him you'd go. You can be depressed all you want, but you only get so many passes for bailing on plans with your friends and family."

"I don't want to be around Miles right now," I whined.

"It's not Miles's fault that his buddy Damon is a jerk. And anyway, that's why I'm going with you. That way at least one person will be by your side who knows what really happened."

The sheets rippled and thundered as she yanked those up, too, just as she promised. I jerked up and stared at the pile of bedding in the corner. "While you're at it, can you strip the fitted sheet and throw all of this into the wash?" I teased.

"I just might. As soon as you get your butt up and get in the shower."

There wasn't a bone in my body that wanted to go out that night, but when I walked into the bathroom and saw myself in the mirror, I knew Zoe was right. I needed to pull myself together. I was half-heartedly job hunting through the week, but evenings and weekends were reserved for wallowing in self-pity. It had taken its toll. My hair was matted, and my skin looked like crap, with dark circles under my red eyes as the cherry on top. Plus, I felt somewhat sick to my stomach. I'd never eat chocolate or ice cream again. Or peanut butter cups. (I'd have wine for sure).

After washing up and drying off, I found Zoe in my living room sorting through a stack of mail I had been neglecting.

"You might want to take a look at this," she said, handing over one of the envelopes. The return address read "Humphries Proper-ties" with "Damon Copeland" printed underneath.

For a second, something that felt like an electric bolt ran through my stomach, but I quickly recovered. "No, thank you," I responded, tossing it down to the coffee table.

She sighed and picked it up to tear it open. Her eyes widened as she read over the paper. "No, hon, you *really* want to take a look at this."

She forced it back into my hand long enough for me to see it was a hefty check noted as "severance pay." I rolled my eyes and stuffed it back into the envelope.

"I have half a mind to rip this up. We never discussed any sever-ance pay. What an asshole. He feels guilty and is only trying to make himself feel better for forcing me out of my job."

"Unless you want to go crawling to your dad to beg for money until you find another job, you better not rip it up." She glanced down at the postmark. "Anyway, this wasn't much of an afterthought. Looks like your 'asshole boss' sent it the morning after your falling out."

I took a quick glance at the date. "Even better. He couldn't wait to punctuate that horrible chapter and put it behind him." I scowled, suddenly feeling even sicker, not at my stomach this time. As if Damon hadn't done enough, now I had to imagine him trying to put the whole thing behind him as fast as he could. He had prob-ably already moved on. "I wonder if he's already sleeping with the new head engineer. I saw the company's announcement. Guess what? It's a woman."

"You must not have looked too closely." Zoe laughed. "I don't think she's exactly his type..."

"Enough about him, Zoe."

"Okay," Zoe shrugged, "let's go pick out what you're going to wear."

She dragged me into my closet and started rifling through my clothes. I realized my luggage from our trip to Portland was still sitting in the corner, unpacked. I'd been too excited that weekend when we returned to bother with it, and by that Tuesday night, everything was upside down, and I was slipping into full neglect of all my household chores and my to-do list, except on restocking my lifesaving secret candy and wine stash.

Now the stupid bag was just sitting there, taunting me. It was a horrid reminder of how happy I'd been when I thought I would stay on at Humphries, and that somehow everything with Damon and me would work out.

"How about this?" Zoe popped out of my closet with a dress in each hand: one turquoise, one purple. "Or this? Pick one."

"You pick."

She was more than happy to. Anything to get me dressed and out the door with minimal chances for objections or complaints.

*B*efore I knew it, my hair and makeup were done, and I was finally looking like some version of my old self again. Zoe had picked the turquoise sparkly dress with a plunging neckline—which by the way, made my boobs look on point—and cute, sparkling hoop earrings. It was really too dressy for a casual night out with my brother and her, but hell, after the past few weeks I had, I figured I'd take any excuse I could get to be fancy and feel alive again. And anyway, the short, tight shimmering number looked great next to her sequined black cocktail dress. And we both had on killer heels to accentuate our legs. I resisted the urge to reminisce about how many times Damon had complimented them.

We took a cab to a trendy club, Marcel's, on the other side of town.

"See. Isn't this much better than hiding out alone in your apartment?" Zoe asked as we walked in past all the young, happy-looking people in their nice clothes with cocktails in hand.

I observed the crowd, remembering how much I used to love going out. But now everything felt different.

"It's not better yet," I told her. "But I do know one thing that will help."

I made a beeline for the bar, breezing right past Miles. Before he could even say hi, I was ordering my first drink.

"Someone's thirsty," he quipped.

"Yup!" I sniped, snatching up the shot glass to throw it back, followed by a sip from my accompanying cocktail.

Zoe just smiled and tried to go along with it, ordering drinks of her own.

"You wanted to have drinks. So, I'm having drinks," I defended.

"Hey, Zoe, my sister's best friend and pain in the ass." Miles chuckled as she stood on her tiptoes to give him a hug. Zoe smiled after swatting my brother.

"Rose says hi." Miles said to us. "Unfortunately, she couldn't make it tonight. She has to work overtime. It's just the three of us."

"There's a thought. Maybe I'll just quit engineering altogether and move into a career in cosmetics instead." I chuckled.

"Let's not give Dad a heart attack if we can help it," Miles said, motioning to a nearby table. "Come on. Let's go take a seat. This bar's too crowded."

Zoe and I followed him over to the table. I was already waving the waitress down for my second round by the time we sat down. Conversation drifted into small talk. Miles avoided talking about work projects like he normally would, likely for my sake. But he had a lot to say about a new motorcycle he was planning to buy and fix up.

It took the pressure off of me, so I didn't have to play social butterfly and keep the conversation going. And it gave me more of a chance to drink, which was all I wanted to do. My sole mission for the night had devolved into getting splendidly drunk. Maybe then I could manage to have a good enough time, so I'd forget about Damon for a while.

But a couple of drinks later, I realized my plan was flawed. The more I drank, the sadder I got. And with all the sadness came more relentless memories of him—a swirling, blurry mess of all the hot, steamy moments we shared, along with those cringe-worthy final moments before I quit and walked away.

"How are you holding up?" Zoe asked me after a while when there was a lull in conversation.

"Fabulous!" I slurred with a bitter tone, ignoring the awkward expressions on everybody's faces.

"Hey, should I invite Damon?" Miles asked. "I mean, you two are cool now that he's found a replacement, right?"

"*No*," Zoe answered for me quickly.

I tried to hold it in, but I knew I looked like someone had just stabbed a knife in my gut. If I were sober, I could have let it roll off without making it painfully obvious that I now hated Damon with a burning passion. But in my drunken, depressed state, I was no match for hearing his name roll off my brother's tongue.

"Uh, why don't you go get Aria here some water," she suggested. "And another cocktail for me."

"Sure thing." He shrugged, sliding down from his seat. "I need to hit the bathroom anyway."

"Deep breaths, Aria," Zoe encouraged me, rubbing my back.

"I missed the truth right before my eyes, which is that my old boss, namely the grumphole Damon Copeland, is a *complete* and *utter* alphahole who sleeps with his employees and then fires them."

"Okay, Aria," Zoe begged nervously. "Take it easy and keep your voice down. That's not exactly what happened, and if the wrong person hears you saying that, it could be bad news for everyone."

"But isn't that what he did? He didn't even give me a chance. He just threw me away like I meant nothing and ripped my job out from under me while he was at it."

"But it was *complicated*," Zoe explained. "I agree he's not exactly my favorite person for the way he handled everything, but come on, Aria. It was a tough spot. I don't know if there was any right way to come out of that one. It was a disaster just waiting to happen."

I stared at the table, shaking my head. I could feel the hot sting of tears threatening to burst from my eyes, but I swallowed them down with the last of my drink.

"It *was* complicated," I agreed. "And it still is. I'm in love with him. I have been since that first night, I think. At least a little. Then working with him, it just kept getting more and more intense. But none of it matters now. Damon Copeland broke my heart."

"Okay, again," Zoe pleaded, "let's maybe not keep saying his name so loud."

"No, why don't you say it again." Miles was suddenly behind us, staring with a furious expression. "I didn't quite catch it the first few times."

I spun around so fast I nearly fell off my stool. "Say what again? What are you doing back so fast?"

"I forgot my wallet. Did you just say you're in love with Damon? *My* Damon? As in my fucking best friend who works for our father? Your old boss?" His voice rose with anger, growing more heated with each word.

Zoe looked back and forth between us. "No. She means a different Damon Copeland. You don't know him."

I scrunched my face at her in disbelief, but it was too late.

Miles wouldn't even look at me.

He pulled out his wallet and several bills.

Before I could say anything, Miles had already snatched his things from the table and headed toward the door. I tried to chase after him, but I was stumbling and falling all over the place.

*Z*oe took my arm and shuffled me off into a cab.

"Take me to Damon's!" I shouted to the driver. "Quick! Step on it!"

"I don't know who Damon is or where he lives, lady," the cab driver said calmly, shaking his head with raised WTF-eyebrows.

"O-*kay*, I think we're done with the crazy." Zoe interjected, sitting beside me, giving him my address instead. "You've had one too many drinks. It's time to get *you* home, sweetheart. I really should have stopped you from throwing back cocktails."

"But Miles is going to kill him!" I cried.

The last thing I remembered was imagining my dad and brothers ganging up on Damon to beat him up (or *murder* him. Oh, God!), just before my eyes closed, and I slumped over onto Zoe's shoulder. "Aren't you glad you got me out?" I mumbled.

"Don't you know it," she replied, patting my shoulder, and giving me a "I should have left you at home" look. "Can't wait to do that, again."

36

DAMON

*K*nock! Knock! Knock!

I was just nodding off when a loud knock sounded at my door.

Bang! Bang! Bang!

What the *fuck*?

I was going to ignore it, but the banging turned into an ongoing rattle that threatened to wake up all my neighbors. I shuffled through my living room to answer. It was Miles.

"Miles?" I rubbed my eyes in a begrudging grumble. "What the hell are you doing here? Is everything okay?"

It was a stupid question. I could clearly see everything was *not* okay.

His fists were clenched at his sides, and his nostrils were flaring. He had this crazy, rabid look in his eyes like he was ready to kill somebody.

Like he was ready to kill *me*.

He *knew*.

While I debated in my head how to handle the shit that was about to hit me, I noticed him rearing back. In less than a second, his fist tore through the air, straight toward my face. I caught it just in time to step aside and dodge the blow, sending him stumbling into my apartment.

"What the fuck?" I barked.

"I swear, Damon," he snarled, gearing up to take another swing at me. "I'm gonna beat your ass to a bloody pulp."

"Okay. I can see you're upset," I stated as calmly as possible, moving around the living room in circles to avoid each one of his attempts to clock me. "Why don't you start by telling me *why* you want to beat me to a bloody pulp, and we'll go from there." I didn't need him to tell me why he was there. I knew why. It had been only a matter of time before he'd find out. Although I didn't know how he'd found out, I knew exactly where this was headed.

I needed to tire him out, and to get the aggression out of him.

"You know damn well why, fucker," he said.

"I might. But just for the sake of clarity—"

"Shut up," he hissed, still lunging at me. "I'm not in the mood to talk. Just beating your ass."

After a few more missed attempts, he went stumbling into my kitchen. Thank God he'd been drinking, and I was stone-cold sober. He spun on his heels to come at me again, but I threw my hands up and tried to get him to listen to me.

"Look, man," I said. "I'm not going to fight you. Why don't you sit the fuck down and talk. If you still want to fight after that, we will. I'm more than happy to kick your ass just for waking me up."

"Do you know where I was, asshole?" he hissed.

"How the fuck should I know?" I asked.

"I came from the bar where my baby sister was crying her eyes out." His face was twisted up with rage. "And guess who put her in that state?"

My head dropped. My heart was heavy.

Fuck.

She'd cried her eyes out?

I couldn't bear the thought of her sad and crying.

I'd never meant to make her sad, let alone cry.

All this had gone on long enough. Being without her had been hell. I suffered like a dog, and I didn't want to live without her. The way she had turned my world upside down made my heart sore with longing for more. I wasn't kidding when I said she'd hit me like a lightning bolt. She was the woman I wanted, needed on my side to thrive.

Fuck polar opposites. She was the missing piece of my puzzle. She was surprising and challenging and full of life. She brought fun, spontaneity—and for whatever crazy reason that absolutely didn't make sense—calm into my life. Her unhinged way of living life was liberating. I needed more of it, more of her.

She was the woman for me. Nothing had any meaning if I didn't have her in my life.

I couldn't live without her.

I wouldn't.

My blood thundered, and for the first time in a long time, I made a split-second decision.

Time to come clean.

This time, I wouldn't back out. "Okay, I see," I said, calmly. "I can explain everything. Do you want a cup of coffee first?"

"No, I don't want anything," he ground out through clenched teeth.

"How about a beer?"

"What?"

"Let's have a beer first, for fuck's sake," I growled.

"Man, you're just trying to butter me up. Nothing's getting you out of the ass kicking you've got coming your way."

"Fair enough. Beer first, then fighting," I offered, pushing past him to the fridge, and getting annoyed. "But remember. I'm your friend. We're friends. Best friends. Remember? Think about all the shit we went through."

"Damon! That's the fucking problem!" he hissed, breathless.

"Let's just sit down and talk."

I could tell that was the last thing he wanted to do, but he resentfully snatched the cold bottle from my hand and followed me to the couch with a scowl.

"Did you fuck my little sister?"

"Yes," I said without a second thought.

Silence.

Miles' face twisted in disappointment and anger. Suddenly, he was winding up to come after me all over again. Such immature bullshit.

"But it's not what you think," I defended, but it wasn't enough.

Rather than stopping his next hit, this time, I stood up and faced him. "I love her," I confessed just seconds before his fist struck my cheek.

His fist stopped midair, just hanging there as we both heaved a breath, fueled on adrenaline and anger.

"What did you just say?" he hissed.

"I fucking love her. I didn't just 'fuck' her, okay? Some stuff happened, yes. But it wasn't just about sex," I said. "Let me fucking explain."

He let out a long breath and walked over to the couch, finally flopping down to listen. After throwing back a huge gulp of beer, he stared at me expectantly. "This better be good."

I sank down next to him, raking my hands through my hair. "I didn't know who she was—she didn't know who I was. I had no idea she was your sister. I never would have gone down that road. We'd already hooked up before she ever came on at your father's company."

"When?"

"About three months before she started."

"Huh?" His features wrinkled in confusion. "At Talia's? *She* was the girl you were all bent out of shape over?"

I nodded. "I never got her name that night. I had no idea she was your sister. But I guess she pieced it together the next morning, and that's why she took off."

"You expect me to believe that?" He chuckled incredulously.

"Of course I do, Miles. Think about it. Why the hell would I have talked to you and Oliver about her and that night, if I knew who she was?"

I paused, letting him consider it, as we both took a few more much-needed drinks of our beers.

"You fucked up."

"I wasn't thinking straight," I told him. "I'm still not thinking straight, man. I tried to make it right, but it only made things worse. It all went to shit. I feel like scum. I broke her heart and her trust."

"You *are* scum," he quipped, letting out a slight laugh. He still looked pissed, but finally, he was calming down some. "Did my father threaten to fire you? And more?"

"Yeah. I'm telling you, it all went to shit. I didn't know what to do."

"That's not like you."

"None of this is like me. I don't get myself into these kinds of messes. I didn't want to cause a big fight in the company, in the family, or fuck up everything else."

"So, you bowed out."

"And now she's fucking gone. And I'm miserable as fuck."

Miles was quiet for a long time, staring off at nothing, in deep thought. Every so often he'd bring the bottle back to his lips and drink. I'd do the same.

"Still want to fight?" I asked, half-joking.

"Yeah," he shot back. "But I'm not going to. I'm pissed that you slept with her behind our backs. But..."

I figured a "but" was coming, so I took another drink of my beer and waited.

"But I do feel for you." He sighed. "I know what it's like to love somebody and feel like you're no good for them. Love is like that, I guess. Everybody says it makes you crazy."

"Yeah, I'm not really a fan of it." I turned to face him again, staring at him with a serious expression, hoping he might see that no matter how much I fucked it up, my intentions weren't to screw this up. "But I'm a fan of Aria. I'm kind of glad I didn't know she was your sister. Or else I never would have given her the time of day, and I wouldn't have felt..." I trailed off, shaking my head.

There was only so much I could bring myself to say to him.

"I'm a fan of her, too." He nodded. "Let's just say that she hasn't made the best decisions about men in the past. Let's say that might be the reason Oliver and I are not playing. The last dude she was with really fucked her up. He told her shit no man should ever tell a woman. Just to cover that *he* fucked it up, the fucking narcissist."

I tried to keep my anger at bay.

Something in me wanted to crush that dude's skull.

"She plays the tough chick, but Oliver and I know how he ruined her. I'm not a violent man, but I swear, if I ever catch that motherfucker, he'll regret the day he was born. Oliver and I wanted to rip his fucking dick out and shove it down his throat when she first told us. The fucker's been hiding, but Oliver will get him sooner or later, no doubt. At least he's gone, and she can heal. Which is why I can't have dicks like you breaking her heart."

"I know," I agreed. "I'm afraid if I go anywhere near her again, I'll just make it worse."

He stood up. "She deserves better. Better than what exists. Nobody's good enough for my little sister."

Fuck. "I know I need to stay away, but—"

"Just shut up and listen to me, okay? Nobody's good enough for her, but if you really love her—"

"I do."

"Then there's nobody else in the world I'd trust enough to treat her right. You'll have to make this right with her."

"Miles, for Christ's sake. Don't you get it? If there was a way to do that, I would have by now. Believe me. I've been torturing myself over here. It takes everything in me not to go see her, but if I do that, it'll start a shitstorm. By the end of it, she'll hate me. This will be a fucking disaster."

"Don't want to be in your shoes and face her wrath when you see her again," he said with a pitying laugh. His chuckle faded as he scratched his chin, racking his brain for a solution. "I'll talk to my dad."

"I'll come with you."

"No. It'll go over better if I explain everything to him as a sort of mediator. He might still fire you."

"I don't give a fuck. I know I made the wrong choice. I should have stood my ground with him and chosen Aria."

"We'll see what he says." He shrugged. "I'll do what I can."

"Thanks, man."

"While I'm here, you got anything to eat?" he asked, switching gears suddenly, slapping my shoulder.

"Yeah," I chortled. "Leftover pizza in the fridge. Come on."

"*You*...eating greasy delivery pizza?" He gaped. "Damn, you really have been going through it."

"Laugh it up. I've been more than making up for it in the gym at least, but something's gotta give."

"Looks like we've got to give you our blessing before your six pack turns into a beer and pizza gut," Miles said.

"Halfway there," I agreed.

"I can tell."

"Shut the fuck up."

37

ARIA

For the second day in a row, I heard someone entering my apartment after I ignored their incessant knocking. *Can't a girl have some peace and quiet around here?* I wasn't sure if it was knocking this time, or just the pounding in my head growing disproportionately loud. But I was really freaking regretting giving my brothers and Zoe keys to my place. What was the time anyway?

It was Miles that appeared at my bedside this time. "Drink this," he said, holding out a to-go cup of some orangey-greenish gunk.

"Just looking at that makes me want to wretch," I groaned, turning away. "I can't even fathom putting it in my mouth."

He set it on the nightstand anyway. "You'll do it if you know what's good for you. Then you'll get yourself together and come into the living room. I brought breakfast and coffee, too."

He walked out, leaving me to peel myself up and try to wrap my head around what happened the night before.

I remembered everything with Zoe dragging me out of the house.

I remembered the swanky spot where we met Miles.

I remembered the bar and my hasty order of a shot and drink.

After that...everything got blurry.

But I insisted on retracing the events of the evening in my mind, anyway. I had this nagging feeling like there was something important I needed to recall. Something that had gone horribly wrong.

Sitting up and rubbing my aching head, I pulled off the covers and went into the bathroom to splash some water on my face before slipping into my comfiest robe, muttering to myself the whole way.

I looked hot. Zoe looked embarrassed. *God, probably because I drank too much.* Miles wouldn't shut up about his stupid bike. Then he had the nerve to bring up Damon...*Damon.*

Oh, my God!

Damon.

Miles knew about Damon!

The memories of my drunken crying fit came rushing back to me with a fury. My eyes grew wide as I gasped and bolted out into the living room. Miles was sitting there, spreading croissants and coffee cups out on the table.

"Damon!" I shrieked. In my hazy shock, it was all I could manage to get out.

"I didn't kill him," he stated plainly. "Calm your tits, woman. Geez."

I let out a sigh of relief, clutching my chest, but it was quickly overshadowed by a million other concerns.

"You went and talked to him?" I winced, hating myself for blurting everything out.

He nodded, and I sank onto the cushion next to him. Still cradling my pounding head, I remembered going on and on about

Damon fucking his employees and firing them. *Ugh, why did I have such a big mouth. So stupid.*

"Miles, I don't want him to get in trouble," I pleaded. "I hate him for what he did to me, but I was just as guilty for going along with it. It's not what you think."

I was quickly spiraling into a full-grown panic, thinking that Damon might lose his job because of me. But the scorned woman inside wanted not to care. *I* did lose my job because of him, after all. The back and forth of anger and pity toward him had my head spinning and my stomach tying itself in knots. I was starting to get nauseous, and suddenly realized accepting Miles's hangover cure drink might not be such a bad idea.

"I know," he told me.

"Huh? You know? How?"

"I talked to him."

"You did what? When?"

"He told me everything."

"Everything?" I cringed. I was silently praying he had enough sense to leave the bulk of the details out. Like the vibrator he gave me and our little rendezvous in the conference room, just as two examples. "*Everything?*" I repeated.

"He told me more than he told you," he answered. "I know you dislike him now, and I don't blame you. But the poor guy was in a tough spot. Dad threatened him."

Dad threatened him? This just kept getting worse and worse. The killer hangover would have been enough, but I was crashing deeper and deeper into a dark hole of dread.

"Dad threatened him," I murmured. "You mean he knows? Dad knows?"

"Geez, woman. Of course he knows. Apparently, he saw you two together and figured out there was something going on. He pulled

Damon into his office and not only threatened to fire him but also probably guilt-tripped him over the whole damn thing, and issued warnings to ruin his whole future career."

"When?"

"Right before Damon started trying to find somebody to fill your position."

It was all starting to make sense. No wonder he changed so quickly—like night and day. On the trip, he seemed hell-bent on convincing me to stay on at Humphries. By Monday, he was unreachable. And Tuesday...that was such a terrible day I wished I could forget altogether. All because our dad had threatened him.

"That jerk," I hissed through clenched teeth.

"Come on, Aria. Don't be too hard on him. I might have done the same thing in his position. No, he shouldn't have been messing around with you, considering he was your boss and a friend of the family. But—"

"No! Not Damon!" I flew to my feet and started pacing the room. "I mean, yeah, he's a dickhead for making that decision for us. He should have talked to me! He had no right to make that judgment call on my behalf. But *Dad. He's* the jerk. I can't believe he talked to Damon instead of talking to me!"

"What was he supposed to do?" Miles argued. "Say 'Hey, only daughter of mine, I hear you've been sleeping with your boss, my employee. Care to chat about that?'"

"Yes!" I cried back with an irrational shrillness. "I have to go."

"What?" He gawked at me as I raced back into my bedroom and started digging through my clothes, slinging shirts and pants through the air. "Aria, what the hell are you doing?"

"I have to see Dad. He had *no* right to interfere with my life and threaten Damon like that!"

"Aria, don't. *I'm* going to talk to Dad for both of you, okay? I already told Damon I would."

He kept pleading with me, but it was too late.

I had spent *weeks* feeling completely heartbroken and used. Sure, Damon was to blame for not telling me what happened. But it all fell on Dad for butting into my life and using his power to intimidate and get his way.

I was sick of him never trusting me and letting me decide what was best for me.

It was time for it to stop.

Judging my life decisions was one thing. But sticking his nose into my love life and playing all of us like puppets—that was crossing a major line.

I huffed out of the house with Miles chasing me. Ignoring his begging for me to stop, I whistled down a cab and ordered it to go to my parents' house.

38

DAMON

*H*ow could I have let her go? What had I done? I should have never allowed her to leave. Instead of showing her that there were men worthy of being trusted, I had made her feel alone. Made her feel unwanted. I had let her go. *Idiot.* I should never have allowed her to make a single step from my side. I should have proclaimed to the whole world that she was my girl, with a big proud smile, from the start. That she was mine, now and forever. Seeing her happy eyes would have been worth any shit that might have followed.

Instead, I fired her. I screwed up massively.

I barely fucking slept after Miles left. Maybe that's what was altering my judgment the next morning. It might have been crazy, but I was convinced him talking to his father for me wasn't the best solution. It was weak. It was shit. No, it was the worst possible next step in the whole scenario.

One of my biggest regrets was not standing up to Mr. Humphries and telling him how I really felt about his daughter.

Cowering behind his son and leaving it up to him to explain everything would only be making that same mistake all over again. No. Not happening. If I expected him to have any ounce of respect for me, enough to actually give us his blessing, I had to face him like a man.

Putting on my nicest casual clothes: a white dress shirt, a pair of jeans, and a brown blazer, I made the drive out to the Humphries' estate. A gut feeling told me that Miles hadn't spoken to Mr. Humphries yet. He was probably still in bed, snoring. Good. I stopped halfway to the door, not second-guessing myself, and kept putting one foot in front of the other. There was no telling how it would go, but it was my only shot at redemption. And the only way I could secure both my dignity (what was left of it) and the woman I loved, assuming she would even have me after being such an asshole. It was worth a shot. Not that I had other options.

I knocked and waited.

After a minute or two, the door flung open. I had expected staff to open the door, so I was surprised to see the man I'd come to see at the door himself. Mr. Humphries was smiling when he answered, but it faded the moment he saw my face. He'd tolerated me after our talk, but things hadn't been the same. He still hated my guts.

"Mr. Humphries," I said. "I need to talk to you. May I come in?"

His mouth tightened, and I knew he was gearing up to say no. But his wife appeared behind him and quickly pulled me in.

"Damon! So good to see you! It's been *ages*. You look very handsome if I may say so. I bet you have women lined up all around the city. Or do you have a girlfriend? I bet a man like you is never single. Heartbreaker, you! Come in, come in!" Mrs. Humphries yanked me into the house and ushered me into the living room, ordering me to sit. "To what do we owe this pleasant surprise?"

Mr. Humphries came in behind her, looking tense and pissed. His eyes met mine with a knowing death glare. Yep, he already knew why I was there.

"I hate to barge in on your Sunday afternoon," I told her, "but if I could just have a moment with your husband, I won't take up too much of your time."

"Of course. When duty calls." She laughed. "I'll make you boys some coffee and snacks. Or something sweet maybe? I've baked these wonderful brownies."

"No need, honey," Mr. Humphries objected, holding his hand in the air. "Damon says he won't be long. Just give us some privacy."

Still oblivious to the tension between us, Mrs. Humphries carried on cheerfully. "Certainly. You sure you don't want any brownies?" She looked at me with a bright smile.

"No, thank you, Mrs. Humphries."

"Please, call me Helen. But okay, I won't get in your way. I have some gardening to tend to anyway. Let me know if you change your mind about the brownies. They are gooey and probably still warm. Also, *love* that blazer. Your girl is sure a lucky lady." She double-winked at me. "*Cheeriohoo.*"

With that, she breezed out of the room, humming to herself as she went, just as happy as ever. I wished some of her energy could have stayed in the room. But no. It was just me and an enraged Mr. Humphries who probably would have killed me right then and there if he thought he could have gotten away with it.

"Mr. Humphries. Again, I'm sorry for dropping in unannounced. But I need to talk to you about your daughter."

He immediately groaned and sank his face into one hand. "Damon. We discussed this already." His voice was cold and impatient. "I don't know that I can forgive you for messing up Aria's potential future with my company, but we'll get over it. What's done is done. You did the only thing you could have done to right your wrongs."

"It wasn't the right thing," I argued sternly. "What I should have done is what I'm here to do now. And that's to tell you I'm in love with your daughter."

"Ha, ha, ha." He laughed in disbelief.

I kept going anyway. "I'll gladly surrender my position at the company if that's the only way to be with her."

"That can certainly be arranged," he shot back, no longer laughing. "But it'd be in vain. Because I don't approve of you and my daughter being together. My original position still stands. Leave her alone, or you're fired."

"Fine. Fire me," I persisted. "While I want you to give us your blessing, Aria is a grown woman. If she wants to be with me, she can. I don't mean any disrespect, but I'm not backing down."

He paused. "Good Lord." Then, he leaned forward, burying his face in both hands now, and sighed. And sighed again. "You want a drink, Damon?"

"Yes, why not? Thank you."

He walked over to the arrangement on the mantle and poured two glasses of Scotch, bringing one back to me. His expression was unreadable as I reached for the drink, but at least he hadn't officially fired me yet. Or pulled any shotguns or pistols out of his closet. Though I half-wondered if he kept one hidden behind the bar, and maybe the whole drink thing was just a distraction.

"My wife and I have worked our asses off to try and give our kids every opportunity in the world," he explained, shaking his head. "The problem is—when you do your job right as a parent, your kids tend to take a lot for granted. All of my children are smart and hardworking, of course. We're very proud. But Aria...she's always had her head in the clouds."

"Aria is a—" I started to speak, but he lifted up his hand to stop me.

"If you know what's good for you, son, you'll keep your mouth shut and let me say what I have to say."

Nodding, I took a drink of my Scotch.

He grunted and stood from the couch, walking over to admire the family photos displayed around the room. He picked up one of him and Aria in a cap and gown, smiling at the camera during one of her graduations.

"I always hoped she would find a nice, solid man to keep her grounded," he continued, staring down at his daughter in the photo. "Someone who was responsible. Focused. Grounded and stable. Hell, I figured even if none of that rubbed off on her, she'd at least have someone other than me around to talk some sense into her."

He paused for a moment before setting the frame back in its spot. "How long has this...*thing* between you two been going on?"

I took a moment, choosing my words carefully. I couldn't very well blurt out that we hooked up after randomly meeting at a bar.

In the end, I told him everything—*almost* everything. I explained how I hadn't been able to stop thinking about her after we met. That I didn't even know her name or that she was a part of their family. I only knew she was one of the most amazing women I'd ever met, and it only took one chance meeting for her to make that impression on me. Of course, I left out the part about us having a one-night stand or any other details. "If she could make me feel that way in such a short amount of time," I started, "I was dying to know what else she'd inspire in me, *if* we had the chance. That's how things got out of hand. I knew I was crossing a line as her boss. But no matter what I do, I just can't help the fact that I'm madly in love with her."

He looked up at me.

"And it has me making all sorts of insane decisions."

"Aria can have that effect on people I suppose." He suddenly smiled. "Did I ever tell you how me and my wife Helen met?"

"Not that I can recall."

"I passed her on the street one day and thought she was the most beautiful woman I had ever seen. Then I got to talking to her and realized she was smart and funny, too. I was working my ass off trying to prove myself to my father. I was stubborn and refused to accept any of his help. I wanted to make a living for myself, but at that point, I was practically penniless. Then Helen came along. Her family was wealthy. Boy, did her dad ever hate me. Even after I had made a name for myself, I don't think he ever changed his mind about me."

"I imagine it's hard for fathers to let their daughters go."

"Harder than I thought...as it turns out." He smirked. "I didn't realize it until you walked in here and said you loved my Aria. For a moment, I think I hated you more than I did when I thought you two were just having an office fling."

I rubbed my hands together and stared at my feet, wondering where he was going with this. The waiting and listening were killing me.

Just as Mr. Humphries was about to speak, Mrs. Humphries came in with a plate of brownies. "He's hardworking and dependable. Responsible. Focused. Grounded. Stable. You get my point, Charles?" She gave him a knowing glance.

Mr. Humphries cleared his throat. A moment later, his shoulders fell. "Yes. You're all the things I hoped Aria would find someday. Of course, I never actually expected her to go for the kind of guy I wanted for her. But now here you are."

"I do love her, Mrs. and Mr. Humphries. I've never felt this way about anybody," I explained cautiously. "And I promise you this. If given the chance, I would take care of her. You wouldn't have to worry about her. I'm afraid with Aria being as stubborn as she is..."

"Which, ironically, she got from my husband," Mrs. Humphries said, and Mr. Humphries chuckled.

"I may not be able to stop her from taking off and doing what she wants to do," I said, "But I can at least be there for her whenever things don't work out. I can catch her when she falls. Though to tell you the truth, while everything she does may seem haphazard and random, she's pretty damned good at her job and at taking care of herself."

Mr. Humphries nodded. "I suppose you're right, Damon. That may be just another thing I have to accept. Learning to trust her to take care of herself. But...I suppose there's no reason why she can't have someone by her side while she does it. It's not like she would listen to me anyway. She *can* be stubborn as a mule."

I waited patiently, hoping he was about to say what I wanted to hear. The only thing that mattered—second to what Aria decided. Even after all this, she still may never want to see or talk to me again.

"I appreciate you coming here and talking to me," Mr. Humphries said. "I know it couldn't have been easy, considering our last chat."

"I'm willing to do whatever it takes to win Aria back. I want to be with her."

He leaned over and put his hand on my shoulder, smiling. "I guess you better go get her then."

A wave of relief rushed over me—like a huge weight had been

lifted. But getting her father's blessing was only half the battle. I still had to find a way to explain everything to Aria and make things up to her.

"Thank you, sir. You won't regret this," I said, vigorously shaking his hand as we stood for him to show me out.

"Thank you, Mrs. Humphries."

She waved a hand in dismissal. "Oh, please. Call me Helen, I insist. We're practically family, Damon," she said with a wink. "But now, I really must tend to my garden." With one final smile, she rushed out of the room.

Mr. Humphries walked to the front door but froze the second he opened it. "Aria?"

"Aria?" I echoed.

She was standing there in sweats with a leather jacket thrown over her top. She wasn't wearing any makeup, and her hair was in a messy bun with stray pieces shooting out in every direction. I still thought she looked beautiful, but she was clearly a mess at that moment.

And she looked mad as hell.

"Dad! I need to talk to you." She seethed, pushing her way in. She stopped cold when she saw me standing there behind him.

"What the hell are *you* doing here?"

"I could ask you the same thing." I smirked. God, it was good to see her again. Even if she was pissed at me.

"This is my parents' house," she shot back with a scowl, crossing her arms. "I'll get to you in a minute." She pointed a finger at her dad. "You! You're the one I came to see. I had a nice little chat with Miles. He tells me *you're* the one responsible for all of this. How could you do that? How could you go behind my back and—"

"Aria, wait." I interjected. "Don't take it out on your dad. He was just trying to look out for you. I can't blame him."

Mr. Humphries gave me an approving nod. After giving me his blessing, the least I could do was put in a good word for him when he was the one in the hot seat.

"Well, I certainly *can* blame him," she argued.

"I think I better give you two a chance to talk," Mr. Humphries offered, seeming in a hurry to escape her wrath.

"Oh, no, you don't!" Aria scolded.

"This is my house, young lady. And I'm still your father. Now go in the other room and hear what Damon has to say." He walked away, not giving her a chance to argue any further.

By the time she turned back to me, her expression had changed from fiery rage to something softer—and almost worried. We were both breathing heavily, coming face-to-face again after long weeks apart. I wanted more than anything to take her into my arms right then and there, but it would have to wait.

"I've missed you," I said, not knowing where else to start.

"Did you now?" She pursed her lips to the side and nodded toward the living room. "Come on."

Nothing had changed a bit. I was still just as eager to pull her into my arms as I had been that night on the street corner in the rain. I knew from the look on her face it wouldn't be that easy. I couldn't just kiss it away—at least not yet.

But this time, I did have something more to offer her. A way we could be together where we both got what we wanted.

I followed behind her, realizing this was the only chance I was going to get.

It was now or never.

I had to get past all of her anger and make her understand how I felt. Mr. Humphries wasn't standing between us anymore, which meant if I messed it up, I had no one to blame but myself.

39

ARIA

*J*ust seeing Damon again made my knees go weak and my heart flutter. The way he looked at me. I felt myself softening up to him no matter how badly I didn't want to at that moment. *But, no-oh, nice try, missy. Have to wake up way earlier to fool this bitch over here.* I stuck to my guns and stared him down with a look that made it clear he wasn't getting out of this that easily.

"Okay, why didn't you tell me my dad and brothers threatened you?" I scowled.

"Why do you think?" he rumbled. "I didn't want to cause any trouble with you and your family. Aria, I care about you. I want you to be happy, and the last thing I wanted was to stir up any shit that would result in you hating me."

"And you thought giving my job away without talking to me was a better solution?" I crossed my arms and raised my brows.

"Yes. The lesser of two evils maybe. I don't know."

"You don't know?"

"I know I made a mistake."

"No kidding." I huffed out a breath.

"I'm not just talking about a fucking job, Aria." He took a few steps forward, approaching me with caution. "I made a mistake by losing you."

I felt my lip tremble and wanted to break down from relief, happiness, and lingering anger all at once. But I bit it down and stayed stern.

"You're right," I said. "You *did* mess up. Big time. You're a prick."

He laughed. Actually laughed! A deep, sonorous laugh that made my heart flutter.

"Are you ever agreeable?" he asked, his eyebrows raised. "Or do you always have to argue about everything? I'm agreeing with you, I'm admitting to shit, and you're still calling me a prick."

"I call 'em like I see 'em," I shrugged. "But...I didn't say you were just a prick. You may have a few other redeeming qualities."

His eyes darkened (strangely enough, I liked that dark gaze very much), and he tilted his head.

"Okay, fine. More than just a few." I sighed. "That doesn't change the fact that you should have been honest with me. We could have tried to figure it out together. If you weren't such a control freak..."

"A control freak and a prick," he quipped, moving even closer. The safe gap between us was rapidly shrinking, right along with my resolve. "Aria, I need to tell you something—"

"What are you doing here anyway?" I cut him off. "I thought Miles was going to talk to Dad for you."

"He offered, but not owning up to my feelings myself is what got us into this mess. And if you'd just listen for a minute, I could explain. Aria, I came here to tell your dad and to tell you—I fucking love you. I love you."

Did he really just say that? OMG. No, I must have misunderstood.

"*That's* why you came here?"

"Guess I got my chance to tell you sooner than I was expecting. What are *you* doing here?"

"I came to yell at Dad for threatening you, obviously," I fired back, finding it hard to breathe. "But wait. What did you just say?"

"You heard me."

"I didn't," I lied.

"Aria, I love you."

OMG. This is real?

I searched his eyes for any sign that this might be one big sick joke. I couldn't believe what he was saying...and yet I could, I wished, I wanted to, because I felt the exact same way. Hearing it out loud was still more jarring than I expected, though—like the moment I had the relief of seeing him again, someone punched me in the gut, knocking all the wind out of me.

He inched closer and closer, wrapping me in the warmth of his body and scent that I'd been craving for weeks. His dark eyes, behind his glasses, searched mine, and they were just as mesmerizing as ever. Maybe more so thanks to the words spilling from his lips.

"I...I don't know what to say." My voice cracked.

"Woman, tell me you love me, too," he suggested. "Unless you don't. But I know you do."

"You do?"

"I do, babe," he grumbled sternly. "If you don't, I'll just haul you over my shoulder and—"

He pivoted toward my legs, sending me shooting forward. "Don't you dare, you big stubborn brute."

My words caught him and his smiling face, just in time for me to crash into his chest (literally *crash,* as in ram into gracelessly), letting his big arms sweep me up. I nuzzled my face into his neck under his strong jawbone, feeling like I could just curl up and sleep there forever. Not actually *sleep*, sleep, but rest, relax, let go of the freaking huge boulder that'd been squishing my poor heart. He made me feel so safe, and his air was like a drug I'd been withdrawing from since the moment I stormed out of his car that rainy night.

Everything in the world felt right again. Well, maybe not everything. I was still painfully unemployed, but we could sort all of that out later. All that mattered right then was being in his arms again.

"I love you, too," I whispered, and he squeezed me even tighter.

"I know, babe," he murmured. "I told you I know."

"You're going to break a rib." I couldn't help but laugh.

"Nah." He kissed my hair.

It was the perfect moment. Maybe even good enough to make up for the hell I had been in leading up to it.

It felt like nothing in the world could tear us apart again.

Nothing.

"What the fuck?"

A voice suddenly cut through the room, causing both of our heads to whip around to catch Oliver standing there with wide eyes (so much for nothing in the world could tear us apart). "What the hell is going on here?" Oliver barked.

Before we could answer, the front door opened. Rose and Miles rushed in just as my mom came down the hallway. "Oh, how wonderful! A surprise visit from all of my kids! All on the same day! What are the odds? I've made brownies. They are gooey and probably still warm. Well, I can warm them up if they're not. Miles, Oliver, come here, give your mama a kiss and a hug. *Beautiful* dress, Rose!" But then she saw the fuming expression on Oliver's face, and the confusion in Miles and Rose's eyes. "Did I miss something?"

"I obviously did," Oliver growled. "Mom, take Rose and Aria into the other room."

"What on earth for?" My mom looked puzzled.

Oliver started rolling up his sleeves and popping his knuckles. "Because I don't want you to see me breaking Damon's nose."

"Oh, good lord," I muttered to myself, rolling my eyes.

"No noses are getting broken," my dad said, joining in on the major traffic jam piling up in the entryway of my parents' home. "I can explain everything."

"What the fuck are you doing here?" Miles asked Damon. "I thought you were going to let *me* talk to Dad about this shit."

"What *shit?*" Oliver barked.

"The better question is—what is *Aria* doing here?" Damon argued. "It's a good thing I came when I did. She came barging in, spilling everything, thanks to you."

"She got away from me, and I figured I'd better bring Rose as backup," Miles explained. "I figured I'd be walking into a shitshow, just didn't know it'd be this big of one."

"Everyone, just calm down," my father pleaded, stepping in the middle of it all, holding his hands in the air. "It's okay. Damon talked to me. I gave them my blessing."

"Blessing for fucking what?" Oliver turned bright red, clenching his fists tighter. His eyes dropped to Damon's and my fingers, still hooked together between us. "Damon...what the actual fuck? You never told *me* anything?"

"Oliver, watch your language," Mom said.

"It's all right, Oliver. Chill." Miles stepped in, trying to hold him back.

"Oh, great," Damon groaned. "Here comes protector Oliver, acting all tough like he's saving some damsel in distress."

"Damn straight," he growled, looking back to Miles. "You knew about this?"

"He accidentally heard Aria talking about it," Rose said quietly.

I took a deep breath and braced myself, moving in front of Damon. "We're in love."

Oliver's brow wrinkled with denial. "Who's in love?"

"Damon and me, you idiot." I reached back and held his hand tighter—like it was us against the rest of them.

"Aria!" Mom scolded. "Don't call your brother an idiot. And Oliver, leave your sister alone."

Good grief. It felt like a live taping of Jerry Springer. *Geez.*

"Christ Almighty." Dad sighed, leaving us for his minibar on the other side of the room.

We watched as the reality of everything settled in with Oliver, and then he was rearing up all over again. "That's it," he said as a millisecond warning before flying across the room, tackling Damon to the carpet.

I screamed while Miles laughed. Rose looked like she might never want to come around us again. Dad poured his drink, but it was Mom who marched right over and grabbed Oliver by the ear. She yanked him up to his feet and dragged him away from Damon, like he was a five-year-old kid all over again.

"Just what is your problem? If Damon and Aria are happy together, you should be happy for them. Not trying to beat up your best friend," she raved before finally setting him free.

"Does no one care that I approved all of this?" Dad whined.

"You approved all of this?" I shrieked, putting my hands on my hips. "What about me? Doesn't anybody care about what *I* think?"

Everyone fell silent. I stepped toward my mom with an earnest expression. "Mom?"

"Yes, dear."

"Do you like Damon?"

"As a matter of fact, I do. Always have." She smiled over at him.

"Good. Because we're in love. I love him." Saying the words out loud still sent a chill down my spine and made my entire body light on fire with a tingling feeling.

Mom smiled wider, looking like she might tear up. But Oliver still wasn't having it.

"You slept with my sister," he snarled.

"All right." Dad jumped up, making a prompt exit. Talking about love was one thing. Who I slept with was more than he could take. He took his bottle of Scotch with him on his way out.

"Yes, well!" Mom blushed. "Since everyone's here, I might as well make us something to eat. I assume you can stay for dinner? It's the least you could do for me after barging in with this big scene so unexpectedly."

"Yes, Mom. Of course." Miles chuckled, grabbing Oliver by the arm. "Come on, buddy. Let's go take a walk and cool off."

He wrapped his arm around Oliver's shoulder and guided him out the front door, with him muttering under his breath the whole way, "Damon slept with our little sister. I told him not to and he did it anyway. I'm fucking pissed. But what I'm even more pissed about is that he didn't tell us."

"Man, he didn't know she was our sister," Miles said. "Let me explain..."

Rose was left behind with an awkward look on her face. "I'm just gonna...go help your mom in the kitchen."

Finally, Damon and I were alone again. But I was so overwhelmed, I didn't know what to do or say. His lips were parted as he stared off toward the foyer where everyone had just been standing moments ago, looking stunned but amused.

"Do you regret all of this now that you've seen how nutso my family can be?" I laughed, going over to rest my hands against his chest.

"Totally. You can just tell your dad to revoke his blessing. And I'll have to quit my job anyway to get away from Miles and Oliver, so no need to worry about that."

"Shut up."

"Make me." He winked, leaning his mouth toward mine.

I was more than happy to crash my lips against his, flooded with everything I'd been missing—his firm and gentle lips and the taste of his tongue on mine. His strong arms. The scratch of the stubble on his chin and the cedar scent in his hair. It was enough to make me dizzy.

I was so wrapped up in our reunion kiss, I didn't hear the door open yet again. I turned around just in time to spot Oliver glaring at us, but thankfully Miles was still with him, keeping him calm.

"Hey, guys, the blinds are wide open," Miles warned us. "Maybe let me get psycho here farther down the street before you start kissing in plain sight."

"He's going to have to get used to it," I shot back.

"Yeah, but one thing at a time."

"It's not like Miles was any better when he came charging into my place last night," Damon teased. "Which by the way, you could have given me a warning before you drunkenly spilled everything to him."

"Really?" I asked. "You want to lecture me about giving people warnings? Hmm... Let me see... Let's count the endless number of things Damon could have had the decency to warn me about like—"

"Let's not." He kissed me again to keep me quiet. It was a tactic I more than approved of.

"I guess I'll have to make it up to those guys somehow," he added a moment later. "They did ask about us, and I didn't tell them. I understand why he's pissed."

"Yeah, but who could blame you after seeing the way they were acting?"

"Your dad, though, he was a class act. Very understanding. At least, today he was. So was your mom."

"He's probably planning to fire you first thing Monday morning," I said sarcastically.

"Then we'll both be out of a job."

"Not funny yet!" I sang, throwing my arms around his neck so he could hold me tight.

"I guess I better go talk to Oliver." I sighed. "Poor guy really gets bent out of shape over this kind of thing. All the girls flocked to him in high school, because he'd beat up any guy who didn't treat them with respect."

"As I recall, that's not the only reason they flocked to him." He smirked. "But do you think I should go talk to him instead?"

"Eventually, but not yet. Let me ease him into it. This is all for show anyway. I think he was secretly kind of relieved we kept him from beating you up. He's just making it clear that he would, if you ever hurt me...again."

"No chance in hell I'm letting that happen, if I can help it." He gave me a soft kiss before I turned to walk outside. I flashed him a sly smile as he playfully smacked my butt on the way out.

·　·　·

$\mathcal{M}$om whipped up a nice dinner for everybody, and I was finally able to get Oliver calmed down enough to join us—including Damon—at the table to eat. No matter how much he glared at us, I couldn't keep my hands off of Damon. It had sucked bad enough to flee from his apartment after that first night together. But then to get so much closer to him, only to have him taken away from me all over again? It was reason enough to keep clutching his hand under the table or shooting him longing looks all night long. Oliver would just have to get over it.

Afterward, we told everybody goodbye and goodnight. Damon ushered me straight to his car and took off in a hurry. "I can't wait to get you back to my place. We've got lost time to make up for."

"Who says we have to wait until we get back there?" I suggested, grazing my fingers along his upper thigh.

He tensed and shook his head. "You're going to make me wreck the car. Why do you take such joy in teasing me?"

"Who said I was teasing?" I asked, dropping my voice even lower. I leaned across his lap and circled around everything I'd been missing so much.

I knew whatever I did to Damon on that ride home, he would *more* than make up for when we arrived at our destination. And hopefully, outside of the occasional romp in the car (or a public place just for fun), we would never have to keep our attraction and feelings for one another secret ever again.

$\mathcal{W}$e crashed into Damon's bedroom with the same heated passion we had on the night we met. Our hands kneading into each other's skin, ripping away whatever clothing dared get in our way. Each time our lips parted, and our eyes met again, they were full of fiery longing and something deeper than that—we weren't hiding our feelings anymore. No more running from them or what we really wanted from each other, which was far, far more than an office fling.

Damon moved inside of me in all the right ways, using his expert touch across my folds to guide me to climax right along with him. He knew all the right buttons to push and when to push them. Before I let myself crash over the edge with him, I dug my nails into his skin and breathlessly whimpered, "I love you."

"I love you too, babe," he grunted into my neck with his raspy voice that I loved, trailing kisses down to my breasts as he fucked me.

"I love you," I repeated. The words felt so good to say, it was the last push I needed to send the orgasm ripping through me. He kissed me until we couldn't manage it anymore and succumbed to our mouths breaking apart just long enough for us to cry out through the mounting pleasure.

The second it started to fade, he kissed me again. "I love you, babe."

I had a feeling his lips would always return to me like that, maybe even for the rest of our lives.

We hadn't managed to get away from each other yet, despite all of our best attempts. And I didn't see that changing any time soon.

We stared at each other in the dark for a long time, resting in the comfort of everything we'd finally overcome. "I love you" was a good start, but his eyes were full of promises of a million other things he could express, if I gave him time.

Finally, it felt like time was something we had plenty of.

40

DAMON

I was hard at work, when my inbox chimed with a new message from Mark Castell. I clicked it open and looked at the pictures of the groundbreaking of the construction site. Their new headquarters was underway and going well. My heart swelled with pride, knowing that Aria had played a big part in making their vision for "Eco Workspace Power" come true.

But with that success under her belt, Aria had already moved on to several new projects for Humphries Properties. The woman we'd hired to replace her had quit after a few months. Apparently, not everybody was as well-equipped to handle the insufferable demands and controlling attitude of the company's Chief Technology Officer as Aria was (their words, not mine). At least, that's what I'd heard some of the office gossipers were saying. I'd had a personal sit-down with Dana, so I knew that she and her husband had decided to move back to New Orleans to make their dream of opening a brownie bakery a reality. The bonus check we handed Dana for her work would be a good start for them.

I reached for my phone to send Aria a DM.

Me: Babe, meet me at Talia's in an hour.

I glanced over my desktop toward her office, where she was scrunching up her nose, with a smile. An hour seemed reasonable enough, knowing she still had work to do. I was already grabbing my coat and heading out the door, so she wouldn't have a chance to respond and ask what I was up to. I knew she'd wrangle in her excitement and wrap up the rest of her work so she could head over to the bar.

$\mathcal{S}$canning the crowd of customers sprawled out at their tables and bar stools, I saw her searching for me. Perfect timing. I got in position. She turned the corner and nearly ran straight into my chest—but I managed to catch her this time.

"I'm sorry. I didn't see you there," I said, smoothly. "Nice running into you, though. I'm Damon Copeland."

She raised a brow but accepted my very cordial handshake—complete with a gentle kiss to her hand. "What are we doing here, Mr. Copeland?" she teased.

"Just trying to recreate the moment when the hottest chick in the world crashed into my arms, messing up all my plans in the best possible way," I rumbled into her ear.

"And you managed not to soak my shirt for your voyeuristic pleasures this time." She ran a hand down her dry blouse.

I pulled her in close and rasped into her ear, "Although, if you were wearing that same lacey bra you had on that night, I wouldn't be complaining. I planned on us avoiding all the mishaps of the night we met this time around, but if I knew you had on something like that, it might send us off into the men's room together all over again."

I eyed her from head to toe with the same hunger I'd shown that night, only this time around, she made no secret of showing me how much she liked it.

"I don't think the bouncer would buy that whole 'she's my sister' routine if he caught us in there together a second time."

I chuckled. "If he walked in and caught us doing the kinds of things I'm fantasizing about right now, he'd be mortified, especially if he believed you were my sister." Then I remembered our last encounter. "On second thought, actually, he might be inclined to join in."

"Mr. Copeland. Get your mind out of the gutter," she quipped, shaking her head.

"Let me buy you a drink to make up for it."

"I see you found your *sister*." When I turned, I saw the bouncer grinning behind us. *Speak of the devil.* Man. I couldn't help but laugh. He raised his fist, and I bumped it.

"My name is Axel," he said.

"Damon. This is Aria, my girl."

"Have a nice evening, you two," he said before walking off.

Well, that was unexpected. I guided Aria to a seat at the table behind us. She waited as I went to the bar to Gracie, returning a few moments later with a Cosmopolitan for her and a bourbon for me. I sat across from Aria and lifted my glass to hers.

"Cheers. To a new beginning." I clinked my glass to hers.

"One we can tell our kids about," she said, but then her smile faded, and she leaned forward, breaking character.

"Damon, you missed out one important detail," she hissed.

"What's that?"

"The first time we ran into each other, you weren't wearing glasses."

"True. I only put them on half an hour later and completely swept you off your feet."

"I admit, it wasn't just the glasses. There were other factors, too. But your glasses played a crazy role. Speaking of crazy. I still can't believe that you overheard my secret-theory talk with Angie and Lulu."

"I can't believe it either." I chuckled. "You, babe, beauty queen, doll face, Mrs. Goddess, are unmatched."

"Unmatched crazy, you mean?"

"Care to tell me about that little theory?"

"I guess I developed it as a kind of coping mechanism, over time. I got teased and bullied a lot, when I was growing up. Needless to say, the freckles didn't help. Oliver was there for me, so sweet and understanding. Miles helped too, but he's more laid back and just said to ignore the idiots. Oliver was my hero. He hated seeing me suffer. He kicked their asses, and I loved him for it, still do. He knows I have a brittle insecure heart since that time. Then I had a boyfriend who knew about my insecurities and when he found another girl, he just kept poking at them, telling me I wasn't good enough for him."

"He told you you're not good enough because of your freckles?"

"No, not directly like that, but he talked about other imperfections, too. Today I know, of course, he just wanted to make me feel bad because he needed an excuse not to feel shitty about himself. But it left a scar. A deep one. I was so dumb. I really thought there was something wrong with me. So that's how I developed my theory. If a man couldn't see my imperfections, he couldn't use them to hurt me."

"Babe. Wanna know a secret?" I said conspiratorially.

"Sure."

"Men don't give a fuck about fucking imperfections. Grown ass men don't care about any of that shit. Especially not when you don't give two shits about it, yourself. Be yourself. We can't help but fall madly in love."

"Wait. So you're not just *in love* with me, you're *madly in love* with me?"

"Of course I am. With you and all of your freckles."

"Really? You like my freckles?"

"No."

"Oh."

"I fucking *love* your freckles. Every single one of them. It's the first thing I've noticed about you. I also love the adorable little beauty mark on your inner thigh."

"Oh my God."

"And for the record. I don't just love your freckles and beauty marks. I love *every* place on your body."

She humored me, sipping her drink before widening her eyes. "Wait. What did you say your name was?"

I squinted, deciding to play along. "Damon Copeland."

"Oh, my. Well, Damon, I hate to break it to you, but it seems we have some mutual acquaintances. I believe you're friends with my brothers...Miles and Oliver. Best friends, in fact. And you just so happen to work for my father, Mr. Charles Henry Humphries." She let out a sigh. "Which sadly means...*absolutely* nothing can happen between us beyond this drink. Sorry."

"I have it on good authority they'd be more open to me dating their little girl than you might think."

"I wouldn't bet on it." She smirked.

"People can surprise you sometimes."

"I'll say." Our eyes locked together as I drifted closer, leaning across the table. I reached over to brush a strand of hair away from her face and felt her shudder through my fingertips just as she had on the first night we met.

I pressed my lips to hers in a soft and tender kiss. She stroked the stubble on my skin, and I felt her tongue slide into my mouth in a slow sweep. We lingered there for a long time, setting our bodies on fire with a promise of what was to come after that.

Aria drew away and licked my bottom lip. "After these drinks, I think we could use some fresh air."

I nodded and adjusted my pants beneath the table. "Miss Humphries, I've heard that fresh air is code for making out and stumbling into my car, before heading back to my place for one unforgettable night. What would your family say?"

"Unforgettable?" She quipped. "*You* were the one who had trouble forgetting it. Not me."

"Nice try." I winked. "But I'm onto you now, Aria Humphries. You can't get by with those kinds of games anymore."

"Speaking of games—one last question. I've always wanted to know. *All* women want to know. Okay, mostly Zoe, Angie, and Lulu. We discussed this topic. Well, you overheard. There's some, well, confusion."

"Shoot."

"What *do* men care about?"

"Specify."

"You know, how do you win a man's heart? By sucking his dick 24/7?"

"Oh God," I laughed, leaning back. She was hilarious. "The question of all questions. I'm not sure I should reveal our secrets. I mean, snitches get stitches. Yeah, no, sorry, can't betray my brothers, not giving the game away."

"I'm serious."

"So am I."

"Damon! Stop it. What do men want?"

"Relax, Princess. It's easy. Men care about," I raised my hand, counting down fingers. "...Loyalty. Trust. Respect. Values. Warmth. Humor is a plus." I leaned my head down to her ear and lowered my voice. "And we have a special weakness for quirky, haphazard chicks with crazy-ass theories."

She grinned. "I'm not sure who you could possibly mean."

"It's a mystery to me."

"But wait." She blurted. "Your list...you forgot sex!" She shrieked, loudly. Some of the patrons looked at us, as did Axel, all of them giving us curious looks. I chuckled and shook my head, before giving Axel the "everything's under control" nod. Sometimes, I still couldn't believe that we—she and I—weren't just a figment of my imagination. Unfazed, she lowered her voice back down to an almost whisper. "There's no sex on a man's list?"

"Ha." I smiled and inclined my head. "*And* sex. Lots of it. Let's go."

A few minutes later, we were pressed against the same brick wall outside the bar, our lips locked together, and our tongues tangled in each other's mouths—fervently working to recreate that first night. From there, we stumbled into a car and made out until we were back at my place.

What transpired after that was every bit as good as I remembered it being the first time around. Back scratching. Sexy ass slapping. Spanking. Primal, hot, *savage* sex. Sucking. Nibbling. Licking. Fucking. Lots of fucking. Lots of kissing. Lots of staring into each other's eyes. Lots of unforgettable, sweet sappy-ass, us-against-the-world love-making. Maybe even some lengthy cuddling.

She looked so sweet lying next to me, her soft tits pressed

against my chest, her blonde hair covering half of her face and splaying across the pillows. She was an angel. Gently, I raised one hand to brush the locks away, smiling as the moonlight hit Aria's beautiful face and her magnificent freckles. I leaned down to kiss them. She wrinkled her nose, adorably, in her sleep. I nudged her closer to me, careful not to wake her, my arm firm around her.

I could never have enough.

As I said, it was every bit as good as I remembered.

Maybe even better. No. Definitely better.

*D*ing.
My cell, a message popped up.

Stella: Hey Chunkamunk. What up, loser?

Stella: Kiss emoji.

Me: *Jackpot.*

EPILOGUE: ARIA

The *best* part was that when I woke up the next morning, I didn't have to run away.

I snuck off to the bathroom before he woke up and fixed my hair, smudging away the remnants of my leftover makeup under my eyes. After freshening up, I crept back to Damon's bed.

The *second* best part was that he liked cuddling! He was great at it, too. Lying there next to him was always beautiful. *There's a big difference between a man who says you're beautiful versus one who makes you feel beautiful.* I felt safe and protected, as if nothing in the world could ever happen to me. As if I was special, despite all my quirks and kinks and flaws. Damon was special too. It was just us two, and we were a magical place where he was the king, and I was his queen.

The broody Black Dragon King with glasses and his quirky Queen Femme Fatale with freckles.

Damon's tan, muscular body lay there in front of me, draped in his expensive sheets. He still looked like something sculpted by the gods and hand-delivered straight to me. I smiled wide and snuggled up next to him.

"Good morning." I smiled as his eyes squinted open. I couldn't resist trailing my hands along his warm skin.

"Good morning," he rasped in his sexy sleep voice, immediately wrapping me with his arm and pulling me closer to him.

"In case you forgot, my name is Aria." My hand snaked down to the woody he was pitching under the sheets.

Warmth crinkled his eyes. "I'm glad you reminded me. I completely forgot."

"Yes, that's what I thought," I said. "Men aren't very smart, you know."

"So they say," he groaned.

"They only *think* they're smart."

"Yep, and that's not very smart." He paused. "What are you doing with that hand of yours, Aria?"

"As part of our new beginning, I thought I should finally reveal the second act I'd planned to imparting on you before I realized you were forbidden fruit, and I had to flee."

I wrapped my hand around his shaft, but he didn't let me get far.

"Is that so?" he asked and rolled over on top of me, revealing his *own* second act. Maybe he had been right in his jokes through those office messages, and his job with me really was far from finished all those months ago.

But there was nothing stopping us now.

I sank back into the mattress with a moan and let him thrust into me and devour my body however he pleased, and once he was finished, I inflicted the same pleasures on him.

We tangled between the sheets for the rest of the day, ignoring work and the rest of the world. It was the perfect ending to a chance encounter at a bar.

When we finished, I turned to him, feeling him still inside of me, and whispered, "I think we should leave this part out when we tell our future kids about how we met."

"Good call," he replied, nibbling my neck and squeezing my butt.

I spread out over his chest and closed my eyes, listening to the beat of his heart.

For the first time in my life, I didn't feel so restless.

I was happy. Mad happy.

I'd found the perfect job, and the arms of a *real* man along with it. It wasn't my fault that same man just so happened to be my boss —or my brothers' best friend—and father's employee.

I wouldn't have changed a thing—as long as it landed me right there in his arms, where I belonged.

The End

Thank you for reading my novel. The next book in the series will be released soon!

In the meanwhile, if you LOVED *Charming My Broody Billionaire Boss*, make sure you check out book one in the *Oh Billionaires!* series: Billionaire BOSS: Secret Baby is available on Amazon.

I hate him—the man who'd taken my v-card. Now, I'm supposed to work with him–*for* him. What's worse, he doesn't even recognize me! What if he finds out that I have a son...his son?

I've included a sneak peek on the next pages.

BILLIONAIRE BOSS: SECRET BABY SNEAK PEEK

"How about another drink?"

The deep voice sent a shiver down my spine, and I glanced to my left to see who'd spoken. *Holy smokes.* I was face-to-face with the most gorgeous man I'd ever seen. He was tall enough to tower over me, even while I sat on a high bar stool, and his broad shoulders strained against the form-fitting sports jacket he was wearing.

Thick black hair was slicked back from his face, giving me a full view of his dark-blue eyes. They observed me with an intensity I'd never known before, and I immediately found myself drawn to him.

I toyed with the rim of my empty glass. "And ... what would it cost me?"

His smirk widened. He took a seat on the stool next to mine, leaning in close. "Time." He paused, tilting his head. "And sleep."

"Sleep?" I rose a questioning brow at that.

"Well, we won't be getting much sleep tonight, so you're probably going to be tired in the morning."

I couldn't help but blush. Normally, a blunt come-on line like that would have been a major turnoff, and I'd have headed for the door without a backward glance. I'd been hit on before, and I was *definitely* no stranger to men with large ... egos, but his confidence seemed well-earned. I could sense there was something ... breathtaking about him.

The bartender slid a full glass in front of me before removing the empty one.

Hooking up with a strange man was *not* something I'd planned to do tonight, in fact, not something I'd *ever* done before or had ever even intended to do. I could feel the refusal I'd prepared dying in my throat. I'd been working so hard for Christ's sake! I deserved to blow off a little steam and have some fun for a change.

"Convince me." I accepted the drink and felt rather daring—like a bit of a *femme fatale*.

He raised his eyebrow in amusement and gave me an "I would think looking at me would be enough" gesture.

"Well, you *are* attractive," I admitted. "And you seem nice enough so far, but I don't know you."

"What better way to get to know someone than by getting naked and exploring each other?"

"Maybe, I don't know ... a name *first*?"

He laughed, his rich baritone sending a ripple of desire through me. Those deep eyes sparkled as he leaned in closer. "Jonah."

"Hi, Jonah. I'm Naomi."

Jonah's eyes softened, and he reached out to take my hand. "It's nice to meet you, Naomi." The way his mouth wrapped around my name made my entire body feel flushed. "There, now we know each other. So, we're going to finish our drinks, leave together, and spend several pleasurable hours discovering each other."

I had to admit, all of it sounded amazing. When the collar of his jacket moved, I could see the hint of a tattoo on his neck, trailing away under his neatly pressed shirt. It surprised me. He didn't seem like the type—then again, what did I know? The one thing I was sure of was that I desperately wanted to see just how far down that tattoo went.

And, then I remembered ... Oh, *no*! Well, damn it! Today, of all days, why was I wearing the Halloween monster underwear that Lily had given me as a gag gift? To be fair, they were pretty comfy (so comfy, in fact, I wore them on days to cheer me up, or when I wanted to be reminded of Lily's unwavering self-confidence), but that wasn't going to stop me from killing her later. And—double damn—the reason she'd given them to me in the first place was now more hilarious than before. She'd presented them to me, saying, "There you go. For the only virgin left in our circle over the age of twenty-one! They'll keep your mind *below* your waist for a while." She'd laughed hysterically at her own joke, and at the time, I'd laughed along with her.

Finally, finally, there was this hunk of a man, seemingly hell-bent on deflowering me ... having him see me in these panties would beat all awkward moments I had *ever* been in (and trust me, there had been quite a few). I imagined his face dropping as he undressed me, and instead of finding some sweet hot lingerie, he discovered orange panties with an ogre staring back at him.

"There's just one little problem." I could hear the evasiveness croaking in my voice.

"What's that?"

"I—I really wasn't expecting to meet anyone tonight..."

"I guess we both got lucky then," he murmured.

"I'm a virgin," I blurted out. *I know. Completely out of place.* But somehow this seemed a *slightly* better confession than telling him about Shrek. *So much for femme fatale!* I wanted to crawl under the bar stool and hide. I regretted my words as soon as they fell out of my mouth. If that didn't put him off, nothing would. To my surprise, it didn't.

Jonah showed no signs of surprise, only curiosity. "Why would that be a problem?"

"Well..."

"Is it a problem for you?"

"What do you mean?" *I couldn't even think straight.*

"I mean," Jonah leaned in so close, our thighs touched—the solid heat of it drawing my attention, "is your virginity a conscious decision, or are you using it as an excuse not to get close to anybody?"

"I think maybe a little bit of both?"

Jonah studied me carefully, his gaze drifting from my eyes down to my lips and then back up again. "What are you afraid of?"

That was a loaded question. *If you only knew.* But seriously, with everything going on in my life, romantic relationships were very low on my list. And I mean *very*. Those panties were proof enough of that. I had my parents to worry about, which meant I never had time to get close to anyone. If I did, my virginity was always something I could use to push them away when things became too serious. Mostly, I just didn't want a relationship or the emotional ties that went along with it.

I probably would have done the same thing tonight if another man had shown up, but, now, in Jonah's presence, it seemed I was throwing caution to the wind—my usual excuses were flying out the window at record speed. I mean, it wasn't like I planned on staying a virgin forever. And this guy, well, he was freaking hot. And his pick-up lines didn't make me want to run for the hills. So, why not give him a shot? What was the worst that could happen?

Right. I could lose my virginity in Halloween underoos. Maybe I should just play it cool and see how it goes.

"There are a lot of things to be afraid of."

Jonah gave a nod of agreement. "But if you're always afraid, you're never gonna live."

"A nice sentiment, I could *almost* believe it, if I didn't think you were just saying it to get in my pants."

"I wouldn't say it if I didn't believe it." Jonah gave me a mischievous smile. "Besides, I don't need to resort to cheap lines to get *anyone* in my bed."

"I'm sure you don't." I took a sip of my drink as he took one of his, and our eyes locked.

We wound up in an expensive hotel across the road from the bar. When I heard the price of the room, I almost fainted, but Jonah paid it without batting an eye. His expensive clothes and Rolex had already tipped me off to his wealth, but seeing him drop hundreds of dollars for one night made me feel a little uncomfortable.

I didn't have time to dwell on it. The second we slipped inside the room, he shoved me against the door and kissed me. He tasted like expensive whiskey and smelled like laundry detergent, soap, and musk. It was an intoxicating combination of scents and tastes, and I quickly became addicted. I melted against him, grabbing his jacket to pull him closer.

"Let me know if it's too much and I'll stop," he whispered into my ear as he nipped at the lobe. His tongue lapped at the spot his teeth had grazed, before he traveled down to feast on my neck.

"Don't you dare."

Hands groped at my clothes, pulling and tugging to remove them. I did the same to him, eager to feel his hot skin against mine. By the time his hands were removing my skirt, I really didn't care about the "panty problem" anymore. Now, they were just a small barrier between me and my fabulous and pleasurable destiny.

I felt him hesitate, and then a smirk crossed his face. "Why, Naomi, you make me sorry my *Three Little Pigs* undies are in the wash!"

"I'll forgive you as long as you brought the Big Bad Wolf." I actually heard him snicker like a schoolboy.

The rest of the night was a blur of new feelings and sensations. We did so much and touched each other for so long, I lost all sense of time.

He was dominant and rough, but never with malice. I matched his roughness with my own eagerness, and when we finally collapsed, spent and satisfied, I was changed forever.

"What are you thinking about?" he asked as we lay face-to-face with him stroking my hair, and me, lying against his chest.

"Nothing," I said with relief. "For the first time in years ... I'm not thinking about anything. Just this moment. Just us."

Jonah cupped my cheek, bringing me into a surprisingly tender kiss. "Nice."

I tucked my head under his chin, listening to the steady drumming of his heartbeat. My fingers traced the tattoos etched into his skin, and I followed the black lines until my eyes began to droop.

I dozed off before I could stop myself.

With a sleepy groan and the beginnings of a hangover, I returned to some semblance of consciousness hours later. My surroundings were unfamiliar, and it took me a good thirty seconds to remember where I was. Memories of firm hands and a distracting mouth flooded my muddled brain, and I smiled at the naughty images. I'd never anticipated that sex could be *that* intense. Sure, I had read my fair share of romance novels and heard my friends go on and on about their sex lives, but I'd always assumed the stories had been greatly exaggerated.

Pushing my messy hair out of my face, I rolled over, reaching for my, well, Jonah, only to touch cold sheets. My heart sank. I sat up and looked around the room. The only source of light came from the bustling city outside the large window.

Had he left a note? *No.*

A business card on the pillow? *Nope.*

A message on the bathroom mirror? I kicked off the blankets, went and checked. *Nada.*

Frustrated, I let myself fall back onto the bed. I should have known he wouldn't stick around. He'd been way out of my league. Rich, muscular, hot, tattooed, *and* mesmerizing? I *knew* it was too good to be true. I'd acted out of character and, sure, I definitely enjoyed it, but there wasn't going to be a fairy tale ending. *No, that's not me, I'll never be prom queen* lyrics sounded in my mind.

I could feel myself starting to become self-conscious and a little guilty. I pushed it away. Why should *I* feel bad? Why should *I* let him have that power over me? It wasn't as if I'd fallen in love. Me? Never. Not with him. *Please, Naomi,* I scolded myself, *you can't be in love with someone you just met.*

I decided that what I felt for him was "first sex affection." A simple mixture of lust and gratitude! Angry, I stood from the bed. The room was paid through the night, but there was no way I was going to stick around. If he could bang and leave, then so could I.

I got dressed as quickly as possible, and despite my disappointment and determination, I couldn't help but feel ashamed. I hadn't expected us to exchange numbers or anything (I had), but, I at least deserved a goodbye.

Before I left, I took a moment to calm myself. *What's done is* done, I thought. *It was fun and now it's over. Once you leave, put him out of your mind and move on.*

That's exactly what I did.

At least, I tried. I really, really tried.

...

End of the sneak peek.

"Billionaire BOSS: Secret Baby" is now available on Amazon. Also available as audiobook.

ALSO BY JOLIE DAY

Kiss a Billionaire **Series**

In this steamy-hot series, alpha billionaires working in the same company will catch your eye and drive you wild. Just some good old fashioned romance, comedy goodness, and sexy fun. *All novels can be read as single books.*

Crushing on my Billionaire Best Friend

She's my best friend. Of course, I'd never think about touching Laney. Not today. Not tomorrow. Not ever. Then she moves into my penthouse.

(Book 1: Oliver Humphries)

Faking It with the Billionaire Next Door

He's my next-door neighbor. My mortal enemy. Cocky. Infuriatingly hot. The biggest jerk I've ever met. Imagine my jaw drop when he asks me to be his fake fiancée. Imagine his jaw drop when I agree.

(Book 2: Miles Humphries)

Charming My Broody Billionaire Boss

He's the devil himself: Damon Copeland (he practically carries a pitchfork). He's the top dog at my father's company and my brother's best friend. Oh, and someone I *accidentally* slept with.

(Book 3: Damon Copeland)

More books coming soon!

Join my mailing list to be notified when the next book goes live: www.joliedayauthor.com

Oh Billionaires! Series

If you love a man in a business suit during the day and biker gear by night, this series is for you. *All novels can be read as single books.*

Billionaire BOSS: Secret Baby

I hate him—the man who'd taken my v-card. Now, I'm supposed to work with him–*for* him. What's worse, he doesn't even recognize me! What if he finds out that I have a son...his son?

SOLD: Highest Bidder

I bought her at an auction. My best friend's sister.

Billionaire Baby DADDY

OMG...I'm pregnant with a billionaire's baby!

Fake Girlfriend

He's my worst enemy. He's about to acquire my family business. But, he's got a solution for me: My company in exchange for an *arrangement*. He needs a fake girlfriend, and I fit the bill. Fine, I'll pose as his girlfriend. Problem is–What if I don't want to stop pretending?

CONNECT WITH JOLIE DAY

From a sexy bad-boy hero and laugh-out-loud moments to the happily-ever-after. If you stay up way too late reading steamy romance novels, you've come to the right place!

Jolie Day is a romance author with a knack for steam. She invites readers to abandon inhibitions and melt into the pages. Alpha men, boyish charms, rugged good looks—her books take you on a thrill ride of suspense and seduction. Do you want to read about the knight in shining armor willing to do anything to protect his woman?

Then her books are for you.

Follow Jolie Day on Instagram
@joliedayauthor
and on TikTok
www.tiktok.com/@joliedayauthor

Read More from Jolie Day on

Jolie Day's Website:
www.joliedayauthor.com

amazon.com/author/jolieday
instagram.com/joliedayauthor
tiktok.com/@joliedayauthor

Printed in Great Britain
by Amazon

10088039R00173